**MU**

Chapter 1

In the run up to Christmas, Crofts and his team had dealt with seven sudden deaths in a week. It meant long, tiring days and many missed Christmas parties and meals with friends and families, but they had made it. Now the big day had been and gone, Crofts looked around the still and empty office.

Boxing Day wasn't everyone's favourite day of the year to work, but Crofts didn't mind one little bit. It meant that he had been able to spend Christmas Day with the family, and still manage to be available for work at some time over the festive period. As with everyone who worked for the emergency services, working over that time of year was part of the job.

Duties would have been worked out many months ago, trying to make it as fair as possible. Those who had worked the previous years would have been taken into consideration, then volunteers would have been requested.

There were many reasons for people to want to work over this period. For some it was all about the money, as Bank Holidays could be lucrative, double pay and time off in lieu. Others may have a partner who also works over this time, and they would be celebrating their own Christmas in a day or twos time.

Whatever happened, it meant that Crofts would have to work this Boxing Day. He had thoroughly enjoyed his Christmas Day. Watching Oscar, his young son, opening his presents had been great. The next hour or so had then been spent putting together all the toys which needed assembling. Then both sets of his and Deborah's parents had arrived, and after a couple of drinks it was time to sit down for their sumptuous meal. Deborah had, as usual, cooked a wonderful lunch, giving everyone far too much food as usual. This culminated in everyone sitting down to watch The Sound of Music, yet again.

To save costs, the force had always set a low number of staff over all the bank holidays, Crofts was the only Senior SOCO covering the whole of Sussex and Surrey for the day, and would be on call overnight, as well. He had a total of four SOCO's on Early shift, and four on the Late shift, spread around the two counties. They would be tasked for serious crime only. Although that doesn't seem too bad, experience had told them that every year there was a murder over the Christmas period. Whether it was because families were couped up together for too long, or because it was a time when alcohol consumption was at its highest, tempers were lost, fights were started and before they knew it, someone was dead or seriously injured. Christmas wasn't always a happy time for everybody.

However, so far, it had been the dreaded "Q" word: quiet. No-one in their type of work ever said the full word in case it tempted fate.

Crofts had started alone in his office. The only SOCO from his office in Eastbourne, Ellen Parsons, had booked on duty in her hometown of Hastings and was out dealing with a couple of burglaries. Crofts had then spoken to the other three staff on duty and worked out what they were all going to deal with for the day. He had then read all the main logs from the last two days when he had been off, to keep abreast of what had been going on. It seemed, so far, that they had covered everything. Some would say that they had 'got away with it' again. Many of the SOCOs complained that there weren't enough people rostered over the holidays, and that it was all to do with money. This period would be quoted in any arguments for and against any changes in minimum staffing levels in the future. The fact that all work had been covered so far wouldn't help the cause of those seeking more staff on duty.

Crofts was quietly happy with the amount of work over the period. It meant that he had plenty of time to finally get on top of the mounting paperwork that his job produced. It was hard to find a happy medium. All the practical work that was needed during the examination of crime scenes took up a lot of time, but it all had to be logged properly as well, as it was this side of the work that defence barristers would try and attack. They couldn't question the physical exhibits found at scenes, they would just try and find fault in the rest of the work carried out by the investigation team, hoping to find faults which would then sew the element of doubt in the Jurys' eyes.

There was so much for him to do, and today was going to be a fruitful one with no interruptions.

Chapter 2

It wasn't a quiet Boxing Day for Julie Goldson, and her husband John. They owned a restaurant called Sundowners in the town centre of Eastbourne.

Although they had both been in the catering trade in one form or another all their married life, Sundowners had only been open for a year. They had just had their first Christmas Day dinner, followed today by a Boxing Day special. Both days had been sold out for weeks. It was something they had dreamt of, but it was also demanding work.

When they took over the restaurant, it had been a premises that had changed hands every year or so, never seeming to really make it. All diverse types of food had been tried over the years, and various names had been used, but it did seem like it was always going to be a failure. No-one could work out why. It was in the busy South Street area of the town centre of Eastbourne, where there were plenty of pubs and other eateries, but this one had never quite become part of it.

That was what attracted John and Julie in the first place. They wanted a project like this, that they could build up from scratch. They had been successful in most of their previous ventures, but they had always taken over an existing business.

It started with the name, Sundowners. It was the name of a nightclub where they had met on the outskirts of town, back in the eighties. The club no longer existed, in fact it was now part of the modern Sovereign Harbour, where they now lived in a large, detached property. Boating and catering were their two main loves, only surpassed by their love of their only daughter, Natalie, now aged twenty-six, who had recently married and moved out to her own place.

They had chosen a menu that would attract a clientele of their age group, knowing that the fifty-year olds were quite often the age group with more disposable income. Nearing the end of, or finishing their mortgages, with children grown up and having fled the nest, this age group were there for the taking. Having been in the business for so long, they knew what worked and what didn't, and they knew that keeping abreast of changing tastes of food was important. They had been around when the vegetarian revolution had started, and they had been there when Nut Roast was the only option available in most food outlets. This had now really changed. A third of their menu was vegan or vegetarian, with some tasty options on their menu. Together with a wide selection of grills, pastas, and pizzas, it had really taken off. They had also made sure that their bottles of wine were much cheaper than local competitors and added the cocktail bar providing the perfect theme for a Mediterranean style restaurant called Sundowners.

Its popularity had caught them by surprise. Having opened in the previous May, they had expected a slow build up to their first Christmas. The preview night with the local MP, the Mayor, and other dignitaries had been well publicised on Facebook, another tip they had learnt over the recent few years. The actual opening night for the public sold out weeks in advance, and then so were the first few weeks after the reviews on social media. It carried on throughout the summer, hardly ever having a quiet night. Even in the slowest of months, November, they were still busy. Then came the month of December. Their festive party nights were so popular, they also sold out. Adding a DJ and clearing an area for a dance floor, really worked, and many asked why they weren't opening on Christmas or Boxing Days at all.

The truth was that when they had started, they hadn't realised how popular it would become, and having worked many times on those days over the years, they were looking forward to a relaxing time for a change.

That changed this year though, as they had a full sitting booked on both dates for seven course festive lunches. So having just finished a month of long, late nights, they were now halfway through two busy days. Julie was so looking forward to the twenty eighth, when they had decided to have their family Christmas dinner at home with Natalie and her husband Jimmy. The money they were making was great, but Julie wished it were all over, and she could relax, at last.

Chapter 3

It was about ten o'clock when his office phone rang, making Crofts jump, as he was immersed in a laboratory submission which had taken over an hour so far.

The ring tone told him that it was from an internal number on the police network.

"Hi Simon, its Ellen. I've just finished one of the burglaries and popped into Hastings nick to grab a cuppa. Even you wouldn't have accepted one at the house I've just been too!" she laughed.

"Anyway, just talking to Mick Bernard, the duty DC over here, and he thinks he may have a job we might be needed for. I thought I would just give you the heads up."

"What is it?" Crofts replied.

"It's a bit of a strange one. A chap has just phoned in to tell us about his daughter and her boyfriend. They don't have a lot of contact with them as they live away. The couple are only nineteen, and had a baby together six months ago, which they have never seen. Anyway, what with it being Christmas and all that, they decided to try and visit them to see the baby. They called their daughter, Zoe, and they said that she was a bit odd on the phone, and was trying to talk them out of visiting? When they probed further, she told them that sadly the baby Joshua had died a couple of weeks ago, and that they had already had a funeral, with just the two of them attending. They hadn't wanted anyone else to get involved. She then terminated the call, and turned her phone off, and had left it off. They had decided to come down today, anyway.

They got to the flat and the daughter and her boyfriend weren't there. So they spoke to a neighbour who knows the couple, and she said that she hadn't heard about Joshua dying, or indeed a funeral? The neighbour knows them well, has seen Joshua lots of times over the past few months, and has a spare key to their flat, but doesn't want to go in, or let the parents in, without a police presence?"

"Okay" replied Crofts "Sounds a bit odd, so who is going down there, then?"

"Mick was just going to let uniform go and have a look, but then thought he might pop along as well, and let us know if we are needed?"

"That sounds good to me" he replied, "Remind them if there is anything suspicious, not to touch anything, and leave it for us to record properly."

"Yes, I will do" replied Ellen "I'll hang on here until I hear something from them, either way."

Crofts took a note of the serial number and read the story that Ellen had just told him. It was a bit of a strange tale, but his job had taught him many times over the last twenty years that there was 'nowt as strange as folk' as the saying went. He made himself a cup of tea whilst awaiting an update.

He didn't have to wait long, this time it was a call on his mobile, directly from the detective. "Hello mate, I have only stuck my head round the door, but from what I have seen, you'd better come over and deal with it properly" he said.

"Why, what have you found?" Crofts asked.

"Well" he replied, hesitantly "The neighbours say they haven't heard or seen them for about a week. So I let myself in with the key, and there was no sign of anybody on entry" He continued, "Then I noticed some red splattering all along one of the walls of the kitchen, which I thought was a bit odd. I then had a look in the bedroom, and there is something in the cot?"

"What like?" asked Crofts.

"I didn't want to touch anything or go any further, but it did look as though it was a baby shape, but had a blanket covering it, so I thought I had better leave it for you guys to look at properly?" His voice drifted away as he finished the sentence. Crofts could tell that the detective had been upset by the whole experience.

Crofts thanked him for dealing with it in a professional way, asked him to put a scene guard on the door, and told them that he would be over as soon as he could. He then called Ellen and told her to meet him at the scene in twenty minutes, as traffic would be light today, and then headed out to his car to drive over to Hastings.

Chapter 4

Julie had tried calling her daughter Natalie twice that morning, but both calls had gone to voicemail. It didn't worry her too much, as there wasn't a good reception where they lived out at Cooden Beach, and quite often they would suddenly get several text messages from her in one go. Julie hoped she was having a good Christmas, especially as it was the first one that she hadn't spent with her parents.

Even though she was now twenty-six, she was still her little girl, and Julie still struggled to get used to the fact that she was now a married woman who lived with her husband. Natalie had met Jimmy Fletcher at a New Year's Eve party the previous year. Not normally her type of boyfriend, as he was over twenty years older than her.

He was a 'businessman.' Neither John or Julie really knew what his actual 'business' was, it appeared that buying and selling property was part of it, but he did seem to have his fingers in a lot of pies. There was also murmurings of some involvement in the drugs trade, but neither had ever broached the subject with him. He admitted that he had served time in prison when he was younger but put it down to being a 'bit of a naughty boy' in his youth.

He was, however, a good-looking guy, who looked after his body and kept himself fit. He was a bit of a charmer with the ladies. In fact, Julie would never admit it, but he had even been a bit flirty with her the first time they had met, which obviously won her over easily. At the same time, he had got on well with John straight away too. Their similar age helped, together with their love of football, and the local team, Brighton & Hove Albion. Jimmy had a box at The Amex Stadium, which he would invite John to, whenever he could fit it in his busy schedule. A few beers together, followed by decent food and the highs and lows of watching their team in the Premier League had cemented their friendship.

After meeting at the party, Natalie and Jimmy had then seen each other every day with everyone who knew them noticing how besotted they were with each other. Six weeks later Valentine's Day, Jimmy had arranged for them to stay the night at The Grand Hotel on Eastbourne seafront, the town's only five-star hotel. After cocktails and a sumptuous meal in the Mirabelle restaurant, Jimmy ordered a Brandy for himself and a Tia Maria for Natalie, which they took to the leather sofa beside the large open log fire. They sat staring into the crackling embers, enjoying the moment, and then Jimmy got down on one knee and proposed.

Natalie couldn't have wanted for a better occasion to be asked for her hand in marriage, and accepted straight away, before bursting in to tears of joy, and phoned her mum straight away. Julie and John were both happy with the news. They had at the beginning of the relationship, worried about Jimmy's age and his background. They had later decided that he was better than some of Natalie's previous boyfriends, that he was obviously affluent, and would be able to keep Natalie in the lifestyle that she loved.

Jimmy had bought a large detached four-bedroom villa on the beach at Cooden, the cost was undisclosed, but was not cheap. Natalie had then involved her mother in the preparations for her upcoming wedding. They both decided that the Cooden Beach Hotel, not far along the road from their house was going to be the venue.

Weeks of planning had culminated in one of the best weddings that had ever been held at the hotel, something that was hard to contemplate, as they held weddings most weekends during the summer.

The sun had shone throughout the day, which was always a bonus. The ceremony itself was held on a small stage in the gardens, decorated with pink ribbons and matching pink roses. The guests sat on rows of white covered seats on the lawn, all finished off with pink ribbons. There was also a five-piece string orchestra to one side, all dressed in white, which completed the beautiful vision. The ceremony culminated with white doves being released on completion of the vows.

The banquet that followed, and the evening function were both fantastic. The fact that there was a free bar all day helped. Some of Jimmy's friends looked a bit shady at the beginning of the day, but by the end of the evening, everyone was having a wonderful time. Especially Natalie. The joy on her face was obvious to all, throughout the day. It was better than any wedding she could have dreamt of when she was a little girl, she was so happy.

## Chapter 5

The drive to Hastings was one that Crofts was used to, although today was a lot quicker as there was less traffic on the road. He was glad that there had recently been a bypass built near to Bexhill which meant that he didn't have to drive past the Ravenside Retail Park.

That would have been a major hold up today, as it was the start of the Boxing Day sales, and the queues of traffic would have hindered his journey. Crofts thought of the crowds and the sales and smiled to himself; he would much prefer being at work than being a part of that. Even though the scene he was going to didn't sound as though it was going to be much fun.

He didn't need a satnav to guide him to where he was going. It was an area of large terraces of houses, dating back to Victorian times. When initially built they would have been owned by the rich but had slowly over the years been converted to flats, and now housed some of the poorest members of the Hastings community.

Crofts and his team had been to countless crimes in this area. Whether it was burglaries, assaults, murders, or suicides, they all seemed to happen in this area. The inhabitants were usually of the lower end of the scale, whether it was through unemployment, mental health, drugs, or other addictions, it wasn't a place that most people would want to live. As usual in these areas, most were not there by choice, and found it hard to escape.

Crofts pulled up outside the house. A marked police car was parked close by, but there was no obvious scene guard or crime scene tape outside at this time. Ellen was already there, having only driven a short distance from the police station, she had already put on her white over suit, known as a bunny suit by the SOCO's. She walked over to Crofts and started talking to him while he changed.

"I told them not to put any scene tape outside at this stage, and for the scene guard just to wait outside the actual flat in the building for now, until we know exactly what is going on, is that OK?" she asked.

"That's great" replied Crofts "You know what it's like around here, one piece of scene tape, and the whole neighbourhood would be nosing around."

"That's what I thought" Ellen said, sounding relieved "The flat is actually on the top floor, so it does seem a waste putting a scene guard down here as well."

"Yes, definitely" Crofts continued "Anything else to add since I spoke to Mick?"

"No" Ellen replied, "They have manged to take the visiting grandparents away to the nick to take statements, but there is still no update of the whereabouts of the parents."

"It's all a bit odd, isn't it?" Crofts continued "Let's get in there and have a look."

He grabbed some overshoes, gloves, and a mask, waiting to put them on once he was in the building. He also grabbed the video camera and his notebook, and Ellen grabbed her camera, and they walked to the main front door of the building.

He knew that in the sort of area that they were in, more than a dozen people were watching him, and that word would be spreading, but that luckily most of them wouldn't know what they were doing there. The SOCO vans were in the area so often, no-one was that interested.

The front door was open, so they let themselves in, and started ascending the stairs. These type of places had their own, unique smells. It was a mixture of dampness, old cooking, and smoke, both cigarette and cannabis. As they passed each landing, they could hear the sounds from some of the flats, music, TV, children, and even a dog barking, all of which, together with those smells made a concoction that would put people off visiting, let alone living there. They finally arrived at the fourth floor, where they found a young PCSO, who looked very relieved to have some company in such a building.

He said a nervous "Hello" before asking them their names for the scene log, adding the time and date to their entry. Crofts and Ellen put on the rest of their protective clothing, Crofts started the video, and told Ellen to wait there whilst he recorded the scene and had a look around. He took a deep breath in and opened the door to the flat.

Chapter 6

Just as the doors opened for the Boxing Day special lunch, Julie received several texts from Natalie. They had had a lovely Christmas Dinner in the Ivy in Brighton, followed by a few drinks at one of Jimmy's many business associates houses, and then eventually getting home late that night. They were having a few friends round today, and Natalie was sorting out the food, obviously well taught by her mum and dad. Tomorrow they were going up to London for the day, a visit to Winter Wonderland, and seeing a pantomime. Even though she was now in her mid-twenties, Natalie would never miss attending at least one panto a year, and the London performances were always better, with well-known celebrities as the stars of the show. They would get back late that night, and then they would be attending John and Julies house for their special delayed festive dinner on the twenty-eighth, something they were both looking forward to immensely. Natalie finished with the usual "Love and miss you both," which pulled at Julie's heartstrings, but she had no time to get emotional, as the first guests were arriving. They had decided on a set menu, with several options, with the bonus of free wine. This meant that some of those attending would be trying to drink as much as possible, but it evened itself out with the gross profits, and taking it all into account, was a great deal for the customers, as well as being a good earner for the Goldsons. The staff were all on triple pay, which also helped make the day go smoothly, as happy staff meant a happy atmosphere. They had been lucky with most of their crew having been with them from the beginning or from previous places they had worked. They had trained them all well, and looked after them personally, too. It meant that their staff were not only good at their perspective roles, but they also enjoyed their work, and were loyal to the restaurant.

Within the first hour, all guests had been seated, and the wine was flowing. The food was beginning to come out, and all was going well. Julie walked over to where John was re-stocking the wine bottles and said, "Look at it."

"Look at what?" said John quizzically.

"Forget how busy we are, just take a step back and look at what we have achieved. It's what we have always dreamed of."

John put down the bottle of merlot that he was carrying. He stood with his hands on his hips and surveyed the room, nodding slowly, a smile starting to show. "It certainly is, just think of all the hard work we have put in over the years, and this is our reward" His smile turned into a grin, he winked at Julie and pulled her towards him for a quick hug.

"No time for that round here!" They heard from Kathy, one of the servers "We need more garlic mushrooms, we're running low!"

The Goldsons stepped back from their quick embrace and laughed.

"Hi ho, hi ho, it's off to work we go!" said John trying to sound like a cartoon character but failing miserably. Julie and Kathy, both gave him a strange look. "At least Natalie always laughed at my jokes!" he replied with a sad face. "Yes, but now she's all grown up as well" replied Kathy, which made Julie laugh even more.

John shook his head, although still smiling. It really was true. His lovely daughter had doted on her dad, as all girls do, but had now found a man of her own. He was also a little sad, but happy at the same time. Pleased that she was happy but missing having her around all the time. However he had no more time to ponder, as it was getting busier by the minute.

Chapter 7

As the tattered front door opened, Crofts looked inside at the cramped, scruffy little flat. The door led him straight into the living room containing a grimy brown corduroy two-seater sofa, a single seater chair of the same material, and a large screen TV. Toys were dotted all around the place. In the corner was what an estate agent would call a kitchenette. It was a sink and a cooker, with a small slab of worktop which didn't look as it had been cleaned for weeks. There were dirty plates in the sink and half empty packets of food stuffs all around the area as well. Beside it was an overflowing bin, which had dirty nappies, contents of ashtrays, and more left-over food. Not that there was much in it, as most appeared to have landed on the floor. The walls were covered in woodchip paper which had been painted a shade of yellow at some time in the past. Crofts couldn't work out whether the current colour was a remnant of that or was just that hue due to nicotine staining. He noticed the red splattering on the wall beside the cooker which the detective had seen, it was directional splattering, but at this stage he was only videoing the general scene, so would come back and look at that in more detail later.

It was eery in there. Silent, yet he could hear sounds from the rest of the building, people going about their daily lives, unaware of what he was doing. He headed over to the one bedroom and opened the door.

There was a double bed and a cot in the corner. The unmade bed was covered with a duvet that looked grey, although it was hard for him to tell whether that was the original colour, or just grime. Only one of the pillows had a cover on it, the other was a beige colour with loads of stains which could have been one of many fluids at some time or other.

He filmed the room as it was and then turned his attention to the cot, there were several teddy bears in it, but there was also one large shape in the top half of the mattress, covered by a blanket. It was, indeed, baby shaped. Crofts tried to tell himself that it was just another teddy, but in his own mind, he knew that he was only trying to kid himself, trying to make it seem not as bad as potentially could be. He filmed it all in situ and then walked towards the cot for a closer look.

As he approached, he could almost feel the tension in himself, imagining music in the background starting to rise to a crescendo, as if he were in a thriller movie. He got to the cot and noticed that the blanket was a hand-made crocheted blanket, quite unusual nowadays, and Crofts quickly imagined an elderly gran or auntie, lovingly spending hours making it for the impending birth of a baby.

He lifted the blanket, the music in his head was getting louder and louder, and then he saw it.

Laying there was indeed a baby, obviously deceased, looking as peaceful as they always did after they had died. Something was wrong with the face that Crofts couldn't quite make out, as it was quite dark in that corner. He turned on his lamp and could then see the gruesome sight. The mark he could see was that the nose and mouth were decomposing.

Crofts wasn't sure but he later remembered that he physically took a step back. He was used to most things in his job but had never seen anything like that before.

The music in his mind had now stopped, and he had another look. He was right the first time. It was the grey of decomposition that meant that the body had been here for some time.

It also meant that the parents were now potential suspects, their story having been completely blown out of the water.

Crofts put the blanket back and walked back to the door and called Ellen. He didn't want to tell her what was in the scene within earshot of the scene guard. He had looked worried enough as it was, he didn't need any more upset, and anyway it wasn't his role.

Ellen looked at Crofts as she entered the room "It's not good, is it?" she asked.

"What makes you think that?" Crofts enquired.

"I can tell by the look on your face" she answered.

Crofts was surprised that she had noticed that without him saying anything, but then realised that what he had just seen would have upset most people, no matter what they were used to. He talked Ellen through what there was to see in the scene. He could see the colour drain from her face as he described the deceased baby. She then started taking photographs of each area of the flat as directed by Crofts, until they arrived at the cot. Having taken several shots of the blanket covering the baby, Crofts then pulled it back and Ellen saw the face for the first time. Crofts thought he heard her give out a little cry, but she then put her professional head back on, and continued taking photographs as if she were dealing with any other job.

"Let's go back out to the vans" Crofts said on completion "I need to make a few phone calls."

Ellen had never looked so relieved, Crofts thought, as they headed back down the stairs, and out of the building.

Chapter 8

Having had their little moment earlier, neither Julie nor John had time to do anything like that again for the rest of the day. Julie did wonder whose idea it was to have a seven-course meal on Boxing Day, but then remembered it was hers. Whatever, the chefs were coping brilliantly, all the courses were on time, hot, and all cooked well. The waiting staff were as efficient as ever, looking slightly harassed at times, but keeping on top of their duties delivering the food, and then clearing the tables when needed, all with a smile on their faces as much as possible. It wasn't a difficult day for them. Yes, it was busy, but none of them were fazed by that.

Most of them enjoyed being busy as it made the time go quickly, better than sitting around bored and watching the clock. Added to that was that it was a great atmosphere on the day. It was always a good place to work, but today was even better than usual, on top of that, the triple time was a great incentive, and they also knew that the tips would be good today. All that free wine helped on that front.

Julie and John were non-stop, both helping when needed, whatever the task. There were a lot of restaurateurs who would stand and direct their staff, but they weren't like that, they were both very much hands on. They had both worked at some time or other in all the separate roles within the business, and would help when required, whether it was kitchen porter duties or even the pot wash, neither were scared to get their hands dirty. It was obviously something that their staff noticed, as well and further cemented their loyalty to the Goldsons. Good team members were hard to keep in the catering world, they seemed to have got it right. That proved to be a bonus on days such as this.

Having started with canapes, the meal then went on to various starters including everyone's favourite, the prawn cocktail. The main course had been cold meats, bubble and squeak, roast potatoes, together with all the accompanying pickles and sauces. There was also a large seafood paella on one side of the room, and a large fully dressed salmon displayed on mirrors on the other side of the room, for everyone to help themselves to. After a short respite, the two puddings were banoffee or apple pie, both served with lashings of cream. Another respite then left time for the cheese and biscuits, not just dumped on a plate as most restaurants did. They were well known for their cheese and biscuit trolley. It would come round to every guest individually. They could then choose from a dozen different crackers and biscuits, together with the same number of cheeses. It was a winner. Coffee and mints followed, but few had room left for them.

The staff were still busy clearing away and tidying the restaurant after all the different courses. The customers slowly started to leave, by now it was seven o'clock. John and Julie endeavoured to say farewell to all their guests, something they had always tried to do to make customers feel as though they were getting a full personal service and would want to return later. There was no need for that today. There wasn't a single person who had not enjoyed the occasion, there were two couples who asked if they could book for the following year. As pleased as she was about it, Julie had to say that she hadn't even bought a planner for the following year but would let them know when it was available.

The final guest left, albeit a little gingerly, as he obviously had a little too much to drink. He thanked everyone three times and then bumped into the desk near the entrance, hiccupped and said thank you to that as well.

Julie slid the bolt across the door and turned around to the staff and gave a little cheer. The staff all stopped what they were doing and returned the gesture. "Right everyone, stop what you are doing and get yourselves a drink" Julie continued, heading to the bar "What does everyone want?" She then started to pour out the drinks as requested. She finally poured herself a large glass of rose wine and a large merlot for John, who had now joined her at the bar. He then began a speech "We would both just like to thank you all for all the great work you have put in. Not just today, but the whole of the Christmas period. Without you we wouldn't be able to continue. Some of you have been on the journey with us for many years, and we can't thank you enough for your service. We are now looking forward to two days off. The restaurant will be completely closed for those days, so please help yourselves to some food, anything that you want before we must throw the perishables away. Also, does anyone want another drink?" There were cheers from the staff, all proud of their roles at this wonderful place to work, and the mini party started. It continued until about eleven when everyone started to flag, a sign of the long day they had put in.

Julie and John finally left at just after midnight having sorted out the left-over food, emptied the bins, and tidied up. The taxi driver was a regular, he had arrived from Poland twelve years before, and quite liked the night shift, especially when it was such a nice couple. The fact that they always gave him a good tip also helped.

On arrival at their home, they were both in bed and asleep within half an hour.

Chapter 9

Crofts had spent the next half an hour on the phone. The first call was to the Control Room to ask them to get the Duty SIO to contact him directly. The phone rang straight away, as the on-call Senior Investigation Officer responded. Crofts was glad to hear the familiar voice of Tom Mead, one of the easier SIOs to deal with. They had worked on many major crimes together over the years and held a mutual respect. The Major Crime Team had six different SIO's, some were easier to work with than others. Crofts explained to Mead what he had found at the scene. Mead listened intently and then replied, "What happens now with regards a post-mortem?"

"I will contact the on-call pathologist, and it will have to go to a specialist paediatric pathologist up at Great Ormond Street Hospital. I can't imagine that will happen today, but I might be able to get it organised for tomorrow?"

"That sounds good to me" replied Mead, "I imagine it's all videoed and photo'd, so is there any need for me to come to the scene today?"

"Not really" Crofts answered, "I wouldn't wish this scene on anyone who doesn't need to attend, it's not nice."

"It doesn't sound it. Make sure you and your staff are all OK with it when you are finished" Mead stated with real concern.

"We will do" Crofts said, "I'll let you know how I get on with the Pathologist. Enjoy your day."

"As if I can" Mead answered with a hint of irony.

Forensic Pathologists were different from the general pathologists found in hospitals and mortuaries. They were highly trained and experts in injuries caused by criminal acts. They were able to advise on the cause of death at specialist Home Office post-mortems. Normally, Crofts would have rung Forensic Pathology Services, the company that ran the dozen pathologists who covered the South of England, and they would have organised one of their doctors to deal with this job. However, due to it being Boxing Day, none of the office workers would be in. So he had to contact the pathologist direct. He checked the rota and found that it was Andrew Eaton, so gave him a call direct. The phone rang for some time but was eventually answered by a harassed sounding Eaton. Crofts introduced himself, and Eaton replied with a cautious sounding

"Hello." Obviously aware that this might be the end of his Boxing Day celebration with his young family.

Crofts repeated the story again, Eaton listened intently and then replied with relief "This is obviously something that will have to be dealt with by Prof Waddington, the paediatric specialist at Great Ormond Street. Are you able to get the body up there today, and I will contact him, and we can all meet at say, eleven tomorrow? That gives us all time to travel up."

"That's Ok" replied Crofts "I'll get it all in motion and see you at eleven tomorrow."

Crofts then contacted the Coroners Officer, John Snow. "Hello Snowy, sorry to butt into your Boxing Day party, you'll have to sober up now, as I have a job for you!"

"I should be so lucky" he replied, "I've been on call enough times over the festive period to know that it's easier not to organise anything, as it'll always get ruined, and as for drinking, I've just had a cappuccino, so I should be okay, what have you got?"

Crofts repeated the story once again, but also now needed his old friend to organise the undertakers to transport the body up to London. "I imagine we'll need a couple more hours at the scene, so I'll leave it up to you when you call them?" he asked.

"That's okay, I'll put them on standby, and you can give me a call when you are finished? Also can I jump in with you tomorrow for the journey up? It seems pointless us all going in different vehicles."

Crofts gave a mock horror "Oh no!" before continuing with "I suppose so, but only if you bring some biscuits to give to the mortuary staff. It always makes them offer us a cuppa if we do."

"I'm not sure if I can afford that" Snowy replied with a chuckle. He was a retired police officer on a pension, now supplemented with a decent salary in his current civilian role. Probably better off than most of his colleagues.

"If you're going to be awkward, you'd better make sure they're chocolate biscuits then" Crofts replied, "I'll be leaving about seven thirty tomorrow morning."

"That'll be more overtime, then" Snowy replied "Not sure what I'm going to do with all this money I'm getting thrown at me!"

"I'm sure you'll find something to spend it on" Crofts told him.

Chapter 10

Whilst he had been making the calls, Ellen had managed to rustle up a couple of coffees, which they sipped on as Crofts briefed her on what they were going to do. "I just want to go back into the scene and carry out a few tasks before we remove the body and send it up to GOSH, are you okay with that?"

Ellen nodded "That's fine. I feel a bit better since I've had a coffee. It really wasn't a nice sight was it, poor little thing."

"I know" replied Crofts "I've never seen anything like that before. It must have been there for a while. What were the parents thinking of, leaving him there, dead?"

"When I was back at the nick getting the coffees, one of the DC's who had spoken to the grandparents said that the mother, Zoe, had 'learning difficulties' and that her boyfriend was similar. Not sure what that means?"

"Could mean anything really, although Social Services would have been aware of that during the pregnancy. It will be interesting to hear what comes out of that" Crofts replied, stretching, "Right, let's go back in there and get this done as soon as possible"

They grabbed some equipment and headed back up the stairs and met the PCSO at the door, they then signed back into the scene. The poor lad looked even more frightened than when they had first arrived, thought Crofts.

The first area that Crofts wanted to look at was the red splattering that was on the wall as they entered the room, as it didn't look right. As it had all been photographed, he could now test the staining. Ellen took out a KM kit. This was a presumptive test for blood. She took a small circle of blotting paper and folded it into a cone shape and then rubbed the corner in to the red staining. She then added the three chemicals, firstly Phenolphthalein, then Ethyl alcohol and finally Hydrogen peroxide. If it were blood, it would then turn pink. It didn't.

"I didn't think it was" Crofts claimed, looking closer, "I know what it is."

"What" replied Ellen, staring intently at the stains.

"It's ketchup! Someone has shaken the bottle when the lid wasn't on properly, and it's gone all over the wall" Crofts answered knowingly "If it was a home where the occupants cleaned up a bit more, that would've been wiped down straight away. Because they are not, they didn't bother. If it hadn't been for us investigating the crime, no-one would have seen it."

"So it is" replied Ellen "If it weren't such a serious scene, it would have been funny!" she added.

"Right, now we've cleared that up, let's move over to the body" he replied.

They then gently removed each piece of the bedding and exhibited it individually, packaging it in brown paper bags. All of this would be going to the Laboratory to test for traces of drugs, fibres, and anything else which may give an answer to what had happened to the child.

Having removed all the bedding they were left with the body of the baby. They slowly swabbed all areas of exposed skin, which would be used for DNA analysis. They then fibre taped every part of the body, using low adhesive tape, which was then laid onto clear acetate sheets. This would recover hairs and fibres which may be used later in the investigation.

Once they had finished all the required exhibits, Ellen unfolded the small child size body bag, and laid it on the floor. Crofts gently picked up the tiny little body and placed him into the bag. Finally taking one last look at the small face spoilt by the decomposing nose and mouth, before zipping the bag closed. They both looked at each other with a sad grimace. There were times that their job wasn't pleasant, and this was one of them. They didn't need to say anything, they both knew.

They then recovered the bottom sheet and the mattress, before examining the cot for any damage. It was now that the bedding had been removed that Crofts noticed something had fallen down the back of the cot. He reached over and pulled it out. It was a Winnie the Pooh poster which had dropped down. He looked on the wall and could see the marks where the blu-tack had originally been. He then checked the back of the poster and could see that they corresponded with those on the wall. He looked on the poster and spotted a lot of tiny spots which didn't look right. "I think we'll recover this, there's something on that poster I think the Lab should look at" Crofts decided.

Once they had packaged the poster, Crofts told Ellen that it was a suitable time to finish for the day. There would be more to do at the scene after the post-mortem, but for now, they were ready to go. He called up Snowy and told him to get the undertakers enroute, and they packed their equipment up while they waited for them.

When they had arrived, Crofts called them in and told them "We have the baby's body bagged, but I think you should carry it out on a full sized trolly? Maybe add some blankets either side, so that it's not obvious to onlookers that it is so small. I'm sure we are being watched by many now, and if they see that it's an infant it will all kick off. If they just think it's a random dead body, no-one will be interested."

"Sure, it's your call" replied the undertaker "I'll get the gear."

They returned with the trolley, put the body bag in the middle, and then added blankets before covering it with a maroon elasticated cover. It did indeed look like an adult sized body when they finished. They carried it down the stairs and out to the black van with 'Private Ambulance' on the side. Crofts watched from the upper window as they loaded it into the back. He could see a few net curtains and blinds moving, but there was no other reaction in the otherwise quiet street.

Crofts and Ellen then headed back to Hastings police station, where Ellen made some coffee, and Crofts found them a quiet office. "Are you okay?" he asked.

"So so" Ellen replied.

"I know, it wasn't a wonderful job to deal with, but try not to dwell on it" he continued "As with any jobs that are upsetting, you may get flashbacks over the next forty-eight hours. That is a normal human reaction, your mind does that with good or unpleasant events. However, if you keep getting them after that, you may need to see someone specialised."

"I know," said Ellen. She had heard this before but was also grateful for the reminder.

"I can organise a de-brief in a couple of days' time if you want one?" Crofts continued

"I'll let you know" replied Ellen. She hadn't said anything, but he could tell this one had upset her. No matter what they dealt with in their line of work, they were only human, and certain jobs affected some more than others, and it was usually those involving children.

Crofts left the station and got into his van to drive over to Eastbourne. After such a crap day, he was looking forward to seeing his family. Although he was also on call for the night, so anything could happen.

Chapter 11

The following morning was bright and breezy on the seafront at Bexhill and Tam Mackenzie was happily walking along the promenade taking in the lovely fresh air. After two days of being stuck indoors, eating, and drinking, it was great for him to get active. The fact that he was being paid for it was a bonus. He was a Police Community Support Officer, or PCSO as they were better known. They were also known as 'plastic police' by some members of the public, but the truth was that they were nowadays carrying out many tasks of the real police due to the cut in numbers of officers.

It didn't bother Tam, he had been there and seen it all, anyway. He had joined the police as a young man in Strathclyde. His early days on the beat in Glasgow had opened his eyes and prepared him for anything the human being could throw at him. After ten years he had moved down to the Met Police in London, where he had served in several departments, including the Flying Squad, after which the infamous Sweeny TV series had been named. He had thoroughly enjoyed his time in the busy metropolis, but had decided to head for more peaceful surroundings, and transferred down to Sussex, and spent his last ten years working the streets of Eastbourne.

He had always loved talking to people and the interaction with the public that came with being a local beat bobby fitted him to a tee. On retirement, he really didn't know what he was going to do, as he only ever known police work. He had tried a couple of delivery jobs but wasn't happy. He then saw that they were recruiting PCSO's, and that he was in the required age range, and put in for it. He sailed through the process, and a couple of months later found himself back on patrol, albeit in a different uniform.

Tam didn't mind that a bit. He found that his role now was more like his early days as a beat bobby. He had time to talk to the public and get to know everything going on in his patch. It also had the bonus that there was little or no paperwork. It was the one part of police work that he hadn't liked near the end of his career. Over the years it had increased more and more until officers spent a substantial proportion of their shifts filling in forms. The type of jobs he was sent to as a PCSO invariably didn't warrant that type of reporting. So Tam was free to continue with what had always been the best bit of the job. Talking to people, and he was particularly good at it.

Having booked on at eight and been briefed on what had happened over the Christmas period, Tam had then been given a couple of simple tasks, to complete on his patrol. As they were both in shops which wouldn't be open until nine thirty, he decided to go for a walk from the station, through the busy commercial area until he came out on the seafront near to the De La Warr Pavilion. This was a large white art deco building on the front which housed a theatre and restaurant. It always looked very grand, but this morning, with the bright low December sun having just risen, it looked at its best.

Tam had walked along the path beside it and down to the lower promenade, to an area where a few shops and cafes had sprung up over the past couple of years. One coffee shop down there was owned by an old mate of his, Fletch, an ex-cop who had retired a few years before Tam. Fletch always wanted a chat and a catch up on all the latest news from the nick, and for Tam there was always a free cup of coffee. His Scottish upbringing meant that he was always up for a freebie, but the orders nowadays meant that police staff should never take anything for free, in fear of bribery or corruption. Having an old friend give you a drink didn't fit into that criteria, at least not in Tam's mind.

Fletch had only just opened when Tam arrived, he told him that it was a waste of time getting there earlier, as he didn't have any customers before about nine thirty. As he fired up the coffee machine, Tam started taking some of the upturned chairs off the table and setting them on the floor. The premises smelt of damp, partly because of the time of year and because it had been closed for two days, so Fletch opened all the doors and windows to let the sea air and sunshine in. At this time of day, due to it facing towards the east and being sheltered from the wind, it made it a little sun trap, something you wouldn't expect in late December.

Coffees at the ready Fletch and Tam sat down to chat about their own Christmases and to chew the fat about the latest gossip going around the nick.

Chapter 12

Crofts had got up a bit earlier, since he knew that he needed to get up to London that morning. As he sat and ate some toast, he contemplated on how the day ahead was going to be hard for them, and how few people preparing for work that morning would have such an awful event to experience that day. His thoughts were interrupted by a large pounding noise, which was the sound of his ten-year-old son, Oscar bounding down the stairs to see him. "Hi Dad, you're up early" he called as he jogged into the kitchen. Crofts smiled, boys of his age didn't walk or stroll anywhere, everything was done at speed.

He explained that he was going into work early as he had a meeting up in London, avoiding what he was attending. "Whereabouts in London? Is it nearer Arsenal or Chelsea's grounds?" Crofts smiled, in the mind of his football mad son, it was all that mattered in life, "I believe it's closest to Loftus Road. Any idea who plays there?"

"That's an easy one, it's QPR" shouted Oscar, "But they're only in the Championship" he continued. Crofts smiled and replied "The Premier League isn't the be all and end all of everything you know, QPR used to be in it, as did a lot of other teams" Oscar smiled, his dad was always telling him about the old days of football.

Crofts finished his breakfast, said goodbye to Oscar and Deborah, his wife, and then got out his pushbike, put his headphones on, and cycled off with the sound of Meatloaf's 'Bat out of hell' accompanying him on the way.

Snowy was waiting for Crofts as he cycled into the patrol centre just before seven o'clock.

"Blimey, you're keen!" shouted Crofts above his music.

"Couldn't wait to see you dear boy" replied Snowy sarcastically and set the tone for the next couple of hours of banter between the two of them, something they both enjoyed for the humour, and for the fact that it took their minds off the job they were heading to.

They arrived at Great Ormond Street Hospital in suitable time, just after ten. The light-hearted conversations on the journey ended abruptly as they parked up and headed into the mortuary. Crofts had never been a fan of mortuaries in general, but this one he disliked the most.

As GOSH was a children's hospital, everything in the room was child size. That meant the slabs were much smaller and the freezers were also of a lesser capacity. It was all geared up to the fact that they only dealt with youngsters. That was the thing that upset most visitors, as children weren't supposed to die. Sadly, they did, and this was where they would end up.

They rang the bell, and the door was opened by the mortuary assistant, who introduced herself as Linda, and led them through to the waiting area. Snowy produced two packets of Hobnobs, one chocolate and one plain, and Linda smiled "You've been here before, haven't you?" she said as she picked up the kettle and filled it up from the sink in the corner.

"Oh, yes" Snowy replied "Years of attending mortuaries and not being offered tea or coffee leads you to remember the biccies." Linda laughed and explained to them that she was a locum. They didn't need full-time staff there as it wasn't busy enough to warrant them. Every time a special PM was arranged, they would bring assistants in from other hospitals. The bell rang again, and Linda walked over and let Andrew Eaton, the Forensic Pathologist in. He walked into the room with his ever present worried look on his face. This eased once he saw Crofts and Snowy, two old faces he could trust. Crofts wondered whether Eaton ever went anywhere without that expression on his face. They all enjoyed a coffee and a biscuit until the bell rang again, and the final visitors, Ellen Parsons and Alison Williams, the deputy SIO arrived. They had travelled up together from Hastings. That now meant that the whole team were there, just awaiting the main man, Professor Roger Waddington to arrive.

He came in through an internal door as this was where he worked. Prof Waddington was a Paediatric Forensic Pathologist, one of only several in the country. Now approaching his seventies, a largely built man with thin grey hair, he had a serious disposition, but also a kind manner when dealing with officers and staff.

Crofts had met him several times and liked working with him. He declined a coffee, as he had just finished one in his own office and asked for the details of the case. Alison started off by telling him the story as it had initially been reported, and then handed over to Crofts to explain how the baby had been found in the scene. Ellen handed him an album of photographs for him to follow the updates.

"Hmmm" was all he said, as Crofts concluded his account. He looked through the images several times more before adding "Looks like the poor little mite has been there for some time." The others nodded in agreement "Right, let's get to work" the professor stated, standing up and heading for the mortuary room. He then asked Snowy if he was happy to carry out the note taking, and once he had agreed, asked Crofts to tell him who everyone was, and what their roles were, so that it was all recorded for him.

Linda then retrieved the small body bag and laid it on to the mortuary slab. Ellen took some images and the professor asked who would be identifying the body. Snowy answered that it would be him, and then noted that.

Once it had been photographed, Linda slowly opened the bag, and eased the little body out and laid it gently on the slab.

Chapter 13

Julie woke up with a start. She felt as though she had overslept but was surprised to see it was only eight o'clock, and she didn't have any reason to get up early that day. The realisation that they had a day off was a strange feeling. The last few weeks had been so busy, that they hadn't taken a single day off together. John had gone to a couple of football matches at The Amex, and she had met up with the girls a couple of times, but in both cases, they had rushed back to continue the work in Sundowners. She just laid there and thought over the recent events while John lightly snored next to her, still oblivious to the new day.

Her first thoughts were of how successful it had all been. Now that it was all over, she knew that it had gone better than they could have dreamt of. Lots of food had been served, and it had all gone down well with their customers. The few complaints that they had received, weren't even anything to worry about. Julie had learnt over the years that there was always a small percentage of the public that would never be happy whatever they were given, and to not worry about their moans, especially when they were well outnumbered by the positive reviews. There were one or two things that she would change next year, but overall, everything had gone well. Why was she thinking about next year? It would be all happening next week as they were holding a New Year's Eve Special night, followed by a New Year's Day dinner, like their Christmas events. She would have time to correct those problems then.

Now, however there was time to have a lie-in and have a couple of days to themselves. Today was a lazy day. They had planned not to do anything, and they did not want to go anywhere, either. They would have a slow, late breakfast and then chill all day, catching up on all the Christmas TV they had missed. The only thing she had to think about was tomorrow's Christmas day lunch with Natalie and Jimmy, which meant that a meal for four people would be a doddle after what they had recently been preparing.

She drifted back off to sleep again, until she was awoken, this time by the shrieking seagulls. She smiled to herself, she loved to hear them, as they made her remember that she lived by the seaside. She could not believe that people had been complaining on social media about the gulls, what did people expect when they lived by the coast?

John coughed and woke himself up. He looked at the clock, saw that it was nine, and smiled to himself at the realisation that he too was having a day off.

"Not quite sure what woke me up, your snoring or the seagulls" Julie said, nudging him in the ribs.

"It must be the seagulls as I don't snore!" he exclaimed.

"I beg to differ" Julie replied. "Have you remembered it's our day off today, sweetie?"

"Of course I have, I'm going to grab a quick shower, and then I will make you some breakfast in bed, before I settle down for the football" John answered, sitting up on the edge of the bed.

"What football?" Julie asked with a pained expression.

"There's a couple of games originally from yesterday's programme, which were moved to today for TV. I can spend the afternoon just watching them" he replied. "I told you that several times."

"Oh, ok. It looks like I'll be watching my programmes in the other room then, doesn't it?" Julie replied trying to sound annoyed.

"Yep!" said John with a smile, as he jogged off to the shower, ducking out of the way of the pillow that Julie had thrown at him.

She didn't mind really, it did mean that she could watch her own programmes in peace without John moaning about the 'idiots' in East Enders, or 'that prat' on the cooking programmes. She smiled to herself as she heard John singing 'Good old Sussex by the sea' in the shower. It was an old first world war song that the Brighton team ran out on the pitch to. John was obviously feeling in a good mood today, too.

Chapter 14

Having examined the body very closely and having asked Ellen to take photographs of every little mark or blemish on the baby, Prof Waddington then started to examine the face, and the decomposition that had looked so unsightly. Andrew Eaton aided him. He was a highly trained forensic pathologist, but he would only have dealt with a small number of suspicious deaths involving children, so for him, today was also a lesson, albeit with one of the most famous teachers in his profession. He never felt like he was the pupil when working with this man, unlike some of the older pathologists when he had been training, who seemed to enjoy putting down their juniors in front of mortuary and police staff.

As they examined the grey and blackening mess around the nose and mouth, the Professor asked Andrew his view on how long he thought it might have been there. Andrew replied that he thought it was over a week, even a fortnight." The older man agreed. "It's quite unusual for it to decompose like that inside a house though, isn't it?" he continued, "If it were outside and had been visited by insect life, I would expect it. Indoors, and with no maggots it is unusual." The professor was still examining it very closely "I think I might know what has happened" he said.

"Go on" the junior pathologist replied, questioning.

"I think this poor little child has had some sort of trauma around the nose and mouth, and due to that injury, it has been exposed, and that is why the decomposition has sped up in those areas only."

Crofts looked up and saw the grimace that passed between Ellen and Linda. They were both women who dealt with injuries and death daily, but they both had that motherly instinct that overrode what they normally dealt with on cases like this.

Andrew Eaton agreed, they asked Ellen to take some more close-up photographs. She moved across the room to her camera bag to change to a macro lens and a ring flash to make sure she could get the most precise images possible. She then took a deep breath before turning round to continue her work, Crofts watched her, and knew that she was now ready to continue.

The Prof waited until Ellen had taken about ten images, before he cut open the area around the nose and mouth. "You can now see it" he stated, as they all looked a bit closer, "You can see where the bruising had spread prior to the moment of death" he continued "That made the area more susceptible to the decomposition as it was weaker." Everyone in the room knew what that meant, that the poor little mite had been beaten at some stage of his short life.

There was a silence in the mortuary as they all took in the findings. Nobody really wanted to break that silence for want of making the wrong comment. Finally Prof Waddington ended the awkwardness by declaring "Right, now we know that we will continue with the rest of the PM as normal." They all realised while the saddest of moments was over, and that it was now time to get on with their job.

Crofts started organising the exhibit bags, ready for the samples, Ellen took some more images, and Prof Waddington was handed a scalpel by the Mortuary Assistant.

Post-Mortems of babies are the same as those of adults, but with everything on a smaller scale. Even though the slab was smaller, it still made the body look tiny, like a doll.

The Professor started to cut open the front of the body with a 'V' shaped incision with Andrew Eaton at his side, both assisting and learning at the same time. The reason for this was that although it appeared as though there had been an assault at some time, the pathologist still had to check every other part of the body to make sure the exact cause of death. They still had to rule out natural causes, highly unlikely in this case, but if it weren't checked for at this stage it is something that a defence counsel could use in court.

Having opened the chest cavity, the skilled professor then looked at the tiny ribs, "I will need these x-rayed to be accurate, but I can see several fractures already." Everyone moved closer to look, as he pointed out some of the larger marks. The bones of an infant this young were incredibly soft, but that did not stop them being fractured under pressure.

Ellen took some more images before the two pathologists delved further into the examination. All the internal organs were removed and examined on the cutting board at the end of the slab. As they sliced through each organ, they looked at each other knowingly before the professor stated, "There is trauma to the kidneys and other areas of the internal organs. This poor child has had quite a lot of beatings."

Crofts realised he let out an audible sigh and Ellen whispered, "Oh no."

Again, no-one spoke for a while, as they all took stock of the latest findings. Although there were many years of experience in that room, this sort of job affected them all. The pathologists continued with their examination. Crofts collected the blood and urine samples from them and secured the pots in the exhibit bags. These would be sent to the Lab for toxicology, checking for any levels of drugs in the body. Again making sure that the correct cause of death was established. Depending on any drug habits of the parents, it could show whether they had given him anything.

The rest of the PM did not take long. A few more samples were taken, and more images captured before the Professor stated that he was finished and then added the end time for the records.

The mortuary assistant started gathered the organs together and into a plastic bag, and returned them to the cavity, before beginning to sew the body up. Within minutes it would be intact. Crofts and Ellen gathered all the exhibits together and handed them to the Professor to sign all the exhibit labels. Having completed that, they all disrobed and headed to the ante room, where they all sat with notebooks ready as the pathologist started his summing up. "Well, it is obvious that in this case there has been trauma to the body, damaging the internal organs, ribs, and trauma to the face. The damage to the organs has then led to cardiac arrest which is the cause of death. The body has been left for some time and the bruising around the nose and mouth has started to decompose. I would suggest that this was between a week and a fortnight ago, although we cannot be exact."

It was quiet as everyone finished writing their notes. As they finished and all looked up, there was an uneasy moment as no-one knew what to say, finally broken by Alison Williams saying, "So now all we have to do is trace the parents and charge them with murder."

The pathologist replied, "That is correct."

Chapter 15

John had kept to his word and brought breakfast in bed for Julie. He had made scrambled eggs, and added smoked salmon, and a few mushrooms around the edge of the toast. Just how Julie liked it, added to a cafetiere of fresh coffee, she was in her element. "What have I done to deserve this treatment?" she asked. "Just being you" was the reply with a wink from her husband.

"Only so you can watch the football!" Julie laughingly replied, "Not at all" said John, "I would have made you breakfast anyway; you know that." Julie smiled to herself. Of course she knew that. They really were a happy married couple, and there were few who could say that nowadays.

As she sat there basking in the pleasure of her life, her phone rang, and she saw it was Natalie. "Hello darling, how are you?" she asked. "Absolutely fine, mum, we're currently on the train up to London" Natalie replied. Julie could hear that from the background noise, but she could also hear the happiness in her daughters voice, which pleased her. "How did it go at the restaurant yesterday?" Julie then recounted what had happened from start to finish, with Natalie asking questions at every stage. She had worked with her parents for so long, and knew how the business ran, and all the staff as well, so she was genuinely interested.

In truth, she had missed working there over the festive period, as it had always been a part of her life. She was also relieved, as it meant that she had been able to have a Christmas off for the first time ever, especially as it had been spent with her wonderful husband. This time last year, she hadn't even met Jimmy. How her life had changed.

Having recounted the last couple of days events, Julie then asked what they had been doing. Natalie told them of their fantastic experience at The Ivy on Christmas Day. For a restaurant that was already top quality, they had certainly pushed the boat out. The prices were exceedingly high, but worth every penny. As always, the cocktail bar had been as good as ever, even adding a festive twist to all the usual favourites. They had then all gone to the home of one of Jimmy's business friends, a mansion on the cliffs close to the famous Roedean girls private school near Woodingdean, where the staff, yes, staff, had served them with canapes and champagne all night. It was a different world all together, with a pianist playing in the massive hallway beside the biggest Christmas tree Natalie had seen outside Trafalgar Square. They had finished with a champagne breakfast at about four o'clock in the morning.

Natalie had always enjoyed the best things in life, but even she had been blown away with the luxury on show at this gathering. It was like nothing she had seen before, especially in someone's home. The hostess, Nadia, was an incredibly attractive former model, now in her forties. She had taken a shine to Natalie and was already arranging a few days out with her.

When they had finally got up the following day, Nadia had arranged a spread of cold meats, pickles, and bubble and squeak together with freshly caught seafood for their guests. There were only six visitors, but Jimmy's closest associates. All knew each other and their latest partners well, so it had been a nice comfortable day. Plenty of alcohol, plenty of food, together with some music and then games, it had been great. The charades had been one of the funniest Natalie had ever taken part in, especially as a couple of the guests did not really know how to play, meaning some completely random answers which, after copious amounts of alcohol, were even funnier.

She was now on the train up to London, where they would spend the afternoon at Winter Wonderland and then on to The Hackney Empire to watch Dick Whittington, which she was really looking forward to.

Julie told her about the lazy day that they had planned, and Natalie laughed when she mentioned the football "I know, Jimmy has mentioned several times about the fact that he's given up watching that to go to a pantomime!"

Julie heard Jimmy say something in the background to which Natalie replied, "You know you love them really!" and continued to Julie with "Don't worry, we haven't forgotten tomorrow" to which Jimmy shouted, "I wish we were coming there today!" Natalie chuckled and then asked what time they should get over.

"Anytime really, I'm cooking the turkey overnight, so it won't matter what time you arrive."

"Great, we'll be over about one-ish. I'll text you when we're on our way as soon as we get somewhere with a signal!" she replied.

"I know," Julie said, "it is a pain sometimes, not being able to get hold of you." "Jimmy has been on to O2 again this week complaining about the coverage. All they say is that they 'are working on it.' As he says, he cannot believe he paid all that money for our house, but we can't get the most basic need nowadays, because of its location." Julie agreed. "Anyway, Mum, I must go, as we are just pulling into East Croydon, so the train is bound to get crammed full, so I'll see you tomorrow."

"Ok, have a fun time today, love you" Julie said to which Natalie also replied, "Love you, too."

Chapter 16

For Crofts and Snowy, the journey back to the coast was not a good one. Neither of them felt the need to speak, and it wasn't helped by the fact that because of the sales, London was terribly busy, so the traffic had come to a standstill. Not what you needed when all you wanted to do was get back to the office and then go home to your family. The mood was only lightened when the car in front nearly ran over an octogenarian Rastafarian who had been dancing in the road, to the music from a large boogie box on a shopping trolley and accepting money from drivers in the traffic queue. He had approached the car in front of him, whose driver had obviously not seen him, and carried on driving ahead. The old guy had suddenly found a turn of speed belying his years and managed to jump out of the way, but also continuing his dance whilst making faces at the poor driver, who was now wishing he had seen him.

They both laughed aloud at the sight, which then lead to some light-hearted conversation about what had happened. That then continued with further chatting, but neither of them mentioned the PM, or the case in general. It was just something that neither of them wanted to talk about.

They had reached the Uckfield bypass, with about half an hour to go, when Crofts phone rang, and he answered it by speakerphone. "Hi Simon, it's Tom Mead here, are you free to speak?"

"Just me and Snowy in the car, so go ahead" replies Crofts.

"Thought I'd call you to let you know that we've arrested both parents down in Dorset" The SIO continued,

"That was quick" Crofts replied.

"Yes, I know" said Mead, "Although it wasn't too hard to find them. As you know, they aren't the most intelligent couple in the world, and their favourite place to visit is a campsite near Poole in Dorset called Rockley Sands. It's where Zoe, the mother used to go for all her holidays as a youngster, and always talks about it. One of the actions from what her father told us, was to check the place. One of the enquiry team called the site and found they had booked in there about ten days ago, unbelievably, under their proper names!" Mead concluded.

"Wow" replied Crofts, "I wish all crimes were that easy to crack!"

"I know" continued Mead "You won't believe what the boyfriend, Smithers said on arrest!"

"Go on" Snowy and Crofts replied in unison.

"He said 'We didn't do it' before he was told what he was being arrested for!" exclaimed Mead.

"Well that should make things easier for your interview teams then" Crofts replied.

"Yes and no" said Mead, "Because of their limited intellect, they both require appropriate adults, which will make everything now go into slow time for us, but I don't think it will take us long to get the answers. However, my worry is that they both blame each other. If that happens it will be hard to prove which one killed that poor child"

"I suppose so" Crofts gloomily replied.

"Anyway, how are you two doing? Alison tells me it wasn't a pleasant experience up there?" Mead asked with genuine concern.

"We're okay, thanks Guv" Crofts answered, continuing with "Snowy here, is about to treat me to fish and chips at that place in Polegate High Street, which is one of the best chippys around, aren't you Snowy?"

The older man looked at him in mock horror "I'm only a pensioner" he replied.

They both heard Tom Mead laugh over the speaker "That's the spirit, you two. I'll see you when you get back here. Now you have mentioned it. I haven't eaten all day, any chance you can get me a portion of cod and chips, with mushy peas, too?"

"Of course we will" Crofts replied, "Snowy was only just telling me how much overtime he has earned this month, he'd love to treat his favourite SIO!"

Mead laughed again and thanked them, before finishing the call.

"Thanks for that" Snowy said in a sad voice, although Crofts knew it was all an act.

"I knew you would want to treat me, as I've done all the driving, and had to work through the PM, while you just lounged about and wrote a couple of things down to make it look as though you were busy!" Crofts replied.

"You know you can go off people!" Snowy replied. Crofts looked over at him, and in the lights from the dashboard, could see that the older man was smiling to himself.

Chapter 17

On returning to the Hammonds Drive Base in Eastbourne, Crofts took the portion of fish and chips up to Tom Meads office, and they both sat down to eat them, straight from the paper, using their fingers, old style. They were interrupted several times by random passers-by, who put their heads round the door and said, "They smell good!" Mead and Crofts just sat there, munching away, and smiling at the interlopers, not bothering to answer, as they enjoyed their meal. On completion, Crofts gathered up the empty wrappers and went into the kitchen area, to make them both a cup of tea.

"So, how's it all going?" asked Crofts.

Mead updated him with the latest events. The two parents were now in cells in the custody block just along the road from where they were in conversation. Crofts had already covered what needed to happen to them forensically, when he wrote his original forensic strategy for the job. They needed to be photographed fully clothed, they then needed to have their clothing seized (although in these circumstances it was hardly likely that they would be the clothes worn at the time of the crime). They would also have samples taken for toxicology and DNA.

The two suspects were then put into 'sleep mode' for the night, and solicitors and appropriate adults were currently being arranged, ready for the morning. All their other clothing would be recovered by search teams at the caravan in Dorset, and at the home address, looking for traces of blood from baby Joshua.

Tom told Crofts that he had withheld a Press Release at this time. He didn't want to cause problems in the local area in Hastings until the family had time to remove personal effects from the flat. This wouldn't happen until the SOCO examination had finished. The fact that there were police scene guards outside didn't really matter as they were a common sight in that area and did not arouse suspicion with the locals. However, the moment a "baby-killer" was mentioned, all hell would let loose. It's not how the police would describe it, but that is how it would be talked about amongst the neighbours and in the local pubs. That was enough to incite some already volatile individuals into violence of one form or another. The local neighbourhood police teams would be involved from the start of the press release, trying to keep a lid on the situation.

They talked about the Forensic Strategy and what would now need changing with regards to the flat. As the original version had covered most eventualities, it didn't really change much, but they also agreed that they needed to send the Winnie the Pooh poster to the Lab as an urgent submission. "We need a blood distribution expert to have a look at that and give us their views. Although I think we can guess what it was" Crofts stated.

Mead nodded gravelly. "Are you and your team, all ok, or do you want a de-brief?"

"I asked Ellen, and she said no at this stage, but I will ask her again tomorrow, once she has had time to let it all sink in" Crofts answered.

"What about you?" Mead asked.

"I'll be guided by what Ellen wants. If she does feel that she needs one then I will go, but I'm okay otherwise" Crofts replied, before adding "Don't worry, I'm not trying to be all macho about it. I do believe in the debriefing systems and have attended plenty of them. In fact I was one of the first in my department to push for them. It's just that I don't need to have one after every job that's a bit upsetting. I prefer to leave it to the SOCO's to make the decision."

"That's fine" said Mead, "Just making sure. There are still a lot of the old and bold who don't believe in it."

"I know" Crofts replied, "But I have seen too many staff go off sick with depression or PTSD which could have been prevented by some form of de-brief over the years."

"Exactly" said Mead, "Anyway, it's time for you to get home. You've had a long day"
"Yes, guv" replied Crofts, "See you at briefing in the morning."

Crofts headed down the stairs to the SOCO office. It was empty as all the staff on late shift were out working on scenes. He composed a Lab submission for the poster, together with a sample of Joshua's blood to make sure it was his on the poster. He then sent an email to the Scientific Support Assistant, who dealt with all the admin in the office, to get it sent off first thing the next morning. He quickly scanned his emails, saw that there was nothing that couldn't wait until the next day, before booking off duty and closing his computer for the night.

He went to the locker room, and put on his fluorescent jacket, and cycle helmet. He then set up his music, and put on his headphones, walked out to his push bike, and cycled off listening to Simple Minds 'Alive and kicking.' The irony of the words, on a day that he had attended a post-mortem wasn't wasted on him and brought out a wry smile as he left the Base.

Chapter 18

Julie awoke to the lovely aroma of the turkey cooking down in the kitchen, as she had cooked it slowly overnight. It now made the whole house smell as if it were Christmas Day, which is what it was for her and her family. Having worked so many Christmases, they had always arranged an alternative date a couple of days later to have their own celebrations. As John had said many times over the years, it didn't really matter, the only thing that was wrong was the date on the calendar!

She laid there for a while thinking about the lovely time they had the day before. After breakfast in bed, they had both got up and sat and watched their favourites. Julie stayed in her pyjamas and caught up with the soaps, and John put on a tracksuit and watched the football.

At about six they had sat down to some tapas and wine, before sitting with their feet up watching all the other festive programmes they had recorded. It really was what they needed after the last few weeks.

Now it was time to prepare the dinner for themselves, Natalie, and Jimmy. Julie realised that it was the first time Jimmy had joined them for their special day. She hoped it would be all right for him, especially as all they seemed to do was eat out all the time at nice restaurants. She then assured herself that whenever Jimmy had eaten at their house, he had always been complimentary about the food, so she shouldn't really be worrying herself.

As the turkey was cooked, all she had to do was prepare the vegetables, not a simple task as she had decided on so many, it really was going to be a large table of food once it was all done. As well as all the basic veg such as carrots, swede, broccoli, and peas, she had also decided on making cauliflower cheese, some red cabbage with sultanas, and the brussels sprouts were going to be mixed with lardons of bacon. She was also making a special gravy using chicken thighs that she had seen Jamie Oliver make.

She had plenty to keep her busy, but she was in her element. Being in the restaurant trade meant that she hardly ever cooked herself, in fact, most of their meals were grabbed left-overs, to save wasting food and money. So cooking for the four of them was a treat for her.

John then came into the kitchen and pulled a bottle out from the fridge, and took two flute glasses from the cupboard, "I'm making my mind up, and it's Bucks Fizz!" he joked.

Julie groaned, "That joke was never funny, but you use it every year."

"I know, but I still think it's funny" he replied, "Would you like a glass, or not?"

"I want to keep a clear head" replied Julie, "But as it is one of my favourite things, I shall have just one."

Chapter 19

Crofts was tucking into a bowl of muesli when he heard his son Oscar, charging down the stairs, "Hi Dad, what's for breakfast?" he asked breezily as he jumped up on to one of the stools at the breakfast bar.

"Whatever cereals you want, I'm at work today, so don't have time to cook anything, although Mum can if you can wait that long" He smiled.

"It's okay, I'll have Weetabix, I don't want to hang around, I've got a tournament on FIFA to play in about twenty minutes."

Crofts smiled again, the youngsters nowadays spent most of their lives on video games, something that wasn't around when he was growing up, so it was hard for him and his generation to understand why they were so addictive. He had played on that game a lot when Oscar was younger, but it had got to the point, as his son grew older, that he completely thrashed him in every game. Luckily, more competitive opponents were available online, so Oscar had stuck to that.

Having prepared the cereal for him, Crofts watched as Oscar seemed to eat it within a minute, wiped his mouth on the back of his hand and said "Thanks Dad, see you later" before bouncing back up the stairs, ready for his tournament.

His wife, Deborah, then came into the kitchen, hair still wet from her shower "Morning sweetheart, how are you?" she asked.

"I'm just about okay, thanks" he replied "Shame I must go to work though. Oh, and Oscar's had his breakfast."

"He can't have done he wasn't even awake when I went in the bathroom" she answered questionably.

"The call of FIFA soon made sure he was up and ready" Crofts replied.

"I still can't understand why the boys love those games so much" Deborah said "Although, all the boys are the same about it, me and the other mums were talking about it the other day. Karen has it the worst, as she's got three boys and they are all into it!"

"At least it gives them something to do at this time of the year" Crofts stated, "It's not the sort of weather that they can go out and play football all day, is it?"

"I suppose so" his wife replied, "Are you back over in Hastings for that baby death?" she asked.

"Afraid so" Crofts answered sadly "There are certain times when I wish I had a simple office job."

"You wouldn't be able to cope with something like that, you'd be bored!" she replied.

"I know I would, most of the time, it's just certain jobs do get to us."

"I know, darling, but you mustn't let it" Deborah replied.

"I try not to" said Crofts with a false smile "Anyway, I must be off."

"Okay, I will see you later" Deborah said, giving him a kiss.

Crofts put on his waterproofs against the drizzle, plugged in his music, and cycled off listening to "Beautiful Day" by U2, and noticed that it cheered him up a little as he peddled along.

Chapter 20

Crofts was first in the office, and checked the rota, before grabbing the mugs, and making the teas and coffees for those due in on the early shift. The SSA, Paula Shadwell was next in, Crofts told her about the urgent Lab submission that he had emailed her "That's OK, I've got to go to Brighton first thing with some other submissions. I can hand it to Des who will get it to Guildford before the noon Lab run. They'll have it this afternoon at the Lab" replied Paula. "Great stuff, thanks for that" Crofts answered. He then headed up the stairs to the briefing room.

The atmosphere in early morning briefings was always different. Depending on what stage an enquiry was at, it could range from excitement, normally at the beginning of a job, or when there was good news or a suspect found, sometimes even euphoria. Right through all the other emotions possible. However, todays briefing wasn't one of those. The subject matter, a dead infant, already meant that everyone involved, would be thinking of their own children, which would have brought sadness anyway. The fact that there were injuries to that child, and that these were caused by the parents, made things even worse.

Nobody can put themselves in the awful position that a parent of an infant finds themselves when that child dies. It is something that every parent dreads. However, to find that that poor child has died at what seemed at this stage, to be the hands of his own parents, beggars belief.

Mead started the briefing as always by giving an overview of the previous day's events. Slowly going through all the information, before asking different officers to interject when it came to their part of the story. Crofts had prepared some images to show the scene in general. Before he started to show them, he gave a warning "Some of the images I am about to show you are not the nicest to see. If anyone feels that they don't want to see them, please leave now, or indeed, if you feel at any time during my update, you want to leave, please do." He looked around the table. There was a selection of detectives of varying ranks, there were the analysts and typists from the major crime branch, as well as uniformed officers from the outside enquiry team. He noticed a couple of them were looking down, but most of them just looked back at him, awaiting the images.

He started his narrative, showing the scene, from the outside, and then indoors, and finally baby Joshua in the cot. He heard a whimper from somewhere in the room but made sure he didn't look to find out who it was from. He had learnt over the years to break the enquiry team in gently on a job such as this. Him and his team of SOCO's were used to traumatic scenes as it was their job, but some of those attending briefings were not, and may have been seeing this type of image for the first time. He slowly talked them through the images taken at the post-mortem too. Again, for those officers unused to mortuaries, it would just look like photos from a butchers shop. He had to explain exactly what everyone was seeing. This was especially important as some of those in the room would be interviewing the suspects later that morning and needed as much information as possible.

On completion, he then asked if there were any questions. There weren't any. Crofts guessed that it was because everyone wanted to move on from what they had just seen, and re-focus on their tasks for the day. The detective sergeant in charge of the enquiry room, Kevin Bates, then went through the list of Actions that were allocated to the detectives for the day.

These came from the computer system known as HOLMES, which was an acronym for the Home Office Large Major Enquiry System which was used in all serious incidents. All information from witness statements, interviews, house to house enquiries, and exhibits were inputted into the system, and would then decide what actions were needed as an outcome of that information. It was a system that was first used in the eighties when computers were only just being used in solving crime. Before that, all enquiry teams had used paper records and filing cabinets, all of which seemed archaic in the modern day, but which helped solve all crimes up until then.

On completion of the briefing, Crofts hung around to see if there were any questions that people hadn't brought up at the briefing, but no-one came over. His account, together with the graphic images, had been enough information for anyone.

Crofts grabbed his equipment and headed out to his estate car for the drive over to Hastings. He wasn't really looking forward to another day spent in that flat.

Chapter 21.

Julie was ready to go, everything was bubbling away simmering on the stove, she had carved the turkey, and all that was needed was for her guests to arrive, which would hopefully be shortly as it was now twelve thirty. John had been helping where needed, but had left most of it to Julie, as he knew it was something that she missed doing. It was great having chefs cooking for you at the restaurant, but you couldn't beat home cooking.

He'd spent the morning loading the accounts into the system on his computer and was happy with what he had found. It had been an extremely successful month of December for them. All the challenging work had been worth it. He had gone through to the kitchen to give Julie an update, but she was more intent on the dinner, so he left it for now. He could tell her all about it tomorrow.

Julie interrupted his thoughts, "I don't suppose you've heard anything from Jimmy, have you?"

"No, why?" he replied.

"I haven't heard anything from Natalie, and she would normally have texted to say that they were on their way here by now?"

"That's unusual, I'll try ringing them both now" he called back to her. He phoned them both, and as he had guessed, they both went straight to answerphone. He told Julie.

"It's that bad reception around their house" she replied, "It is so annoying, although saying that, I would have expected them to have left by now, they're cutting it a bit fine" she said as an afterthought.

"It is a bit unusual for them" John agreed, "Especially as they know how much we are looking forward to them sharing our dinner with them."

Julie shrugged and turned all the knobs down on the cooker. "I don't want to overcook it all."

John headed back to the study and fired up his laptop again. He checked on his Facebook account, to see if Natalie had posted anything that morning. She hadn't. There were some selfies of her and Jimmy from London the night before, at Winter Wonderland and then outside the theatre, but nothing from that morning. He went through to Julie and told her.

"That's unusual for her, she's always on it! Maybe they just got back late, and have overslept, I can turn everything off for now, and wait for them to arrive, it's not too much hassle."

"Sounds good to me" John replied.

Chapter 22

Crofts had got to Hastings surprisingly quickly. He imagined that the amount of winter sales now on would mean that it was busy, but it appeared that even if it were, most people were having a lie in before commencing the task of battling through the crowds. He bought a couple of coffees from the McDonalds drive thru, and when he pulled up outside the scene, he told Ellen to get in his car, so that he could brief her on what had happened since she had left London the evening before, as she had driven straight back to Hastings to book off. He told her about having Snowy over for the fish and chips the night before. "I can't believe that you must be the first person to ever get him to buy you something, the tight old git!" she said laughingly, "And to get him to pay for Mead as well, that's a classic!" she continued.

"I know," said Crofts "He couldn't get out of it, which was even better."

"He won't talk to you again" she said mischievously.

"He will, I've known him a long time, and he loves all the banter" replied Crofts.

"I know he does, but only you could have got away with that one, he is well known for never putting his hand in his pocket. The joke is, he's loaded. He's on a police pension, and now a decent salary as a Coroners Officer." No mortgage left to pay either, so what does he spend his money on?" she asked.

"I don't know" replied Crofts, "But how do you know he doesn't have a mortgage?"

"He told me once" Ellen replied a little too quickly.

"Oh yes, is there anything else you need to tell me?" Crofts asked, raising his eyebrows.

"Don't be silly, he's old enough to be my dad" Ellen replied, but Crofts had noticed how quickly her face reddened, but decided not to pursue the subject.

"Anyway, aren't you meant to be telling me what we have to do at the scene?" Ellen replied, changing the subject.

"Of course I am" replied Crofts. He then updated Ellen on what had happened at the briefing that morning. "It was horrible, I could see that no-one really wanted to look at the images, but that at the same time they really did" continued Crofts. "It is that morbid fascination that all human beings have, but police staff even more so" he finished.

"It is weird, isn't it? Anyone who comes out on attachment can't wait to see the gory photos, yet those of us doing the job aren't that bothered about them" Ellen replied.

"I think it's because we have become immune to it without realising it, as it is part of our job" he continued, "I remember a few years ago we had a complaint against us from some woman who had been out on attachment with us. She complained that two of the SOCO's were looking at and discussing some post-mortem photographs while they were eating their sandwiches, she had found it most disgusting, and was worried about the state of mind of our staff!"

"Oh no, what did you say to her?" Ellen asked.

"I didn't speak to her about it. I just gave the boss a load of waffle about them getting on with their job and passed on my apologies" Crofts answered.

Ellen laughed "I do often wonder about our states of mind though, don't you?"

"Don't" replied Crofts, "You start doing that, you'll only cause yourself problems."

Ellen laughed and got out of the car to collect her equipment, "The sooner we get started, the sooner we will finish" she said.

Chapter 23

"This is most unusual" Julie said, "It's now two thirty, and we haven't heard anything from them at all. I'm worried there's something wrong."

"I'm sure there's a logical reason for it" replied John, although he was also thinking the same as his wife.

Julie had another look at all the food on the cooker and on the worktop, which was about cold by now. She had turned it down, and then turned it off, ready to get it all going again the minute they got a message from the couple, or even better, turned up.

"Maybe, they decided to stay over in London last night, and are late back?" John asked.

"If they had, you know Natalie would have messaged us from there, it's only at their place that the signal is bad, she would have been in touch if her plans had changed, and anyway, they could have got back from there in time, this morning" Julie replied, her voice trembling slightly.

"I know" replied John, "I just can't think what is up" he added.

"I don't like this. There is something wrong" Julie stated.

John couldn't argue with his wife on that "Do you think we should call the Police?"

"What do you think? They are both adults, and they are only a couple of hours late, they're not likely to be too interested, are they? It's only us that knows how out of character this is. Natalie always stays connected with us, apart from the signal problems at their place."

"Exactly," said John, "She will always find a way to contact us. I'll ring them on 101, the non-emergency line, see what they suggest" he continued, getting his phone out.

He rang the number, and then went through a series of answer messages before finally talking to a call taker at the control room. He explained what had happened, and their worries. "That's okay, Sir, I have logged it all and can give you an incident number to call back on later. As you have said, it is only a couple of hours at this time, I would suggest that you drive over to their house and see if you can contact them there?" he stated.

"That's a good idea" John answered.

"You'll be able to see whether there are signs of them, if their cars are there, and things like that" the call handler added.

"We will do, thanks a lot for your suggestion" John finished.

"Right, get your coat on, we're going to have a drive over to their place, see what's going on" he told Julie.

"Why didn't we think of doing that in the first place?" she asked.

"That's exactly what I just thought" he said, grabbing the car keys.

Chapter 24

Tam Mackenzie had just got back to the nick and was having a coffee. It wasn't the first of the day, in fact, he had had a cup every hour whilst out on the beat, but that was how he liked it. No pressure, just an amble around the town centre, sorting out a few enquiries here and there, nothing too taxing. It was like going back thirty years to when he had first started, although Glasgow was certainly a different place to Bexhill.

He was about to book off duty when the radio called out his call sign. "Go ahead" Tam replied.

"Are you available for a cause for concern at Cooden Beach?" he was asked.

Tam muttered under his breath to himself, but answered professionally "What have you got?"

"We've got a Mr John Goldson and his wife. They are worried about their daughter and her husband, as they have had no contact from them today, which is out of character. They called us earlier, and it was suggested that they go and call at their house to see if they could contact them."

"Okay" Tam responded,

"Well, they've got to the house, the electronic gates are locked, but they can see both their cars in there. They've tried ringing the bell, but there is no reply, they would just prefer a police presence before they try to find a way in?"

"That's fine" said Tam "Although I will have to get it authorised, as it will take me into overtime, which I'm not technically allowed to do?"

"Wait one" the call handler replied, and then continued "That's been authorised by Inspector Jim Matthews. He says that it shouldn't take you more than an hour."

Tam chuckled to himself, what the call handler didn't know, was that Jim was an old friend of his, they had crewed a patrol car together many times when Jim was still a PC. That little statement had told him that Jim was taking the mickey out of the fact that he knew he would be money grabbing, as always, and living up to his celtic roots.

Tam wandered down to the patrol room, to see if he could find a car to use. All the cars were out, and he guessed that was why he had been asked to cover this job, as everyone else in the area was busy. The only keys left were for one of the larger vans, a Mercedes Sprinter, usually used for picking up prisoners on a busy night. He was lucky, being an ex-cop, that he had all the permits needed for this vehicle, so grabbed them, and headed out to the yard, ready to drive the short distance to Cooden Beach.

Chapter 25

Julie was now in a right state, and John was trying to keep her calm, even though he felt bad as well.

They had arrived at the house about half an hour ago, pulling up outside, and parking on the single carriageway. The style of the house was large Spanish style villa, leading on to the beach. To access from there, they would have to walk a mile to the end of the road, and then a further mile back. From the road, there was a large wall, giving privacy. There were large electric wrought iron gates, mechanically opened from inside. They could see both Jimmy's BMW, and Natalie's VW Golf inside the gates. Even though it was getting dark, there were no lights on in the house at all, which was strange. They had pressed the bell on the intercom at the side of the gate. They could hear it buzz inside, but there was no answer. They had again tried to ring both their phones but were unable to get a signal.

That's when John had decided to call the police again. He got in the car and drove until he could see a bar of signal on his phone. He was told that someone would be with them in twenty minutes, and so they were now waiting.

"There's definitely something wrong" said Julie in a wavering voice.

"Maybe there's a simple answer" replied John.

"Such as what?" Julie asked.

"Maybe they have gone somewhere else, or by taxi?" John replied, knowing that he didn't sound convincing.

"If they had, you know Natalie would have called or messaged us" Julie replied, stating exactly what John was thinking.

Any further conversation was halted by the arrival of the police van driven by Tam Mackenzie. He pulled up just outside the gates, and then jumped down.

"Well, hello there" he said, "Haven't seen you for a couple of weeks!"

Tam knew the couple well, originally from when he had been a beat bobby in Eastbourne years ago, but also because he and his wife, Anne, frequented Sundowners regularly.

"Hello Tam, nice to see you again, but not in these circumstances" John replied.

"Yes, I read the report, I take it there has still been no contact?" Tam asked.

"Nothing" said Julie, "It is really out of character for Natalie, she is always in touch one way or the other, whether it's calls, texts, or messages, she will always contact us."

"So, when was the last time you actually had contact from her?" Tam asked.

John told him about the call yesterday, and the images on Facebook from their trip in London.

"So, you haven't actually spoken to her since yesterday afternoon?" Tam stated.

"No, we haven't" replied John, "she told us their plans for the rest of the day, and that they were coming to us at about one today. If they had changed their plans, Natalie would have messaged us at some stage. The only reason we sometimes lose contact, is due to the phone signal round here. Any other time she always keeps in touch."

"That's fine" Tom replied, "Just wanted to check, before we go any further. You said you rang the bell, and could hear it inside the house?"

"Yes" said John, and then rang it again. The three of them heard it in the distance.

"Okay, do you know how to open these gates?" Tam asked.

"There is nothing out here, but if we can get over the wall, there is a safety release from the inside" John answered.

Tam looked at the wall, sizing it up before producing a solution, "I'm going to drive the van up to the gates, then climb on top and then drop over the wall. I may need a hand from you, though John."

"No probs" John replied, looking at Julie, who was now visibly shaking. He wasn't sure if it was the fact that it was getting cooler as it got darker, or just the fear that she was showing. He thought he knew what it was but didn't want to believe it.

Tam jumped into the van, and manoeuvred it sideways on, as near to the wall as possible. He then opened the rear doors and scrambled up onto the roof. As he got on top, the thought did cross his mind that he didn't know whether it would hold his weight, but that worry disappeared once he was on top. He then stepped over, on to the top of the wall, before hanging down and then dropping the last few feet and landing safely. "Not bad for an oldie, eh?" he playfully asked, but realised straight away that neither of the Goldsons were in that sort of mood, "Okay, where's the release?" he asked, a little more seriously.

"It's on the left-hand pillar" John replied "One of the bricks is not cemented in. You pull that out and the switch is behind it."

"Ingenious!" Tam answered, having found the false brick, and pressing the switch. The gates slowly rolled open. Once in position Tam instructed "We need to get both our vehicles away from the roadside, parking on the single carriageway is dangerous. I'll drive the van in and then you follow in your car, there's room for both."

They did that, and once parked up headed towards the house.

Chapter 26

Crofts and Ellen were slowly working their way through the flat. All examinations differed due to the circumstances of each case. If the scene was one where there was no known suspect, then every single item was examined throughout the scene. When it was a scene where the victim and the suspects all lived together, as in this case, it cut down the amount of work required.

However, it was still the same as always, as Crofts was always reminding his staff: "You only have one chance to examine a scene, so make the most of it. Once you have handed it back, you can't return."

His staff sometimes jokingly reminded him of this before he had a chance to say it, but it was true, and they always followed his thinking.

As well as making sure that they recovered as much as possible, they also had to make sure that they didn't leave any openings for a defence barrister to question their work. If it was found that something had not been examined or hadn't been negated in their notes, then these people may dwell on that in court, making out the SOCO's hadn't carried out their task properly, leading to the question of, "If they didn't do that properly, then can we believe you did anything correctly?" and thus leading the jury to question whether their evidence was believable or not.

Crofts had seen this happen several times over the years and hated the fact that one sentence in court from a barrister could completely ruin days of work by the SOCO team at that scene. Over the years, their role had become harder. Not only did they now need to prove what had happened, they also had to show that there was no other alternative to their findings. It made things harder for them, but at the same time, made it more challenging, which is what Crofts enjoyed.

Their main area of examination was initially around the cot. Now that they knew it had been an area where blood stains had been found, they needed to see if there were any further minute areas of blood. Using a lamp, they closely examined all around the cot, swabbing any marks found. They then continued in the same way in their search for blood. Several areas were found, photographed, and swabbed. None was directional blood splattering, meaning that they might not have come from an actual assault, but they were always recovered, anyway.

Having spent a couple of hours doing that, they then searched all the clothing in the wardrobes, chest of drawers, and then eventually the laundry basket, again looking for blood staining of any type. Any marks were tested, and if positive for blood, were packaged ready to send to the Lab, if needed. The results of the interviews of the suspects would decide what needed to be sent off. They had just stopped for a coffee break when Crofts phone rang, it was DC Martin Buller from the Major Crime Team, "Hello Crofty, can you talk?"

"Yes, I can talk, I can also walk!" Crofts replied sarcastically.

"Thanks for that you old git, I was phoning up to be serious, and you just want to treat it all as a joke!" Buller laughed.

"If it was anyone else's number showing I wouldn't have been so facetious!" Crofts replied.

"I am glad to be so honoured" joked Buller, "Anyway, do you want me to give you an update or not?"

"Of course I do, stop keeping us in suspense" Crofts replied, putting his phone on speaker so that Ellen could hear as well.

"Well, I've just come out of interviewing Jordan Smithers, the boyfriend. Notice I didn't call him the dad" he continued.

"Oh yes, why is that?" Crofts replied.

"It seems that young Smithers wasn't sure whether he was the father or not because they split up for a short while around the time she became pregnant, and that Zoe had several other men friends around that time" the detective continued.

"Didn't he think of getting a paternity test?" Crofts asked.

"Listen mate, we are not talking the brightest button in the box here. He was simply happy to get back with Zoe and was also happy that she was having a child and was ready to support her."

"Go on," said Crofts.

"There had been quite a few arguments in the run up to the birth, which didn't help. Then the baby was born, and he thought it was all going to be hunky dory, but it wasn't. Zoe, who also has limited intelligence, then started to suffer from post-natal depression, leaving young Smithers to deal with the baby. He has also admitted to drug taking, and that together with his intelligence, and lack of sleep, meant that he was unable to cope with the little one. He didn't want to let Zoe know, as he was worried about social services getting further involved. Anyway, one night, the little one wouldn't stop crying, he was out of it on some drugs and tired and decided to 'clip him round the head' in his words, to stop him crying."

"Lovely" Crofts interjected.

"I know" continued Buller "he said it was only a light tap, but the baby started crying louder, so he did it again. He then noticed there was some blood coming from the nose." He paused before continuing, "Zoe was asleep, so he decided to leave him where he was with the intention of telling her the next morning that he must have bumped his face on the cot in his sleep. Anyway, the next morning Zoe wakes up and finds him dead. Since they were on the at-risk register, Smithers talks Zoe into going away for a few days, to think about what to do next, as they were both sure they would get accused of the baby's death anyway. Whilst they were away, they produced the idea of telling everyone that he had died of natural causes and that they had already had the funeral, and then just going back in a week or so time and getting rid of the body and behaving as if nothing was wrong."

"Did he say how they were going to get rid of the body?" asked Crofts.

"No, I don't think they had thought that bit through. Obviously, they didn't expect nosey relatives and police to break into their flat, either!" exclaimed Buller.

"I suppose so" replied Crofts "I will contact the pathologists, and give them an update of that story, to see if that fits in with their findings. I have a feeling that they will say that that poor baby had a lot more than a "little clip." For a start off, the broken ribs. That's not just from one episode, I would suggest that Smithers has become a bit handy with his fists over a period, poor little thing."

"I agree, he thinks that making it an 'accidental' one off episode will mean he'll get away with it" Buller replied.

"Well, we can let the experts answer to that for us" Crofts said, "Anything from the mother?"

"I haven't seen the whole interview with Zoe, but she had indeed suffered from post-natal depression, and was sleeping a lot, and the first thing she knew about it was when she found him dead with blood around the nose and mouth. From then on, she has just gone along with everything that Smithers suggested, as she thought she was in trouble anyway" concluded Buller.

"Okay, well thanks for keeping us updated" Crofts replied, before finishing the call.

"Did you hear all of that?" he asked Ellen
"Yes" she replied "Bastard."

"I know" agreed Crofts "Lets finish the rest of this off and get out of here."

"I agree, the sooner the better" Ellen replied grabbing an exhibit bag and opening it with more force than usual, before repeating "Bastard."

Chapter 27

As they approached the front door, Tam asked if they had a spare key?

"We have, but we've never used it" John replied, realising how stupid that sounded, straight away.

Tam also noticed that but decided not to say anything other than "Okay, give it to me."

He unlocked the door and shouted "Hello, anyone there?"

Silence.

Julie then shouted "Natalie, Jimmy, are you there?"

Still silence.

They entered the large hallway.

Tam then decided coming from the experience of years of police work, "I think it's better if you wait here, while I have a wee look around" he told them reassuringly.

"But we know the house layout better than you, it's better if we come with you" Julie replied, her voice shaking.

"I know, but in this case, it's better if you wait here" he said sternly.

John nodded and put his arm round his wife, protectively, "It's all right, sweetheart, Tam knows what he's doing. We'll stay here," and then said, "Off you go Tam."

Tam turned on the main hallway light. There were two corridors heading off and he could see several identical wooden doors along each. He tried the first door, it was just a cloakroom, containing coats and shoes. The next room was a dining room, a large six-seater table, with ornate chairs and a lovely view of the garden. He moved on to the next door and felt that he couldn't open it freely as something was in the way. He gave it a shove, and the door opened quickly almost causing Tam to fall in the room.

It was a good job he didn't, as what he saw then made him exclaim," Fucking Hell!"

Julie was behind him within a second, "What is it?" she yelled.

Tam turned around quickly to stop her seeing inside the room, but she had already seen the lower part of someone's legs and his shoes, lying on the floor.

The scream she let out was loud and painful, John was pulling her back and Tam was guiding her away at the same time. He used the momentum to follow them both back outside the house. Julie was now hysterical.

"Was that Jimmy? Was that who I saw?" she shrieked.

Jimmy was staring at Tam, not really comprehending what was going on.

Tam said, "I don't want to say anything at this time, as I can't be sure."

Julie was on her knees sobbing.

"What I do need you to do is go back to your car, and sit in it, while I wait for further back up" Tam told them.

"Why is that?" John asked, still not sure what was going on.

"It appears as though something serious has taken place in there, and I will need further resources" he continued "Although I have plenty of police experience, I am now retired and a PCSO, so I am not able to go any further." He didn't want to tell them that there was another reason. He had seen a gunshot wound on the chest of Jimmy Fletcher. It was hardly likely, but there was a small chance that the shooter may still be around. He also needed a firearms team as well as detectives.

He shepherded the Goldsons out to their car and called the Control Room. He told them his update and could hear the seriousness in the tone of voice of the Controller as he replied. Tam asked for CID, SOCO and a firearms team. The local inspector called up and said he would also attend. He had been following the log earlier in the afternoon. He was also glad it was Tam that had attended, albeit by chance. There were a lot of his younger officers who may not have dealt with it quite as well as the old timer.

Chapter 28

Crofts was just putting the last of the exhibits into Ellen's van when he got the call. He listened to what had been found so far, and realised it was going to be quite a large job, and that he would need extra staff. "Can you call the office and get Hannah Jukes and Leighton Phillips to attend the scene and tell them I will meet them there?" he told the Controller.

Ellen was looking at him with a knowing look, "I suppose that's over with me, and you want someone else" she said.

Crofts laughed "You know how it is, you've got enough work to do finishing off this job, I'll need a fresh team for this job."

"I know" Ellen replied, "What have you got anyway, the bits I heard sound juicy?"

Crofts explained what he had been told so far.

"You lucky sods!" she exclaimed.

Crofts grinned, only SOCO's would think that working on a

shooting would be fun.

"Anyway, thanks for your work on this one, I must dash, people to see!" he called as he got into his car for the short drive to Cooden Beach.

He arrived at the address to a scene of activity. There were several marked police cars around, including a 4x4, that Crofts recognised as an armed response vehicle. The crew were just getting their weapons out of the boot as he pulled up. He could also see a civilian car parked, windows steamed up, but he was able to make out two occupants. He guessed who they were, from what he had been told about the job on the phone. He tried not to let them see him, as he also knew them from their restaurants over the years.

Tom Mead also arrived at the same time, as he got out of his car, Crofts asked him "Blimey, what are you doing here this quickly, I thought the local CID were meant to deal with it first and then call for you?"

Mead smiled "I saw the serial come in earlier on and noticed the victim's name and background. When I saw that he had been shot I knew it's something that we would be getting involved in, so decided to take it on straight away."

"No problem" said Crofts, "It's your call. Do you have preference in how we go about this?"

"We know we have one dead from what appears to be a gunshot wound of some sort, so we do need a firearms approach, even though you won't agree, do you? Mead asked.

"I would prefer if it was forensically lead if possible?" Crofts replied.

"I know, but if something was to go wrong, and there was a shooter in there, and it all kicked off, I would lose my job for putting you into that position" the SIO replied.

"I realise that, but how about this. We get one of the firearms team and dress them up as forensically as possible, and we search through together with him, he can clear each room, and then we can video and photograph it straight away?" asked Crofts.

"That sounds okay to me and covers the safety side of things as well. I'll put it in my policy book" replied Mead.

Crofts went over to the firearms officers and was glad to see that their Inspector was Ray Westbrook, as they had both served in the forces together years before and knew each other well. Crofts explained what he wanted to do.

"That sounds good to me, hang on a minute," and he turned to his officers.

"Buster!" he called and one of the men jogged over. "Didn't you once say that you wished you'd been a SOCO?" he asked.

The officer laughed and said, "I did sir."

Westbrook replied "Well now's your chance! Follow Mr Crofts here and he'll dress you up as a SOCO and explain what he needs you to do!"

Buster smirked, and looked over to the rest of his colleagues, who were all laughing at his predicament. Crofts walked over and explained what they were going to do, and why they were doing it. Buster understood, and then went over to Hannah Jukes and Leighton Phillips to get his PPE on.

Hannah had already taken photos of the outside of the house, so Crofts prepared his video camera, and asked for quiet from everyone, as the video always had to have the audio left on to make it entire. Unfortunately, the quietness enabled them all to hear Julie Goldson crying in her car. There were a lot of nervous looks between various officers in the yard, as the realism that the parents were still there, hit them. Tam took that moment to knock on the window of the car and tell John to let him in the driver's seat, so he could drive them a short way outside the scene. This led to even more tears from Julie, but this was soon covered by Tam starting up the engine and driving them a short distance along the road, out of sight of what was going on. For the second time that evening, the Inspector was so glad he had Tam on his team.

Chapter 29

Hannah, Crofts, and Buster walked to the front door, Buster now dressed the same as the SOCO's, with overshoes, white oversuit, rubber nitrile gloves, a mask and hairnet. His brief was to open each door, and clear the room, so that Crofts could then video record, and then Hannah would take the images.

He opened the front door and carried out the check, before motioning to Crofts to follow. As Crofts started the video, Buster then carried on panning the area beyond them.

Having recorded the corridor and first two rooms, he now came to the room that they knew the male body was in. Again, Buster entered and checked the room and Crofts followed. He looked down to see the body of a male, lying on his back, with two red stains on his chest. He was wearing a sweatshirt, so the red stains had spread through the material, however he could see that the holes in the material were about two inches in diameter, making Crofts guess that they were the exit wounds, meaning the victim had been shot from behind. There was a small plastic cling seal bag on his chest, which had a small amount of white powder in. The rest of the powder had been sprinkled over the body. This gave the suggestion that there had been some sort of issue with drugs involved in this case.

The room was a small utility room. Crofts had a good look around for any sign of a weapon on the floor. In some cases where there were two victims from the same household, it could be a murder suicide. Where life had got too much for one, and they had killed their partner and then turned the gun on themselves. That would lead to a complete change in the investigation. He couldn't see one at this time. He couldn't see any empty cylinders either, which Crofts recorded, but there didn't appear to be anything else in play in this room, so they moved on along the corridor.

Crofts had been briefed by Tam on what he had seen in that room, so he wasn't too surprised with anything so far. At the back of his mind was the fact that the wife, Natalie was still to be found, and they had no idea where she was in the house. If she was there at all.

The final door in the corridor led into a large kitchen, overlooking the sea. It had an island breakfast bar centrally, and Crofts could see two coffee cups on the top, both having been used. Nothing else looked out of place, and the kitchen joined round to the dining room on the left-hand side of the room.

On the right-hand side, glass doors led into a large lounge, again looking over the now dark sea. While Buster was clearing the room, Crofts looked out, and his eye was caught by the sweeping light of the Royal Sovereign light tower in the distance on the horizon. His eyes then came back into the room and took in the furnishings, large white Chesterfield leather settees, two plush cream-coloured recliners, several glass coffee tables, and a cabinet full of ornaments that all looked Asian and expensive. The television was the largest that he had seen in a private house. Crofts wondered how much it cost to furnish this room alone. Not cheap, was the answer. The owners of this house were obviously very well off.

Buster then went through the door in the corner, which then led to a corridor, which Crofts realised, would lead them back into the hallway. He now had the layout of the ground floor in his head. The first door led to a home cinema, six white leather armchairs laid out in a row, with a screen that covered most of one side of the room.

Buster then led them to the final two rooms, a shower room, and a downstairs cloakroom. Crofts and Hannah recording everything as it was found. They were then back into the entrance hall.

"Everyone okay" Crofts asked, they both nodded. He didn't need to say what they were all thinking. Where was the wife?

Buster started up the stairs, taking it slowly, checking the landing above him as he went. He suddenly froze, and looked at Crofts, "You'd better come and have a look of this" he whispered. Crofts headed up the stairs, stopped next to him, and looked down at what he was pointing. There was a coffee cup, the same as the two in the kitchen, which had been knocked over on one of the stairs. There was an ashtray, with a stubbed-out cigarette at the top of the stairs. There were also two rips in the carpet on the riser leading to the top step, and a hole in the skirting board. They looked at each other.

Crofts broke the ice, "Look like bullet marks."

Buster nodded before adding "That's what I thought."

"Good spot" Crofts responded, before looking again, and then turning his torch on. "Can you see that? He asked.

"What am I looking at" the armed response officer replied.

"The carpet is dark in colour, but I can make out some staining leading across the landing to the room over there" Crofts said, moving the torch along the landing.

"Oh yes, I can see that now" Buster replied.

"See, if you had been a SOCO, you would have learnt to look for things like that!" Crofts joked.

Buster gave him a strange look, not getting Crofts sense of humour.

Crofts shrugged and continued "Looks like that is where our second victim is going to be. I suppose you need to clear the other rooms before we go in there, don't you?

"Yes, I do" he replied, looking nervously at the door at the end of the landing.

"We will need to get some more stepping plates up here so that we don't step on that blood. Hannah, can you give Leighton a shout, and get him to bring some in?"

Within a minute, the other SOCO arrived with a new box of sterile stepping plates which Crofts put down in front of them as they moved along the landing.

Buster then entered the first door, which was a guest bedroom, and cleared it for the two SOCO's to continue their recording of the scene. They then went through the same routine for two further bedrooms and a bathroom. It was now time to go to the final room. The main bedroom, and where the blood trail led them.

"Okay mate let's get this over with" Crofts announced to the firearms officer.

He didn't reply, he just took a deep breath, crouched, and opened the door. He then looked around the room quickly before calling "Clear!" before turning away and looking back down the corridor.

Crofts doubted whether he had really cleared the room properly, but he wasn't bothered. He just wanted to get in and see what was in the room.

Chapter 30

Tam and the Goldsons were still sat in the car outside. Julie and John sat in the back, Tam in the driver's seat.

Julie was all cried out now, John sat with his arm around his wife. Every now and then she would ask "Tam, it was a dead body we saw on the floor, wasn't it?" Tam had given up trying to change the subject, as he knew she had seen something, but wasn't sure what she had seen.

He knew what he had seen, and despite all his experience he hadn't been prepared for it. He had seen plenty of dead bodies over the years, and they didn't really bother him. However, that was years ago as a serving police officer. He was now retired and in a simpler role, he usually spent the day on patrol chatting and drinking coffee. His days of dealing with this type of crime were well gone. It had really surprised him how much it had upset him. It wasn't helped by the fact that he was having to placate Julie. She had gone through a full range of emotions, initially shocked, then upset, followed by fear, replaced by anger, then back to worrying about Natalie and what had happened to her.

As much as John had tried to sooth her, it was Tam that she was taking it all out on. He knew it wasn't personal, it was just that he was there, and no-one else was coming over to take over from him. He realised that if it had been one of the younger PCSO's in this situation, they would have been relieved by now, but because it was 'Good old Tam,' they had left him with the relatives. He had already decided that he would be resigning after this was over. He didn't need this sort of grief in a job. He had his pension, and he would look for a part time job with no stress or pressure. He needed to spend more time fishing, with the peace and quiet of the riverbank.

Julie let out an anguished wail "Why are they not telling us what is going on?" she demanded of Tam.

"They probably don't have anything to tell us at the moment" he replied.

"But how long does it take for them to look around the house? We've been here for ages" she snapped back at him.

"It's not quite as simple as that" Tam replied, "There are lots of factors involved in this type of job, and they have to make sure they deal with them properly."

"What sort of factors?" she almost spat.

"Look love" John intervened "Just let the police do their job properly, we will get some answers soon."

Julie continued to sob, and Tam wished he had never answered his radio earlier that afternoon.

Chapter 31

Having let the firearms officer step out of the way, Crofts now investigated the room. The trail of blood that had been hard to see on the darker landing carpet, was easier to follow on the cream-coloured bedroom carpet. It led across the room to the figure of a woman, dressed in a pink dressing gown, lying on her side. One arm was above her head, the other tucked under body. There was a lot of blood on the carpet around her head, as well as down her clothing. As Crofts approached, he could see two bullet holes in her head. One in the cheek and one in the forehead. It also looked as if there was another wound on the shoulder. Whatever, she was obviously dead.

He videoed the scene, and then told Hannah to come in. He stopped her in the doorway first and warned her "It's not nice."

Hannah nodded and then gasped as Crofts stepped to one side "Oh no!" she said with a whimper. She took a few seconds to take it all in before taking a deep breath, she then looked at Crofts and said "Sometimes I hate this job" before starting to take photographs of the awful scene with Crofts laying stepping plates on the floor in front of her.

Hannah took the initial general shots from the four corners of the room. This was known as quartering and was used at all scenes. She then closed in for general shots of the body and the blood staining before going in close to take as many photographs as possible without moving the body.

Crofts told her not to move the body for any further photos. He was going to call a ballistics expert to the scene, and they would want everything left in situ so that they could start their own examination knowing exactly how the bodies were found.

Crofts also had a good look around to make sure there wasn't a weapon in this room either, for the same reason as he had in the utility room. He couldn't see one.

On completion, Crofts said "Okay, that's all we are going to do for now, let's get out of here" and the three of them headed back down the landing and down the stairs. None of them said a word, all deep in their own thoughts.

As they got to the hallway, before they went outside, Crofts asked them both if they were okay. Hannah nodded slightly, but not too convincingly. Buster just shook his head and said, "I'm glad I didn't become a SOCO after all" and slowly walked out of the door.

Crofts walked out and spotted Tom Mead and his deputy, Alison Williams, in his car and got in. He then updated him with what they had found. "We will need a doctor to come and pronounce death" Crofts told him. Even though it was obvious that they were both dead in this case, protocol dictated that this was formally done. "I know we can get a paramedic to do it nowadays, but I'd prefer one of our forensic practitioners, as they are more used to the scene issues" he continued.

Mead told Alison, to get that organised, then asked Crofts, "Anything else?"

"I can't see any sign of a weapon near either of the bodies, so it's not looking like a murder suicide, although I can't completely rule it out until we've finished a thorough search. If it was that scenario, a handgun could've been thrown across the room due to the recoil and be hidden, but I doubt it in this case. The position of the wounds on both bodies appears to have been from a third party."

"I'd like to keep the bodies in situ overnight, and I'll organise a Ballistics Expert to meet us here in the morning, together with a pathologist. Neither will want the bodies moved if possible?"

"That's not a problem at all. I'd rather give the experts everything they want in this type of job. It is a Category A murder, so we need everyone on the ball."

He paused before asking "I don't want to put you on the spot, but do you think it is Natalie and Jimmy Fletcher that are the victims?"

"Sadly, I did recognise Natalie from her parents restaurants, I've seen her around them since she was a teenager. I don't think I've ever met Jimmy Fletcher but looking at the photos around the house, I would say that it is him" Crofts replied.

Tom Mead sighed, "It's just that Natalie's parents are outside in their car, as they came down to look for her. They're being looked after by Tam Mackenzie now. As a PCSO that task is way above his pay grade, but as we know him from old, we know that he's good for the task. However, I think it's only right that I go and inform them myself, as I am going to be leading the murder enquiry. I will have to tell them that they haven't been formally identified, but we do believe it is them, for now."

"Good luck with that" Crofts replied, "Don't know how you coppers deal with that sort of thing, at least with my job, I just deal with the dead ones. You have families to see and all sorts of emotions going on"
"I know" said Mead, "Not my favourite task, but here I go" he finished, as he got out and walked over to the steamed-up car parked on the roadside.

Chapter 32

John saw a figure heading towards their car and warned Julie "Looks as if someone's coming over to see us." His wife stopped her sobbing and looked out of the window, unsure of what was about to happen, and looking at Tam in the front seat. Tam got out and nodded at Tom Mead.

"Evening Guv" he said. "Evening Tam, thank you so much for what you have done. I really appreciate it. Could you ask Mr and Mrs Goldson to get out of the car, please?" he continued. He had decided on the walk over that this was done better face to face, rather than cooped up inside a car.

John and Julie got out and Tom Mead introduced himself and told them his rank and role.

He then hesitated before looking them both in the eye, making sure they were concentrating.

on what he was about to tell them. "I'm afraid I have some sad news to tell you" He paused, allowing the words to sink in. John didn't say anything, but he heard Julie gulp.

Mead continued, "We have found the dead bodies of a male and a female, who we believe to be your daughter, Natalie, and her husband." He paused again.

Julie fainted.

John and Tam quickly managed to catch her before she fully hit the ground, they then both tried to revive her, calling her name, and shaking her arm.

It wasn't how Tom Mead had expected this to go, but it did break the moment, of which he was glad.

After about a minute, Julie had come round enough to realise what she had just been told and sat staring at something in the distance before wailing "Noooooo" at the top of her voice. Everyone in the vicinity stopped what they were doing and looked towards Julie in her moment of anguish. There were a lot of experienced police personnel around, but none of them could be unmoved by this mothers torment at this moment. Julie dropped to her knees and started bashing the ground screaming "No" with every slap. John just stood, numbed by the whole situation.

Tam tried to calm Julie down, but it didn't work, so he let her get on with it, until she finally stopped slapping, and just crumpled into a heap, crying. John snapped out of his trance and consoled her as well as he could, while the SIO and his staff all looked around trying to concentrate on something else rather than the poor distraught woman.

After several minutes, and with Julie just sobbing quietly, Tom Mead asked John "Is there anything you want to ask me?"

John thought for a while before asking, "How did they die?"

Mead thought for a second before replying. "We believe they may have both been shot."

Julie screamed again, before wailing "Who would want to shoot my darling Natalie?"

Mead let her compose herself before replying "I have no idea at this particular moment in time, but I can tell you right here and now that we will find out who did it" he stated, "I will give you my promise as the Senior Investigating Officer on this case, that we will bring the killer or killers to justice."

John still hadn't spoken, but now his face crumpled, and his tears started to flow. Tam put his arms around both and tried to sooth them as Mead waited for them to release their collective grief.

It took a while, but when they were both through the worst, Mead continued, "We haven't formally identified them at this stage, as we need to leave everything as it is until we get some specialists in to help our enquiry, but my Crime Scene Manager recognised Natalie from your restaurant and is happy that the other deceased person is Jimmy from the photographs in the living room" He once again paused, before continuing "I will allocate one of my officers to be your Family Liaison Officer. They will be available to you twenty-four hours a day, seven days a week."

The Goldsons were now staring at Mead with tears in their eyes, he couldn't tell if they were hearing what he was saying, or not, but he continued "Now I must get back to the Major Incident Suite, to start the ball rolling on this enquiry. Is there anything you want to ask me before I head off?" Both shook their heads but didn't say a word. Mead hesitated before adding "I think it's best if you go home now. Tam will drive you" he looked at Tam who nodded in agreement. "The appointed FLO will contact you shortly, and you can also call me anytime you want, Tam will give you my number" The couple just nodded again. Mead then finally added "I am so sorry for your loss, and I know it is still a shock right now, but as I said before, we will get whoever carried out this awful act, I promise you." The Goldsons nodded again, and Tom Mead turned and walked back to his car.

Tam Mackenzie guided the couple back to their car and sat them in the back. Neither said a word as he headed back along the coast road to their house.

Chapter 33

After the medical practitioner had been, and confirmed both deaths, Crofts headed back to the office. There was plenty for him to do and several phone calls to make before he went home. As he went into the small recess that was the Seniors office, he saw a cup of tea waiting for him on his desk. He looked out into the main room and saw Leighton Phillips grinning back at him with a thumbs up. Crofts smiled, he was always glad when he had a tea maker on duty, but he also knew that the Welshman was trying to get in his good books, as Crofts would be picking his team for this job shortly, and as blood thirsty as it sounds, no SOCO would want to miss dealing with this murder.

When it came to an investigation like this, the shift pattern would go out the window, and Crofts would pick a team that could work with him on this job for a few days. It helped with continuity, especially when it got to court later. Defence barristers loved to try and accuse the SOCO team of anything that would undermine the evidence they had recovered, and this was an area they had used in the past.

It would mean that the SOCOs were available for those days, too. It was the nature of their role that they were expected to drop everything and commit to working a scene every now and then. Crofts and his staff had to remain flexible, they had lost count how many events they had to cancel in their private lives over the years for the job, but it was what they wanted. Some were more accommodating than others, depending on their personal lives. Those with children, or partners who also worked a shift pattern were sometimes unable to get cover, so all of this had to be taken into consideration.

Crofts took a sip of his tea, and then called Hannah and Leighton over.

"Do either of you have anything that you can't cancel over the next few days?" he asked. Both replied "No!" very quickly at the same time, and all three started to laugh.

"I take it you have already discussed this, haven't you?" Crofts said.

"We wouldn't do that!" said Leighton, and they all started laughing again.

"Well, that's good," continued Crofts "It makes it easier, as you have both already been to the scene. I will let Duties know to take you out of the shift pattern for the next five days, and we will see how we go from there."

They both nodded and smiled to each other. They were both glad to be on this investigation.

Crofts continued "Get as much as done as you need to tonight and get off early. I'll see you in the morning. Book on at eight, and then we can all attend the briefing at nine, okay?"

"No problem" replied Leighton.

"Will do" replied Hannah.

They then went back to their desks, giving a quick 'high five' on the way. Crofts saw it and smiled to himself. Nobody outside the police would understand how murders could make SOCOs happy.

Chapter 34

It was now time for Crofts to get on with his phone calls. The first was to the Coroners Officer. As usual Snowy answered with "I wondered when you would finally get to call me, I am quite important you know!" Crofts laughed, "I know you are. I always make sure I have all the correct information before I contact you" Crofts replied.

"Anyway" the older man continued "As you couldn't be bothered to contact me, I have taken the bull by the horns, and informed the coroner, and he is happy for you to continue with your scene investigation" Snowy continued with his little reminder to Crofts that it is up to the all-powerful Coroner to decide whether a death in his authority is investigated. "I have also contacted the Mortuary at the Conquest Hospital in Hastings, to save you the job, and they are aware, and will be available, anytime tomorrow."

"Thanks mate," Crofts replied "That's saved me some work. I imagine it won't be until mid or late afternoon, though. We've got quite a lot of work to be getting on with at the scene."

"That's okay, they're always up for some overtime. Theirs has been cut right down for their routine work due to savings by the hospital, so police work is a bonus."

"Great stuff" Crofts replied "I'm contacting a couple of specialists to attend. Do you need me to tell you who they are this evening?"

"No, it's okay, just let me know tomorrow. I don't need you phoning me up all night at home. I see enough of you at work" Snowy replied.

"Love you too" replied Crofts with a laugh and finished the call.

His next call was to the Forensic Pathologist Andrew Eaton. Crofts told him about the incident, and Eaton decided that he would attend the scene along with the other experts, meeting there at eleven the next morning. Crofts was pleased. The younger pathologists didn't attend scenes as often nowadays, some even said that they didn't need to as they could rely on photos, and their role was only to decide the cause of death. However, Crofts preferred that they did, believing that there were certain incidents where it was beneficial if they attended, so that they could get a real feel for the scene.

The next phone call was to Cellmark, one of the Forensic Service Providers that took over from the Forensic Science Service when it was disbanded some years before. Having explained to the receptionist what his request was, he was put straight through to their major crime department. Even though it was getting late in the evening, the phone was answered straight away, this was another department that was always ready for murder investigations. It was answered by a scientist called Jo Whatmore, a Lancashire lass who Crofts had worked with before, and was an expert in Blood Pattern Analysis, known as BPA. After the usual quick hello and niceties, Crofts explained the scene and what he required of their department. Jo listened intently and then replied, "What time do you want me there?"

Crofts smiled. He had guessed that she might want to take this on herself once she had heard the story. Again, this type of job didn't happen that often, and all those involved in these investigations would want to be part of them.

"Eleven o'clock will be great" Crofts replied.

"See you there then" Jo answered, also adding "Sounds like a good one."

Crofts agreed, and then made his last call, this time to a ballistics expert. These all used to be based at the FSS in London, but once disbanded, most of them went freelance, and Crofts knew of one who was local to them and called him.

"Hello, Phil Jenkins" was the reply.

Crofts introduced himself and told him the incident.

"Do you want me to come down now?" Jenkins asked, "I'm only half an hour away."

"Thanks for that, but no need" Crofts replied, before continuing "We have closed down the scene with the bodies in situ and are all meeting up at eleven tomorrow, if you can attend?"

"Of course I can" Jenkins replied "It sounds like an interesting case. We don't get many like this, do we?"

"No, we don't" agreed Crofts "Category A murders are exceedingly rare, I'll see you tomorrow."

Crofts put down his phone, and then started to write up all his decisions in his Investigators Notebook. Everything had to be recorded, his actions, and his rationale. Later, there would be reviews into the investigation, and every piece of information relevant to the enquiry would be examined by the review team. Crofts had learnt from experience that the more he recorded now, the better the outcome of the review later. Especially if things did go wrong during the enquiry. This was his insurance.

Hannah and Leighton finished and waved a cheery goodbye as they left, and Crofts quickly scanned his emails before shutting down his computer and then turning the office lights off and locking the door.

He checked the time, it was ten o'clock at night, and it had been yet another long day, with an even longer one to look forward to the following day.

He put his music on his headphones, grabbed his push bike, and then cycled out of the base to the sounds of Simple Minds "Waterfront.' A nice bowl of chilli and a glass of red were beckoning him.

## Chapter 35

The morning alarm woke Crofts from a deep sleep. Whether it was from the effects of a busy day, or the red wine, he didn't know, but he felt fully refreshed for the day. In the kitchen he had turned on the radio and got the kettle going ready for his early morning cuppa. There was no mention of the job on the news, but that didn't surprise him. Even in this day of immediate news, it was sometimes a while before the Force would release a press statement on a serious incident such as this.

His young son Oscar came down the stairs at break-neck speed "Hi Dad" he shouted, before jumping up into his arms "I didn't see you last night!" he exclaimed.

"I know, I was late off" replied Crofts.

"What were you doing?" his eager son asked, wide eyed.

"Just a few bits of this and that" he lied, unable to explain to a ten-year old that two people had been shot in cold blood, and that he was the crime scene manager.

"Did you see the results last night?" Oscar asked.

"No, I didn't have time, what happened?" Crofts replied.

Oscar then gave him the lowdown of the previous evenings matches, even remembering the goal scorers, without taking a breath. Crofts' wife Deborah walked in halfway through and sighed, shaking her head, "Is that all you two talk about?" she asked with mock horror once Oscar had finished.

"What else is there to talk about, apart from football?" Crofts replied, winking at his son. Oscar shouted "Yes!"

"You certainly dropped off to sleep quickly last night" Deborah stated, "You were asleep before I had finished brushing my teeth!"

"Must've been that lovely chilli" Crofts replied.

Oscar giggled.

"Come on you two, let's get breakfast finished" Deborah continued, "What do you fancy for dinner tonight?" she asked Crofts.

"Don't worry about getting anything for me" he replied, "It's going to be a late one tonight, I'll get something at work at some stage."

"Does that mean I won't see you tonight either?" Oscar asked sadly.

"It might do" replied Crofts, trying to sound concerned, "But if you're already asleep, you know I always come and say goodnight to you, whatever the time."

"I know" said Oscar "I nearly always hear you."

"I know you do" said Crofts, happy to play along, to cheer his little lad up. He was getting to the age when he really missed seeing him, but knew it was something that came with his job.

"Right, who wants a kiss before I go?" Crofts announced, before kissing his wife and son goodbye, and getting his pushbike out to ride to work.

U2 still hadn't found what they were looking for as he cycled along, towards the Major Incident centre which also housed the SOCO base. As he approached the outer gate, he could see that the car park inside was already overflowing. If he hadn't been involved in the scene the night before, he would have guessed that something was going on due to all the extra staff who had been called in to join the enquiry team. This was going to be another one of those days, Crofts thought to himself as he swiped his card at the reader and the gate swung open.

Chapter 36

Louise Jacks was a Family Liaison Officer, better known as a FLO. She had been in the role for seven years and was now one of the most experienced in Sussex. It was a role that had been originally just a temporary post, where an officer would be assigned to look after the victim's family, keeping them up to date with the case, and giving them any support they needed. However, it had soon become obvious that this was a role that needed proper training, and a more professional approach, and so the role evolved into what it was now.

Lou and her colleagues would be assigned to the family in any major incident. As well as all the tasks previously mentioned, they also became a major link between the victim's family and the SIO and would be at the family's beck and call, twenty-four-seven as they liked to call it. It was a demanding role, dealing with all the emotions of the bereaved, but at the same time being part of the enquiry team on a major incident. As they were all trained detectives, there were some cases where their investigative skills had spotted things while with the family which may have gone unnoticed without them.

Lou had been called the previous evening by Tom Mead and given a quick precis of the case over the phone. She had then called John Goldson and given him her details. He had declined her offer of going to see them that night, saying that they were too shocked and upset and would prefer to see her the next morning. Lou had then driven into the MIR and read the whole of the serial and had then researched the Goldsons and the Fletcher family as much as she could on intel and on social media, so that she had an insight to everything involved in this crime.

She had then got a good night's sleep, knowing that she might not get much over the next few days, and was now pulling up at the Goldsons house.

Having rung the bell, John opened the door. It looked as though he had slept in the clothes he was wearing and was unshaven. Neither fact bothered Lou, knowing what had happened to them the previous day, but she noted them mentally, as it was already an insight into the state of mind of the victim's parents.

John put the kettle on, the noise of which covered the sound of Julie coming into the kitchen. She seemed to glide in, and she was staring ahead, without acknowledging that Lou was there.

Again, all was noted by the experienced FLO, who then introduced herself to them. The coffees were now made, and so they went and sat out in the conservatory.

Louise started by explaining her role, and how available she was to them. They both appeared to be listening, she couldn't tell how much they were comprehending. She then asked if there was anything they wanted to ask her.

"Yes, I want to know why someone shot my baby" Julie shouted, before bursting into tears and hugging John. "Why, why, why? That's all I need to know."

Lou nodded reassuringly, "I have no way of knowing at this time, but I can tell you now, we will get to the bottom of this for yours, and Natalie's sakes" she let the words sink in before adding "This really is an unusual type of crime, and it will be something that I'm sure we will be able to solve."

"But how, and why our Natalie?" John asked, as Julie sobbed even louder.

"I don't know at this stage, but this wasn't an accident, and somewhere there will be evidence that will lead us to the perpetrators" Lou stated, reassuringly.

"It's got to be something to do with Jimmy" Julie snapped.

"What makes you say that?" Lou asked softly.

"Because everyone has always said he was 'dodgy.' Natalie hasn't got a bad bone in her body, and would never have upset anyone, let alone enough for them to shoot her, it's got to be something to do with him. I wish she had never met him" Julie cried.

John sighed "He's a great guy, he's always been good to us and doted on Natalie, but I always had the feeling that his business life wasn't exactly kosher. I've met a lot of people over the years in our own business and think that I'm a good judge of character. When I met some of his associates, I wouldn't have trusted them."

"In what way?" Lou asked.

"I couldn't put my finger on it, as they were also always friendly to me, and I had some good times with them, but I had the feeling that if I hadn't been Jimmy's father-in-law, I wouldn't have been welcome." John answered.

"The enquiry will cover all of that, they will be looking through his background and business deals, somewhere in the background there will be a reason this has happened" Lou told them.

"I hope so" replied Julie, "I can't believe someone could be so evil as to kill my Natalie. I hope they rot in hell whoever it is."

"I understand" Lou said, "We will catch them, whoever they are."

Chapter 37

Having grabbed a cup of tea, Crofts headed into the briefing room to set up the computer system so that he could show the images and the video at the briefing. The room was usually empty at this time of day, but there were already a few detectives in there, all holding brand new pale blue investigators notebooks, freshly issued for this operation.

Their chatter paused for a while as Crofts entered the room, but the banter started once they saw it was him.

"Hopefully, it's not too damp for your boys today?" someone called over, an age-old joke that was thrown at SOCO's when they were unable to find fingerprints outside due to the wet weather. It caused a ripple of laughter amongst his colleagues.

"Sorry, did I just hear a mouse fart?" replied Crofts to more merriment as he started up the system.

"What are we going to be watching then Crofty?" called another "Laurel and Hardy?"

Crofts sighed and looked at them "There's only one bunch of clowns around here, and they're all sitting over there!" he answered pointing at them.

The mock jeering started but stopped when other members of staff came into the room. As on all major enquiries, the team would be made up of officers from lots of different departments, and they wouldn't all know each other on this first briefing, so there was an air of caution as fresh faces arrived. If it had just been Crofts and the detectives, the leg pulling would have gone on longer.

Crofts was glad in some ways as it meant that he could concentrate on setting up. As usual, someone else had used the system previously, and had left it in a mess. Even though there were laminated signs explaining how to set it up, people were able to completely change the settings. It took him a while, but he soon had everything ready to go. He hadn't turned the main screen on, so that no-one got a shock at the images as they walked into the room. Crofts would only show them after he had delivered a warning to the enquiry team about the nature of the images he was about to show them.

Crofts sat back, checked his phone ringer was turned off, and awaited the arrival of the SIO and his deputy.

The room was now to its capacity, and the level of noise was getting louder when the door opened, and Alison Williams and Tom Mead walked in. Every conversation petered off, as everyone started to concentrate on the job in hand. This was when the real work would start for everyone in the room, regardless of their role in the investigation.

Mead welcomed everybody and introduced himself to them all. He then asked everyone to individually introduce themselves and their role to the rest of the room.

Crofts was first and then it continued around the room. Firstly, there were his team of Hannah and Leighton. There were detectives from the Major Crime Branch, followed by the HOLMES analysts.

Next, there was the uniform sergeant in charge of the house-to-house enquiry team, His officers would be carrying out interviews with neighbours around the crime scene, to see if anyone had noticed anything in the run up to the murders. Then there was the search team sergeant, they would be needed to initially search the outside areas of the property and may be needed for later searches in the house when the SOCO team had finished.

Lou, the FLO, was next, and then Snowy the Coroners Officer. There was a member of the Finance Investigation team, Jill Maynard. Her role would be to look through the finances of the Fletchers, to see if there were any clues as to why they were murdered.

There was also a member of the Media team, they would be controlling what was disclosed to the press. Due to the nature of the crime, all the main newspapers were interested, some had already published details, albeit guess work at this stage.

Finally, Kevin Bates, a detective sergeant, who was to be the Incident Room supervisor and Alison Williams the deputy SIO.

One of the detectives had already been allocated as the 'scribe.' This was to have a written record of everything that was said at the briefing.

Once everyone had introduced themselves, the briefing began.

Chapter 38

Tom Mead started by informing them that the operational name had been chosen as Op Willow. The names were on a list held in the Control Room and would be issued whenever required for a major incident. The name would stick though, and the crime would always be known by that name in the future and would be remembered by those who worked on the case as Op Willow.

Mead then explained briefly the circumstances leading up to the call to the police from the Goldsons. He then asked Crofts to take over the description of the scene, and to show the scene video.

Crofts stood up and told the hushed room "The video I am about to show you has some unpleasant images of the two victims. If anyone gets upset, or feels the need to leave the room, please do. I don't have a problem with that" He paused and looked around, but no-one had moved. "Okay, I will begin."

He started the video, explaining to everyone the outside of the premises, and then heading into the building, describing any significant points as he went along. As he approached the room where Jimmy's body was found he informed the room what they were about to see. As the video showed the deceased, Crofts paused the video and with an infra-red pointer, showed the audience the important aspects of the scene.

Again, not a word was said, as these experienced officers examined the images. Crofts did notice one or two were not looking too closely, as was their want, but all were fully concentrated on his account.

As he approached the area where Natalie's body was found, he again warned the team what was coming. He could feel tension in the room as the camera followed the blood stains from the initial attack area, up the stairs and into the bedroom. As the body came into view, Crofts heard several intakes of breath, and a couple of sobs as the reality of the state of her body dawned on everyone in the room.

He explained what they had established so far, before informing them of all the specialists who would be attending later that morning. He completed the video before asking "Anyone got any questions?"

The room was silent as everyone took in what they had just watched. There were many people who loved watching crime programmes on the television, but none of those could replicate what these officers had just seen.

Mead thanked Crofts and then went through what would be happening that day. The main event was to be the scene examination by Crofts and his team, along with all the specialists. This would then yield the information that decided how the investigation would proceed.

However, there were plenty of other lines of enquiry to get on with. The actions would be generated by the HOLMES system, which was already up and running.

Meads handed over to Kevin Bates to go through what was required of each department.

Detectives were given several leads to start investigating. The lives of the victims over the last few days needed to be scrutinised to establish a timeline for them, where they had been and who they had been with. The answers may be hidden there.

The FLO was given a list of the background information needed from the Goldsons about Natalie and Jimmy. He re-iterated that he knew that some of this would be hard for Lou to find out at this early stage, as the parents were still in a high state of grief, but as well as being a shoulder to cry on for them, it was also paramount that Lou was able to investigate at the same time.

The house-to-house enquiry team were given the list of questions to ask any of the neighbours. In this case there weren't many to question as there were only houses on one side of the street, with the railway on the other. The questions would not only cover what people had seen on the day of the murders, but also anything that they had noticed in the few days before. Unusual vehicles, people, or events would be recorded. In a quiet area such as this, these things stood out. There would also be a request for CCTV from all houses, as passing vehicles may have been caught on their cameras. They would also do the same at the Cooden Beach Hotel, and on the railway station. At this stage of the enquiry, anything could be in play.

The financial aspect would start later that morning once the banks had given permission to release the details of accounts for both victims.

The media side of things was also covered. At this time, it was just going to be reported that the bodies of a male and female were discovered deceased, at a property in Cooden Beach. Nothing was to be mentioned about how they died at this stage. Although some of the red tops had already speculated more. Social media had a lot to answer for in cases like this.

Mead waited for Bates to finish before adding "I can't express how important it is to make sure we do this job right. We have a husband and wife gunned down in their own home, which is not an everyday occurrence. I'm sure we will get to the bottom of the reasons why at some stage, but until we do, we need to keep an open mind. Remember the old detective adage of ABC: Accept nothing, Believe no-one, and Check everything."

He looked around the room at the eager faces watching him, before adding "This is a Category A murder, and we don't get many of them, so make sure everyone of you, and your teams, are on the ball with this one, and do your utmost to give us a successful outcome for the enquiry, and for the families of Natalie and Jimmy."

With that, Mead and his deputy left the room, leaving the rest of the enquiry team to chat amongst themselves about the tasks they were about to commence.

Chapter 39

Crofts wasted no time after the briefing. He was out in his car straight away, heading through the rush hour traffic, as he wanted to get to the scene early, to greet all the visitors. Leighton and Hannah were just behind him in their van. They arrived after about twenty minutes. Since the property had a gated entrance, it made things a lot easier to manage. As they pulled up outside, an officer opened the gate and let both vehicles in. The three of them started putting on their white over suits. This was followed by shoe covers and gloves, and then finally a hair net and mask.

Crofts went over to the officer beside the front door of the villa and asked him for the scene log. This was a crucial piece of evidence as it showed exactly who had been into the scene and at what time they attended. If this wasn't filled in correctly, it could be used as another way of discrediting the evidence from the scene. In the past, cases had been lost when an important piece of evidence to the case had been thrown out of court as the officer who had exhibited the item had not been signed into the scene, leading to the defence that the said item could not be used in court.

Crofts had a quick check through the log. He was showing as the last person out of the building the previous evening, and then it was just the officers who had changed over as scene guard through the night who had updated the log. "That's good" said Crofts to the young officer on the door, "No-one's been in at all."

"Don't blame them" The officer replied glumly.

"You'd be surprised" replied Crofts "Some people will find any reason to have a nose around."

He noticed the younger man looking a little pensive and remembered that he had been told before that those working as scene guards were sometimes the most susceptible to emotional stress disorders. The fact was that those physically attended the scene saw everything that was to be seen, but those outside just got to imagine what it was like inside, and it was that which affected them the most.

His thoughts were interrupted by a Land Rover pulling up outside and the driver pointing at Crofts to the scene guard at the gate. Crofts waved back and beckoned him in, it was Phil Jenkins, the ballistics expert. A tall, dark-haired Welshman who was always loud and cheerful. They had met several times over the years, so after the usual pleasantries he informed Jenkins that he would be waiting for all experts to arrive, so that they could walk through together. Crofts spotted another van arriving, and went over to meet the scientists, leaving Leighton and Jenkins talking animatedly about their hometowns in Wales.

The scientist, Jo Whatmore, was a short, slight young woman, she had bought along an assistant, Heather, who she introduced to Crofts. They had also worked before on several murders over the years, so had a quick chat about that before it was time for Crofts to welcome their final member of this team, the Pathologist Andrew Eaton. As he had travelled from the West Country by train, he would normally have needed picking up from a railway station. As the scene was just across from the Cooden Beach station, he had walked along the road. As usual, Crofts noticed, he was looking worried. When he had first met him, Crofts had found this a little disturbing, but once he had realised that was his usual demeanour, and that it hardly ever changed, Crofts had relaxed. Having worked with him at scenes and in post-mortems, he knew that Eaton was a highly skilled forensic pathologist.

The next few minutes were taken up with them all putting on their individual PPE, before walking over to Crofts and his team, where he introduced them all to each other. He then told them that everything had been videoed and photographed, and that he would brief them properly once they were inside the building.

Crofts had already noticed several other vehicles in the usually quiet road and had seen cameras being set up and microphones prepared, as the members of press arrived. It failed to surprise him how quickly they turned up at incidents. No matter how remote the location, or how vague the details of the crime were, they would attend. Although they were quite a way from the road, he was aware of their zoom lenses and even zoom microphones and would prefer that they didn't overhear his briefing. They would already have taken images of them in their over suits, which were already enroute to their agencies.

Each member of the team then gathered up their equipment and queued to inform the scene guard their details before stepping through the front door and into the scene.

Chapter 40

Louise Jacks again waited outside the front door of the Goldson's house, having rung the bell. This was the time of an enquiry that she dreaded the most. She had only met them briefly and had then gone to a briefing where she had not only learnt a lot about the case, but had also seen the scene video, which, in this case wasn't very pleasant at all. It was the time when all her skills as a FLO would come to the fore. Her empathy with the victims' family had to be measured up with her investigative skills, as this was a murder investigation that could go any way possible. It had been known in the past that the grieving relatives at the start of an enquiry turned out to be part of the reason the victim had been killed. Although in this case, Lou didn't believe that would be the scenario. It was that good old fashioned 'gut feeling' that several of her old mentors had told her about years ago, and which, she liked to think, she had developed.

Julie answered the door looking a lot brighter than when she had seen them earlier. Lou could see she had showered and applied a little make up, although the mascara was already starting to streak. As she made the coffee, John also walked in fresh from a shower. Lou was pleased. Although it would not help their grief, she was glad to see that they were trying to pull themselves together, which would make things easier as the next few days progressed.

Lou sat down with them both in the conservatory and gave them an update on what had happened so far in the enquiry, deliberately missing out any details of the injuries that she had seen. She explained the process that would take place that day, and how each of the experts would be involved. She tried to make the procedure sound as impersonal as possible, not allowing the Goldsons to worry too much about what was happening to Natalie and Jimmy. She then told them that once the scene examination was completed, that the bodies would be removed from the scene and taken to the mortuary at Hastings, where post-mortems would be carried out on both deceased. On completion, they would need one or both to attend the mortuary in the hospital to identify them formally. She looked at them both, before John replied "I will do that. I don't want to put Julie through it." Julie glanced up at him quizzically but didn't argue with her husband's decision.

Lou was pleasantly surprised how they were both holding it together, and decided to ask:

"I mentioned it earlier, but I wouldn't be surprised if this crime has happened because of something in the background of either Natalie or Jimmy? Is there anything that you can think of that either of them has mentioned recently about any issue that they were worried about, or involved with?"

John replied for them both "We have been talking about this all morning, we've racked our brains thinking back to the last few times we met up with either or both of them" his voice wavered as he remembered some of those meetings, but then he coughed and continued "We can't think of a single thing. Natalie has been over to us several times recently, and seemed as happy as she always was, and when Jimmy was over as well, he seemed the same. We can't think of any reason anyone would do this?"

"That's okay, I thought I would ask again" replied Lou, "Sometimes it can be quite obvious from the start that something was going on in victims' lives, but not always." She paused before continuing "However, you did mention this morning that you thought it would be something to do with Jimmy's acquaintances?"

"I know I did," John said with a sigh, "It's just that Natalie was so well liked by everyone, I can't imagine her being the reason. Jimmy was quite a popular guy, too, but as I said before, some of the company I have met with him have not exactly been angels" He paused again before continuing "I couldn't name names, but I just guess that somewhere along the line, Jimmy may have upset someone for some reason" He looked nervously at Julie, which Lou spotted straight away, and focused her gaze on her before asking "And what about you, Julie?"

Julie shrugged and replied "The same as John. It won't have been anything to do with Natalie, it must have been about Jimmy" she paused before continuing "I will admit that Jimmy wasn't the type of bloke that I would have wanted Natalie to get involved with. He was completely different to any previous boyfriends, who were usually her age. When she first told us about him, I did have my reservations, but when we met him, he was so nice to us both, and we could see he worshipped the ground that Natalie walked on, so we were happy for them both. The wedding was amazing, and since then they have appeared so blissfully happy together, so my early worries were overtaken by the fact that everything seemed good between them." Julie let out a breath, as if she was glad to have got that off her chest.

"I understand" Lou told them "We will be checking through their contacts by mobile and computer systems, to see what we can find. I'm sure we will find the reasons behind this."

"If it is all about Jimmy" Julie suddenly blurted out "Then why did they have to kill our Natalie as well?" she continued "Why couldn't they have just spared her?"

Lou knew it was an impossible question to answer at this stage of the enquiry, so told them "There's no way of knowing at this time, but I'm sure we will be able to give you some answers in the very near future."

"I do hope so" Julie replied starting to weep quietly.

John put his arm around his wife and pulled her to him before adding "Please do" to Lou.

Chapter 41

Once they were in the hallway, Crofts gave them all a briefing, starting with an introduction to the scene. He didn't bother showing the video or images because they were there.

He explained how he wanted the examination to proceed, "First of all, I think we should walk through together so you can see everything. No need for any examination at this point, just an overall assessment. Is that okay with everyone?"

Everyone nodded with agreement, Crofts continued "After that we can come back to here and discuss the way forward, and how we will examine the specific areas. We all have distinct roles, but we can't all work in there at the same time, so we need to work out how we will do that. It will mean a lot of hanging around at times whilst others are carrying out their examination, so we will all need to be patient" he paused, "Everyone happy with that?" again nods all round. "Let's go" he said, leading them along the hallway.

As he proceeded with his little group of followers, Crofts gave a running commentary on what they knew so far about each area. Once they got to the room where Jimmy was found, Crofts warned them all, and then stood back, and let everyone go in individually as the room was so small. Each person took their time, surveying what they could see, and working out in their minds what they needed to do. Once they were all out Crofts then led them around the rest of the ground floor, continuing with his commentary. None of these areas were of interest to the experts at this time, but Crofts knew that these may be the areas where they could yield evidence of the suspect with their thorough examinations over the next few days.

They arrived back in the hallway, and Crofts explained what they had found on the stairs, and then led them one at a time past the evidence they had already seen, to the doorway of the bedroom. Outside he gave them a quick run through of what to expect, and then led them in. It was slightly awkward as they all stepped from stepping plate to stepping plate, but they managed it.

Crofts then let them look at the scene in front of them, the dead body of Natalie being the most obvious item, but he knew that the specialists would also be thinking through what pieces of other evidence in the room they would be recovering.

After a couple of minutes, Crofts led them all down the corridor, and back down the stairs to the hallway.

Once everyone was listening, he started "I don't like to hypothesise too early, but my early thoughts are that the killer or killers were let in by the Fletchers. There appears no obvious forced entry to the property, and there are two coffee cups in the kitchen, and one upstairs. The male deceased, Jimmy Fletcher, appears to have been shot in the back downstairs. The white powder that was sprinkled over him tends to lead us to believe that it is about drugs, but we can't be sure at this stage. There has been some sort of altercation on the stairs, with shots being fired, and that the female, Natalie Fletcher has been wounded. She has been able to crawl along the landing to her bedroom and has died there?" he looked around "Anyone want to add anything at this stage?"

Phil Jenkins spoke "I agree with that scenario, and I would like to add that one of the injuries to the female, in the middle of the forehead, was after she arrived in that bedroom, and was the final shot. I'm sure Mr Eaton would agree, she couldn't have crawled that far having been shot straight through the brain?"

They all looked at the pathologist who nodded his head and then agreed "Yes, a shot to the head like that would mean instant death. I agree with all the hypothesis so far."

Everyone else nodded in agreement. Crofts then organised with them how they would go about the scene examination.

Chapter 42

In the Major Crime Suite, everyone was busy. It was the sort of buzz that all members of the team enjoyed. Getting their head around the crime, setting up all the systems, arranging interviews, and starting to arrange all the Actions that the HOLMES system was already pumping out. The man in charge of the room, Kevin Bates was in his element. Having amassed over twenty years in Investigations, this was what he liked most. A murder with no known suspects, a real whodunnit as the crime writers would call it. In a provincial force such as Sussex, they didn't have more than half a dozen a year, and few as good as this one.

He knew that his role was pivotal in the investigation, but he wasn't worried about the pressure that would bring, in fact, he thrived on it. He had a team of highly trained professionals, and he knew they wouldn't let them down.

He had already read all the early statements that had come in, so that he knew exactly what was going on. He would end up reading every single statement that came in during the enquiry. He knew that the HOLMES system could be trusted, but he also liked to read every item so that he always had a full knowledge of the case. He would eat, sleep, and live this job over the coming weeks, there would be no let up, and not much sleep. He'd already messaged his wife to tell her that the New Year's Eve party they were due to attend in two days' time might not be on. She'd just sent a smiley back as she was used to him and his job.

One of the analysts, Anita Marshall, a thin dark-haired woman who had only been on the team three months was hovering in front of his desk. He was so engrossed in a statement that he didn't realise she was there, and it was only a slight cough that brought him back into the room.

"Sorry, Anita, I didn't see you there. You should have said something?" he said.

"I didn't like to bother you" she replied, reddening.

"Don't be silly, I'm ready for any added info, so what have you got?" he asked.

"Well, you know we were looking for any names or information about suspected contract killers in the local area?" she asked, with a worried look on her face, as if she had got it wrong.

"Yes" said Bates, noticing her hesitancy, and trying to put her at ease.

"Well, there are quite a few on the system, as you would expect, although they seem mainly to have connections with London" she continued, again looking nervously at the seasoned detective.

"That's not too surprising" he agreed, trying again to appear open to suggestion.

"I know London isn't too far away, but it's quite hard to leave this area without being seen, nowadays" she continued.

"I'll agree with that too" Bates replied.

"So, I decided to see if there were any that had connections with Sussex, especially the coast?"

"Good thinking," said Bates.

"I've found a man called Tommy Tomlin he goes by the nickname of Hitman. He's ex-special forces, and seems to be working in a variety of jobs, close protection, and the like?"

Anita looked up at Bates, before continuing "Well, I looked up his recent movements, and his Facebook profile was updated as being in The Victoria, a pub in Eastbourne on Christmas Eve."

"Right" said Bates, encouragingly, "Anything else?"

"Yes" said Anita "I have just tracked his whereabouts over the last two years, and he has been in the same area as three other contract style killings" she finished with a frightened look on her face.

Bates couldn't tell if it was because of him, or because of what she had uncovered about this individual.

"Sounds good" he replied "I'll get one of the outside enquiry team to see you, and then we can follow up on that information. Well done for the research, it's attention to detail that always finds this sort of nugget, you've done well."

Anita felt relieved, she was so glad that she had been able to get her information over, and that it appeared that it could be of some use. She went back to her desk feeling happy.

Chapter 43

Crofts and the experts then decided on the strategy for the examination of the scene. They decided that there were three primary areas to examine. The locations of the two bodies, and the area on the stairs where Natalie had originally been shot. These were the only areas that were of interest to the specialists. The rest of the house could be done in slow time over the next few days and weeks by the SOCO team. Today was all about yielding as much information and evidence as possible from the principal areas, and then carrying out the post-mortems.

As everywhere had been photographed, now was the time that the bodies could be moved, and all areas checked for further clues. Firstly, Hannah took samples of the white powder from Jimmy's body, before the pathologist took swabs from all areas of exposed skin to later look for the offenders DNA. Hannah then fibre taped all areas of the body and clothing. She used lengths of adhesive tape, which she lightly patted in all areas and then stuck on to clear acetate sheets. These would later be examined for hairs and fibres which could have come from the offenders. They also took tapings for gunshot residue, to check whether he had fired a gun at some stage during the altercation with the offender.

Once she had finished, the scientists logged all the blood, recording all dimensions, directions of travel, and swabbing all areas. The pathologist and the ballistics expert then examined the wounds at the front of the body, and then rolled him over to look at the back. As Crofts had guessed, those on the back were the entry wounds, two small holes, indicating that Jimmy had been shot from behind.

Having completed their initial examination, they carried on to the stairs, leaving Hannah and Leighton to bag up the body. The hands and head were covered in small polythene bags with string ties. This was to recover anything that fell off during the moving of the body from the scene to the mortuary. The body was then wrapped in a large sheet of polythene which was secured at each end and around the middle using tape, and then put inside an unzipped body bag which was then secured. They then left it in the hallway for the time being.

Up on the stairs, the blood staining was again dealt with by the scientists, logging, measuring, and recording. Once that was finished Jenkins took the lead. Having recorded them as they were, he now took a closer look at them through the carpet and into the wall. He then took three thin metal rods and poked them into the holes as far as they could go. This then gave him the angle that the bullets had been shot, which would then lead him to working out at where the shooter was when they had fired. Together with the bullet marks on the body, he would later be able to comment on where the victim was when she was shot.

Having recorded them fully, he then started digging into the plaster, and the wooden stairs to recover the imbedded bullets. These would be used later to match to any potential weapon recovered. The striation marks left on the bullet head, and the firing pin marks on any empty shell casings would be unique to any one weapon.

He then followed up the scientists, who were by now following the blood trail to the bedroom where Natalie's body lay. They continued right up to the body and then handed back to the SOCOs and pathologist, who carried out the same sample taking procedure that they had earlier on Jimmy. Once finished, it was back to Jenkins who, together with the pathologist examined the bullet wounds on Natalie. She had been shot through the right shoulder and cheek, as well as the one in the middle of the forehead, all were from the front.

Jenkins spoke "It looks to me as if she has been shot on the stairs through the shoulder and cheek, and that she has only been wounded. She has then been able to crawl towards the bedroom but has then been shot at point blank range in the middle of the forehead." Eaton nodded in agreement.

"I wonder what she was doing, or where she was heading?" Crofts asked.

"Might have been going for that" Eaton pointed towards the bedside table where a mobile phone was charging. "She was obviously trying to reach it."

"Do you think that she would have been conscious enough to do that?" Crofts asked.

"If what I am thinking had happened, it looks like she was only slightly injured from the two initial shots, the third shot we saw on the stairs obviously missed" Jenkins replied "It was only when the final shot, in the middle of the forehead was fired that she collapsed where we found her. Do you agree, Doc?" he replied, looking at the pathologist.

"Yes" said Eaton "The shot through the shoulder and then through the cheek would hurt but would not completely immobilise someone. She would have been able to move that far easily. It looks as if the offender has shot her and left her for dead on the stairs, which we can tell from the blood staining?" he looked at Jo, who nodded in agreement, before continuing "She has then been able to crawl along the hallway and into the bedroom, towards her mobile. The offender has then realised she isn't where he left her for dead, and has then shot her in the head, execution style,"

Jenkins nodded in agreement before adding "Perfect explanation, Doc. It really is that style of shot, so close I can see gunshot residue around the wound on the forehead."

Crofts let all the information sink in before asking "Does anyone else need anything from the scene? Or are you happy that we bag the bodies and head over to Hastings for the post-mortems?"

All nodded in agreement. Crofts called the two SOCO's up to wrap Natalie's body the same way that they had dealt with her husband's. He then called Snowy to tell him to contact the undertakers to attend to remove the bodies and take them to the Conquest Hospital in Hastings.

He called the incident room and told them the information that had been gleaned so far. This would be passed down to those who needed it at this stage.

Ten minutes later, the dark coloured transit van with 'Private Ambulance' arrived at the front door. It was the same crew as the day before, so Crofts had a joke with them about stalking him, which they found funny as they all had a similar sense of humour. They then loaded both bodies onto their trolleys in the hallway, and then took them out to their vans under a barrage of flashlights from the waiting press photographers.

Chapter 44

Graham Johnson, known by everyone as Johnno, had been a detective for twenty years, the last ten on the major crime branch. He was a Geordie, and even though he had left home in his early twenties, still had a strong accent. He was fair haired and liked to call himself 'portly' which sounded better than overweight. He was one of the outside enquiry team, which meant that he could be tasked with an action of any description at any time. This could be something simple as interviewing a witness on the periphery of the enquiry, right up to interviewing the main suspect in a murder. That type of interview would take hours of preparation, and could lead to hours of interview, too. This was another role within the police that didn't keep to office hours. He was often required, at the drop of a hat, to work on until whenever.

Depending on what part of the investigation they were working on would establish who he would be involved with. On this, one of the early days of the operation, he knew it could be anything or anyone. He went into the incident room and after a quick hello and a chat with several members of the team, headed over to Kevin Bates. The sergeant had a quick look through the ever-growing pile of actions in front of him, before pulling one out with a flourish "This one has your name on it my Geordie boy" he said with a smile.

"Oh no!" the detective wailed "The sarge has a smile on his face while handing me an action. That's not a good sign!"

"The opposite in this case, you will enjoy this one" Bates replied.

Johnno read the action, and then looked up at his boss "That sounds intriguing. What have I done wrong?"

"Nothing at all, I need you to use your excellent investigative skills to track down this man, and for you to get him interviewed" the sergeant continued, "Nip over to see Anita Marshall, and she will fill you in with the details."

"Okay, I'm on my way" Johnno replied, and headed over to where she was sat.

Anita looked up worriedly, "Hello pet, how's it going" the detective asked in his usual, friendly way.

"I'm fine" Anita replied, easing now, as she realised that Johnno was one of the friendlier detectives on the team.

"Do you want to update me on what you have found so far?" Johnno said, easing himself into a swivel chair and scooting towards her.

Anita then explained her search for suspected contract killers in the area, and how she had found this man. She then explained how she had researched other similar killings and matched that up with the whereabouts of the suspect at the time of each offence. "Of course, it's not an exact science" She said with a worried look, "It just may be a coincidence."

Johnno looked at her and said "It doesn't matter. At this stage of the enquiry, it is the only name we have, and we can soon rule him in or out once we have a word with him"
Anita visibly relaxed on hearing that. "That's okay, at least I'm not sending you on a wild goose chase."

"No, you're not. There's no way of knowing who is involved in these murders, so every snippet of information could turn out to be important." Johnno told her, "Now I just need some information with regards to his whereabouts. Any idea where he lives?"

Anita checked her notes before replying "He doesn't appear to have a home address, but from what I can find out, it looks like he stays with different mates, due to the type of work he does?"

"So, what does he normally do then?"

"It appears that he works all over the country, usually doing close protection work, or bodyguarding different people all the time" she continued.

"That type of work is like that, they just move from contract to contract" Johnno told her "I've got a mate who does it, he was in the Diplomatic Protection team when he was in the Met. Once he left, he just carried on the same role, but getting paid double what he was earning as a cop."

"Really?" Anita asked.

"Oh yes, there's loads of that type of work once you get on the circuit" He continued "It's just that it is not constant, so they tend to flit from job to job, but always on the move. Not a job for a married man."

"I'm sure it's not" Anita stated, "But that also means that they travel around a bit, so no need for a permanent address?" she asked questioningly.

"Exactly!" the detective replied with a thumbs up "So no-one knows where they are either. A wonderful way of hiding your movements."

"That's not a problem, I'll have a check through his social media, and see whether he, or any of his associates mention where he is now?" Anita asked.

"Okay, will it take long?" he asked.

"Depends, but no longer than half an hour" Anita replied.

"Oh. That's good," Johnno answered, "I could do with a coffee. Anyone else want one?"

Several affirmatives from around the room made him realise that he had made that mistake again. He tutted and rolled his eyes, knowing that it would pass the time away while he waited for the analyst to produce some info.

Chapter 45

The journey from Cooden Beach to the mortuary had been broken up by a quick stop at the drive-thru McDonalds at the Ravenside retail park enroute. Huw and Hannah joined Crofts in his car and the three of them tucked into their meals hungrily. It was always a clever idea to have something to eat before attending the mortuary. There had been instances in the past when they had not had time to eat due to the circumstances, and that had led to people passing out.

"How did the pathologist travel over to Hastings?" Huw asked, "I thought you usually get lumbered with him?"

"He travelled over with Phil Jenkins" Crofts replied.

"I can see a bromance starting there" said Hannah, "Did you see them going through their evidence together earlier on?"

Huw and Crofts laughed. "I'm not sure that constitutes a bromance!" Crofts replied.

"You never know" Hannah said in a hushed voice.

They all laughed.

Crofts was pleased. It took a short break like this to get them through the day. Fast food and humour usually did the trick.

They eventually pulled up at the mortuary and parked up in the bays outside. Crofts buzzed the intercom "Hello Darling, come in, you lovely SOCOs" the voice answered.

Crofts smiled to himself, it was the Mortuary Manager, Linda Pearce. She was a larger-than-life character, very loud and jolly, unlike how most people imagined morticians would be. They had worked together many times over the years and got on well. For all her fun and laughter at this stage, Linda would soon become the serious professional once the real work started. Crofts carried some of the equipment in for Hannah and Huw, and then went through to the office. Snowy was already there, with a cup of tea and a biscuit in each hand.

"You don't waste any time, do you?" Crofts stated, winking at Linda.

"That's his third cup, and he's nearly eaten all the biscuits" she joined in the leg pulling.

"No, it's not!" Snowy exclaimed "I've only just got here, and I bought the biscuits!"

"That's what you say" Crofts replied, "I'd rather believe Linda."

They both laughed, as the buzzer went again. It was the scientists.

"Do you know them?" Linda asked.

"Of course, I do" Crofts replied, "Who else would be asking to come in here randomly in the afternoon?"

"You never know" replied Linda with a chuckle "There's a lot of odd people about!"

They looked at each other and then both looked at Snowy before starting to laugh again.

"Now what?" the older man asked.

"Nothing" said Crofts as he welcomed the scientists into the office and introduced everyone to each other, and to Tom Mead who had also just arrived.

The two SOCOs also came into the office having set up their equipment in the PM room.

"Who are we waiting for? Linda asked.

"The pathologist and the ballistics expert" Crofts answered.

"I told you!" Hannah replied.

"What?" said Linda always the one for gossip.

"Bit of a bromance going on there!" Hannah whispered.

"What?" said Linda, her eyes widening.

"Stop it now" said Crofts in a stern sounding voice, although he was laughing.

Linda then said "It's Andrew Eaton, isn't it? I can't imagine him having a romance with anything other than a dead body!"

They all laughed, but the merriment was interrupted by the buzzer announcing the arrival of the last two members of the team.

Linda buzzed them through, and Hannah and Snowy took the orders for teas and coffees.

Andrew Eaton declined, saying that he and Jenkins had stopped for a bite to eat and a drink on the way over. Hannah's eyes widened in surprise, and she mischievously looked at Linda, which caused them both to smile, but nothing was said at this stage as it was time to put on their professional hats.

Crofts shook his head in mock disappointment, but carried on "Does anyone want to say anything, or update us before we get started?"

Everyone looked at each other and shrugged, but then Mead interjected with "We do have a loose suspect."

"What does loose mean?" Jenkins asked.

"Someone local who has a military background and is known as 'Hitman.'

The SIO continued "He also happens to have been in the area of other contract shootings over the last few years."

"That sounds interesting" Jenkins replied. "I was probably involved in one or two of those, I might even get a couple of them cleared up if he is our man."

Mead nodded before saying "It's early days yet, so we'll just have to see what happens if we can find him?"

"That doesn't sound too promising?" Jenkins asked.

"I'm sure we will" said Mead "With modern smart phones it doesn't take long to track someone."

"Okay" Andrew Eaton stated, "Everyone ready to go?"

Everyone nodded and approached the anteroom to put on their PPE. Once dressed they headed through to the more sterile PM room, where they could see two mortuary slabs with body bags on, one smaller than the other.

Chapter 46

Anita Marshall had taken even less time to find the suspect than she first thought. She had checked his social media accounts first. He didn't seem to use most of them at all, which meant that she was worried that this may have been to keep a low profile, but then she found on Facebook that he posted a daily joke to all his friends. They were some of the corniest jokes she had seen, but it didn't matter.

His account was ramped right down on the privacy settings, but that was only for average users. She was an expert on how to get the most from the background use of the system. She investigated the comments section of each posting and was able to expand his network of friends, and through them, build up a family tree of his associates and their locations. From that she could then work out their movements.

She found that he had been working away in the Southampton area in a close protection role for the owner of a mobile phone company who had previously been getting threats from organised crime groups. He had finished that contract and headed back to his hometown of Eastbourne a few days before. Since then, he appeared to have been out enjoying himself in the pubs and clubs with various friends over the festive period. His local pub was the Victoria, a popular pub in the Seaside area of Eastbourne, one street back from the seafront. He was there most days, sometimes for the entire day and usually until it closed.

Anita finished the cup of tea that Johnno had made her and called him over from where he was studying something on his computer screen the other side of the incident room.

"What you got then, pet?" he asked as he walked.

Anita felt herself blush, although didn't know why, then cleared her throat before saying "I think I know where he is right now!"

"What?" exclaimed Johnno, "I heard you were good, but I didn't realise you were that good!"

Anita smiled at the recognition. "It was quite simple really," she continued, explaining to the detective what she had found.

"So basically, he's in The Vic now?" he asked on completion of her findings.

"It looks like it. Two of his associates messaged each other to say that they were meeting him there tonight at about seven" she said triumphantly, before adding "And it looks like they will be staying in there all evening, as one of them commented on hoping there would be a lock-in as he's not at work tomorrow."

"Great stuff!" shouted Johnno, making Anita blush again, "Now all I need is a team to go and arrest him about seven." He looked over at Kevin Bates who had just put his phone down, "Sarge, what's the chances of you giving me a couple of bods to go and arrest our suspect?"

Bates looked up, amused, "You what?"

"I've got a location for our suspect in a couple of hours-time. Can I have some help?"

The sergeant smiled and said, "I'll need a bit more information than from you just trying to be Columbo!"

Johnno smiled and walked over to his supervisor "You'll be eating your hat later, when I have him in the bin."

Bates smiled "So, go on then, what have you got?"

Johnno explained what Anita had found, Bates agreed that it sounded good, but then said, "I'll have to run it by the SIO first and then we can think about the arrest, but it might not be as simple as you think"?

"What do you mean?" Johnno asked, looking deflated.

"Well, we will be trying to arrest someone who we suspect has shot two people, so it will mean that we will need a full firearms team for the arrest" Bates answered.

"Shit, I hadn't thought of that," Johnno admitted, "But we do know his whereabouts, so surely, we can get a team ready. They will be out and about somewhere anyway, won't they?"

"Of course they will" Bates replied "However, an operation such as this needs a full strategy and an amount of planning, they don't just turn up and run into the pub!"

"I know" replied Johnno, "But surely we can get something sorted in the next hour or so?"

"I'm sure we can" replied the sergeant, "Leave it with me."

Johnno thanked him and turned away. Bates was sure he saw a skip in his step as he headed back across the room.

Chapter 47

Eaton decided to start with the post-mortem on Jimmy. It looked as though it would be the easiest of the two. The two bodies had been laid out by the mortuary staff on separate slabs at either end of the room. Jimmy was at the far end away from the viewing gallery, so everyone congregated there. The SIO and his deputy had gone to sit in the gallery, some might say that it was they didn't like attending post-mortems, but there were several other reasons. Firstly, it was just to keep out of the way. It got busy at certain times of the examination, and two extra people didn't help, but it was also because they were likely to be receiving and making plenty of calls during the hours that the procedures would take, and so it was easier if they didn't keep interrupting the process. They could see and hear everything that was going on and could also step into the room if it were needed. As important as the post-mortems were, there were plenty of other parts of the investigation that would need their attention whilst they were there.

Having photographed the body still in the body bag, the mortuary assistants then opened the bag, and more photographs were taken. As all the fibre takings and DNA swabs had been taken at the scene, all that was needed now was to take off the clothing and place it in exhibit bags. As each item was taken off the body it was individually photographed and then bagged in a brown paper exhibit bag. This was then signed and sealed there and then. This would ensure that there were no questions raised by the defence teams in court about what may have happened to the exhibits.

Once the body was completely unclothed, the assistants washed the body down, and further photographs were taken of the exit wounds. The pathologist measured them again, now freshly cleaned, before dissecting them further and, working with Jenkins, made a thorough examination of them. He then started a normal post-mortem, cutting the front of the body open, and checking the organs before removing them. He would have to establish that there were no natural causes of death, although highly unlikely in this case. As he came to the area where the bullets had moved through the body, he and the ballistics expert would then work together to establish the exact path they had travelled. One of the bullets had gone through the heart.

"What a good shot" Hannah said.

"It is a perfect shot, especially from behind" replied the pathologist, "The shooter was either very skilled, or very lucky" he continued.

He then continued with the rest of the internal examination, and having found nothing untoward, he asked the staff to turn the body over so that they could examine the entry holes from the outside. Again they photographed, measured, and dissected the area. Once done, he then told the others "There is no doubt that the cause of death is from the gun shots from behind." He nodded to Snowy, who had been note taking for him, and he duly wrote it at the bottom of the form.

"Right" said Crofts, "Shall we have a quick twenty-minute break before we start the second PM?"

Everyone nodded in agreement. They would all have to change their PPE before commencing the next one to avoid cross contamination. It would give them time to do that, as well as time for a stretch, or a drink or to use the toilet. It was already half past seven, so it was going to be a late finish, a break now would make things easier.

Chapter 48

The Victoria Hotel in Eastbourne, known by everyone as 'The Vic,' was a popular pub.

It was what many people would call an 'old fashioned boozer,' and it was this that kept it busy. There weren't many left of this type. So many chain owned pubs had concentrated on the food market, and all but killed off the drinking side of things, but The Vic had managed to stay a drinking pub, even though they sold great food if required.

The landlord Geoff, and his wife Rosy, had built up a good clientele over the years. All ages and all levels of society were regulars, giving a great community feel, and everyone got on well together. There was hardly ever any trouble, and if there were, it was usually sorted out by one of the many rugby players who frequented the establishment.

It was s group of these who were starting to get a bit louder this evening. Geoff was keeping a watchful eye on them, although there was no need for him to intervene at this stage. The nights between Christmas and New Year were invariably quiet, and these boys were big drinkers, so he was happy to let it go for now. Two of them had been in since lunchtime, he didn't know how they did it, especially as they were drinking Guinness, but he also knew they were on a bit of a celebration. One of them, Tommy, had been away on a close protection contract for a few months, and so was making up for lost time. Like many men in those type of jobs, he spent extended periods of his life not drinking, making sure he made the most of it when he was home. Geoff had earlier asked him if he wanted anything to eat, he was met with the reply "Eating's cheating!" and laughter from his mates. It made Geoff smile as it was the reply he always got from him.

As there were only a few other people in the pub, he let them get on with it for now, making a mental note that he would give them another half hour before checking on them again. He grabbed the TV remote and started to check through the channels to see what sport he could show on the screens dotted throughout the pub. As he looked up at the screen beside the door, his eye was attracted to a movement outside. Before he could register what it was, the door flew open, simultaneously with the other door and figures in black rushed in shouting "Armed Police, everyone on the floor, hands where we can see them" He also heard another shout from outside in the beer garden, where they must have climbed over the wall to get in.

The rowdy customers did as they were told. One of them started a "What the f…." but didn't finish the sentence. Even though they had been drinking all day, they were sensible enough to know that what was happening was serious.

"Stay where you are. Don't move" was the next order.

"What the fuck is happening?" one of the voices on the floor asked.

"I said, stay where you are and don't move" replied the same voice as before, a little louder and with more menace.

There were then a few whispers before one of the officers tapped Tommy on the shoulder, "You, get on to your knees and leave your hands where I can see them."

Tommy did as he was told. He knew that this wasn't the time to mess about. As he knelt, he could see three Heckler and Koch MP5's trained on him and guessed there were others behind him.

"Put your hands in front of you. I am going to handcuff you, so no mucking about" the threatening voice barked through his black balaclava.

Tommy gave him a filthy look but didn't say anything. Now was not the time. He held his hands out in front of him. The handcuffs were applied, and then a man wearing a suit entered the pub and stated:

"Tommy Tomlin, I am arresting you on suspicion of murder. You do not have to say anything. But it may harm your defence if you do not mention when questioned something which you later rely on in court. Anything you do say may be given in evidence."

"Murder? What the fuck do you mean murder?" Tommy shouted at the nearest man in black, who stared back at him without replying. "What the fuck is going on? I haven't murdered anyone. What do you think you're doing you bunch of nobs?"

Again, no reply was given by the balaclava men or the man in a suit. He was then man-handled out of the door and into a waiting van, where he was placed in the back and the door locked.

Graham Johnson waited until the door was secure, before going back into the pub. The other drinkers were still on the floor being guarded by armed officers, as was Geoff behind the bar.

"Okay lads, you can get up now" he said. The armed officers cautiously relaxed their fire positions and took a step back.

"What was that all about?" one of the men asked.

"Never you mind" replied Johnno, "I'm sure it will all be sorted out quickly," he said before walking over to an ashen faced Geoff and saying "I'm sorry Landlord, but due to circumstances, it was the only way we could do it. Hopefully, there won't be any further interruptions to your evening. I bid you farewell" and with a mock bow he left.

The firearms officers also lowered their weapons and said a murmured goodbye on their way out.

Geoff stood open mouthed, not really knowing what to say. He looked over at the others who were also the same. He turned round and grabbed a bottle of Brandy and some glasses, before pouring them all a drink.

"This one's on the house" he said, before gulping his down.

The others followed suit, none of them saying a word.

Chapter 49

In the twenty-minute break, they all had a chance for a drink and comfort break, before heading back into the PM room, in clean PPE.

As with her husband previously, the body bag was photographed and then opened before further images were taken. As all samples had been taken, Linda then carefully washed Natalie's body down with water. The wound marks to the face and shoulder were then examined by the experts. There was a lot of murmuring and nodding of heads before Eaton stated, "I think we are all in agreement," the others stood back as he announced "The wound to the shoulder was a superficial injury, fired from in front of the body, but not causing too much damage, almost passing clean through. She would have survived that one." He paused and looked at the others before stating "The gunshot wound to the cheek was also of slight damage, almost grazing the flesh before exiting just below the ear. Again, on its own, it would have been survivable." The others were listening earnestly now, awaiting the crucial update. "But it is the third gunshot wound which has been fatal. It appears to have been point blank from the front, directly at the forehead. Thus leaving a small, neat hole at the front, and a larger gap at the rear, with some brain material also discharged. We will see more once we get to look at the inside of the skull more closely." he finished.

"So it was like an execution then?" Hannah asked.

"Yes, it was" the pathologist replied, "It looks like our early hypothesis was right. The offender has shot her twice, and thought she was dead. He's then gone elsewhere, and when he's returned, the victim has been able to move towards her phone which was in the bedroom on charge. He has then gone right up to her and fired straight in the forehead to make sure she is dead."

"That must've been awful for her." Linda exclaimed.

"Yes, it would have been" Eaton answered, "She would have been in a lot of pain, but her faculties would have been intact, and she would have known what she was doing, until the offender put a gun to her forehead and shot her again."

"Evil bastard" Linda snapped.

"Indeed" Eaton replied.

He then gave a moment for everyone to absorb the information before continuing, "Right let's get on with the remainder of the PM." And everyone went back to their positions as the medical side of the examination, to establish there were no underlying health problems, commenced.

As expected, with a healthy young woman, there was nothing to suggest that Natalie had anything which would have led to her early death. Eaton then asked Linda to prepare the skull for examination of the brain. Linda had already donned a large face mask and now connected the cylindrical saw to the power supply. "Stand well back everyone!" she called, before starting the device. It was a hand-held instrument, with a round cutting saw of about two inches. It had a loud whirring sound which increased as the blade started cutting into the bone of the skull. It gave off a strong smell of scorching bone, which was not pleasant. Linda expertly cut a line around the middle of the skull. When the line was completed, she stopped the cutter, and placed it down before using a small wedge-shaped tool to carefully prise the top from the bottom of the skull. Once completed, she would normally take the brain out at this stage, weigh it, and put it on the examination table for the pathologist to look at. However in this case, she left it in situ so that the gunshot wound could be examined.

Eaton and Jenkins then measured the remains of the skull, making notes as they went. They also examined the brain, and Jenkins was able to push one of his probes through to show the trajectory of the bullet. Once recorded, Eaton took the brain out on to the slab, and slowly cut through, so that once dissected, they could see the path the bullet had made.

All the members of the team converged on the table when he had finished. It was an unusual sight for them all to see, and something that didn't happen often. It was also something that would be good for the jury to see to explain, when it got to court.

On completion of the postmortem, the mortuary staff continued with their work, which was to prepare both bodies for identification purposes, something they did daily, although in Natalie's case it was much more complicated as she had the wound on her forehead. Linda managed to wrap a bandage around which would cover the mark but would still enable her to be formally identified.

Tom Mead and his deputy met up with Eaton in the office. "I imagine you won't be surprised to know that both victims died of gunshot wounds" he stated seriously. Mead nodded, as the pathologist continued, "Jimmy died of a gunshot wound to the back and through the heart, and Natalie from a gunshot wound to the head."

Mead thanked him and the other specialists for their work, and then headed off back to the MIR.

Crofts looked at his watch, it was nearly midnight. He realised everyone had been on the go for a long time. "Thanks to you all for today, sorry it's a late finish, but we have got a lot done, and we have had some satisfactory results" he looked round and could see tired eyes looking back at him, "Are you all okay for getting home tonight?" everyone nodded "Right, you can all get going. The SOCO's I will see you tomorrow morning, the briefing is at nine. I will update the rest of you with the details from that later in the day. Thanks again for all your input, it has been invaluable. There were murmured goodbyes, and everyone left to drive home. Crofts got in his car and headed back to Eastbourne.

Chapter 50

Tommy Tomlin arrived at the Custody Centre in Eastbourne. He had had time to sober up on the short journey, and was telling himself to remain calm, something he was struggling to do due to the circumstances he found himself in. He had been arrested several times over the years, for assaults, but had never been accused of murder, and realised that he needed to keep switched on over the next few hours. He knew he hadn't done anything wrong but had no idea what they were going to throw at him, and he needed to be sharp.

On entry to the block he was taken to the Custody Sergeant where Graham Johnson read out the reason for arrest. When asked if he had anything to say, Tommy remained calm and replied "Yes, I do. I have no idea what this is all about, but if you can give me some details, then I can help you see that I am innocent?"

The sergeant looked at the detective "Are you able to give the prisoner any information at this stage?"

The detective thought a moment and then replied "We have a medical and a forensic strategy that needs to be followed, and so we can't interview you until after that has been done. That's the policy."

Tommy remained calm, "But surely, if I am able to negate your suspicions of me, I won't need a medical, will I?" he replied, trying to sound as helpful as possible.

The Custody Sergeant agreed, and added "It does seem a waste of time, if the prisoner is able to prove he wasn't involved?"

"Of course he would say that" Johnno answered, "All prisoners say they are innocent when nicked."

Tommy seized the moment and said calmly" Look, I understand what you are saying, and I am happy to go ahead with the full procedure if required, but I am telling you, I have no idea what it is I am meant to have done? I finished a work contract a few days ago and have been on the lash since then."

Johnno thought for a moment, and then replied "I need to clear it with the SIO. If you can just wait in that interview room over there, I will see what I can do?"

Tommy was led over to the room and waited while the detective called Tom Mead. He returned to the room a brief time after and told Tommy that it had been agreed that they could ask him a few questions about his movements over the last few days before deciding whether to continue with the procedure. "Thank fuck for that" Tommy replied "Someone with some sense at last" he added.

Johnno ignored the dig, and sat down with Tommy in the interview room, and started the tape machine. "Why are you doing that, I'm not in an official interview?" Tommy asked.

"I know that, it's in case anything comes up during this chat, which may be needed for use in court at a later date" the detective replied, before continuing "It can also be used to your advantage to prove your innocence at a later date, so I would play the game if I was you, you're lucky to be in this situation" he reminded Tommy.

"Okay, cool, let's get this over then." He replied.

"So, can you tell me about your exact movements over the last few days?"

"Yes, that's easy" Tommy replied "I finished a close protection contract on Christmas Eve and headed down here to Eastbourne. I spent Christmas Eve at my mate Nobbys' house. Woke up the following morning, watched his little ones open their presents and then went to The Vic for a lunch time session, before going back to Nobbys' for Christmas dinner. Stayed there all evening, played some games, and then got my head down" he stopped, and looked at Johnson, who nodded. "Boxing Day, I was down The Vic all day, got shitfaced, and then back again to Nobbys' house. Is that enough?"

"No, keep going" replied Johnson.

"Ok, so the next day, the 27th, I went to The Vic all day, drank a lot, and then headed back to another mate, Jacko's house, where his missus had made us a curry, ended up sleeping the night there. Today was another session, which was ruined by your lot!" Tommy ended.

"Can you tell me why you are allegedly sleeping at these random addresses, when you have a house of your own not far away?" Johnno asked.

"Yes, because I am always away on jobs, I rent my house out, so it's easier if I just cadge a sleep whenever I'm back. I'm due away on the second for a new contract down in Dorset." Tommy replied.

"You've obviously got very good mates, and even more understanding wives" Johnno remarked.

"They all love me!" he replied, "Seriously, we have known each other years, and have all helped each other out over that time, so it's never a problem."

Johnson read the notes he had made before replying "According to what you have just told me, you were in the company of either of your two pals throughout the last few days, is that right?"

"Yes" replied Tommy, "Why, what was I meant to have done?"

"I'd rather not go there at this time" replied the detective, "I need to make a couple of phone calls and speak to your mates to verify your story before we do anything else. Do you want anything to drink while you are waiting?"

"I suppose a pint of Guinness is out of the question, so I'll settle for a coffee he replied with a grin.

Chapter 51

Crofts got back to the Eastbourne office quickly. It was so much easier to drive around when there was nothing else on the roads at that time of the night. As he parked up, he could see plenty of lights still on in the offices of the major crime suite. The first few days of murder enquiries always meant long days for most departments, and he knew that this case would involve more, due to the nature of the killings. It wasn't a run of the mill job that could be dealt with quickly, as many of their other major enquiries were.

He went to his own office first, just to check through his emails to make sure he was up to date with any added information or any updates from the Labs, before seeing the SIO. There was nothing too exciting in his inbox, generic emails, and a couple of annual leave requests, so he quickly approved them before heading up the stairs to the MIR.

It was, indeed, a hive of activity. Even though it was approaching midnight, it looked to Crofts as if nobody had gone home. Hardly anyone looked up as he entered the main office, all were engrossed on their computer screens or reading statements. One or two were still on phones. Nobody looked the least bit tired; all were enjoying the excitement that a murder brings to the detective world.

Crofts saw the pile of pizzas that had been ordered in, and grabbed a slice, realising how hungry he was. Although ordered hours before, it was surprisingly still warm, and he ate it as he headed round to Tom Meads office.

The door was open, but Crofts could see the SIO, his deputy Alison and Johnno in conversation, so stood outside as he finished off his snack. Tom Mead spotted him outside and waved him in. "Hiya Crofty, Johnno here is just telling us he has lost our only suspect" he said with a straight face, but with a wink towards Crofts.

"That's not true at all" exclaimed Johnson "He's got an alibi which checks out for the last few days."

"Really?" asked Crofts "How does that come about?"

The detective sighed and went through the whole statement again. He then went on to explain that having spoken to the two friends, both Nobby and Jacko had corroborated the story. He had then returned to The Vic, and checked the CCTV, which had also backed up Tommy's story. Indeed, looking through the recordings, not only was he in the pub at all the times he had said he was, the amount of Guinness he had consumed over the period, would have meant he wouldn't have been capable of firing a gun, let alone hitting a target. They could also prove from his phone records that he had been at the houses when he said he had been.

"I also asked him why he was known as "Hitman?" Johnno paused before replying. "It was because he used to be a boxer, and one of his favourite fighters was the "The Hitman, Thomas Hearns," and he just liked it as a nickname."

Crofts laughed "I must admit, I didn't really see a professional contract killer calling himself "The Hitman" on Facebook!"

Meads and Williams joined in the laughter, and finally, Johnson, failing to keep up the hurt look of someone who had just lost his main suspect from a murder case, also joined in. It was that loud that the incident room supervisor, Kevin Bates, popped his head around the door.

"Everything alright?" he asked with concern.

"Absolutely fine" replied Tom Mead "Apart from the fact that we no longer have a suspect in this case!"

"Oh no," Bates replied, "So what's so comical?"

"I'll let Johnno explain!" Mead replied.

"Not again!" Johnno cried, making the other three start to laugh again.

"While he does that, I think it's about time that the rest of us stop for the day, don't you? I'll see you all at briefing in the morning."

Crofts left, as he walked down the corridor, he could hear Johnno earnestly explaining why he no longer had a suspect in the main room, and it made him smile again at the thought.

How many other jobs could have such a serious day ending like this? He thought to himself, as he went to the locker room, and got himself ready to cycle home. He put his headphones on and pressed the play button on his phone. Meatloaf's 'Dead ringer' started to play, as he headed off along the cycle path to home.

Chapter 52

The briefing room was a buzz of excitement as everyone started arriving, all carrying their blue investigators notebooks, and most of them carrying a cup of something. There was plenty of friendly banter between officers from the different departments, some of whom hadn't seen each other since the last enquiry they had worked together on.

The forensic experts had headed over and sat next to Crofts and the SOCOs, so there was some general chat about what time they had all got to bed, and what time they had had to start. Although there was an obvious lack of sleep, none of them looked tired. The only person missing was Andrew Eaton. As an on-call forensic pathologist, he had already been called to another part of the country for a stabbing. In general, it was unusual that they would attend a briefing anyway, as their report would be given by the Deputy SIO or the crime scene manager.

Mead and Williams entered the room at the stroke of nine, and the crescendo of noise faded away as they took their seats.

Mead started "Good Morning ladies and gents, and welcome to the first full briefing for Operation Durham" he paused a moment, knowing that nearly every person in the room would write that down on the front of their notebooks, "We are now heading to the Northeast for our operational names" There were a few laughs around the room.

Mead then introduced himself and his team, before going round the room, to let everyone introduce themselves and their role. As it was a full room, this took a while. Once finished, Alison Williams then took over with a potted guideline of the events, enabling everyone on the enquiry to know what had happened. Depending on their role, some would have known more than others, but there may have been officers who had come in straight from a rest day, unaware of what had been happening.

Crofts was then asked to show the scene video. As usual at this point, Crofts gave a warning to everyone in the room that the images they were about to see were not nice, and that if anyone felt that they needed to, they could leave. As well as seasoned detectives and forensic experts in the room, there were also some who would have never been to any crime scene due to their role, let alone a double shooting.

On completion of the warning, Crofts started the video he had taken the day before and started a commentary. He could feel the nervous tension in the room, as the video slowly showed the walk into the house, only easing when the image of Jimmy Fletcher was showing, and he could almost feel the sense of relief as officers took in the details on the screen, almost glad that it wasn't too gruesome a sight. Having paused the video while he explained what they had deemed had happened to Jimmy, Crofts had started the video again, and he could feel the tension rise as they approached the second body. Having explained what they thought had happened on the stairs, Croft's video then slowly traced the route that Natalie had taken, until it arrived at her body. There were a few intakes of breath, and even an "Oh no" from someone, as they all came face to face with the sad vision of Natalie.

Again Crofts paused the video and explained what the experts believed had happened. As he stopped to let the information sink in, he looked around the room, and could see the upset and anguish his scene video had caused. He had a quick sense of guilt, as his role meant that he was used to this type of thing, but many in the room weren't, but there was nothing he could do about it. They all needed to see the scene, as it would help them understand the investigation better. At the end of the video, Crofts asked if there were any questions. There weren't. He was used to that. Crime scene images had that effect on people as they were all letting what they had seen, sink in.

Crofts then introduced Phil Jenkins and Jo Whatmore, and they gave a more detailed brief on what they had deduced so far. On completion, Alison Williams read the notes from the post-mortem.

All the way through, officers were writing down notes as they listened, trying to take on as much information as possible. The nature of their roles meant that at any stage, the tiniest morsel of information could be the clue that eventually solved the case, and none of them wanted to miss it.

On completion of the forensic side of the investigation, the other aspects were then briefed. The backgrounds to the victims, with the FLO explaining their family backgrounds and relationships. The Finance Officer, Jill Maynard, gave a quick overview of the business details she had been told about so far by the family. These were quite scant at this time, but she was sure her team would be able to find a lot more information once they had access to his accounts.

The house-to-house team sergeant had already produced a document which would be used by his officers when they visited all the neighbouring properties. They would be asking owners if they had seen anything suspicious or different in the last few days or even weeks. There would also be similar enquiries around both Jimmy and Natalie's places of work. No-one knew what the motivation for these murders was, and every avenue would have to be explored. It would all be collated, as anything could be the key to unlocking this investigation.

After finishing with an update from Kevin Bates on how all statements and reports, both electronic and paper, should be submitted to the incident room, Tom Mead thanked everyone for their time and work so far. He then reiterated how important every scrap of evidence and every piece of information was. He also went on to say that every single one of them were needed to help solve these murders, and that they would eventually crack this case. He then sent them on their way.

Chapter 53

Crofts waited around to see if anyone had any queries, but nobody approached him. They all had plenty to do at this stage of the enquiry and were all eager to go. He had a brief chat with the SOCO's and experts and told them what to get on with for the time being, until he had agreed with the SIO about what the strategy would be, and then headed up to the SIO's office.

Alison had just made the drinks as Crofts walked in, rolled her eyes, and said, "I suppose I had better make you one now?"

"Go on then" Crofts replied, "You've twisted my arm" he joked.

The meeting consisted of the SIO, his deputy, the office manager, and the exhibits officer. Once they had all settled down, Tom Mead began "So, Simon, it looks as though your team maybe the key to this one, don't you think?"

"It might well be" Crofts replied, "Although there's not a lot of evidence so far, and if it's a professional hit, then those guys are good, and won't leave much evidence behind" he noticed the glum looks around the table and then added "But that's how we like it, the smallest amount of evidence the better, and we'll find it!" He saw the smiles return around the table.

Mead recalled what they had learned so far. We are still awaiting results on any phone triangulation in the area, although it is a crap signal around there. Also checking whether their Wi-Fi picked up any alien signal." He looked around the team before continuing "The offender was known to the Fletchers, as there appears no forced entry, and indeed, they had a coffee together. "I take it that will be priority to get to the lab?"

"Indeed" Crofts answered "The SOCO's are recovering it as we speak, and after this meeting I will prepare the lab submission form, and we'll get a motorcyclist from Traffic division to take it directly to the Lab. They will start working on it this evening, so we could have a result by tomorrow afternoon."

"I didn't think they would do that anymore?" Williams interjected.

"They don't normally, as they feel it's no longer part of their role." Crofts replied, "However, I spent a lot of time on a fatal RTC recently with their sergeant so he owes me one, and anyway, the potential evidence from these exhibits could solve the case, and would then save thousands of pounds, so justifies our use of them."

"Good thinking" Williams responded.

Crofts continued "So we will be looking for DNA from saliva on the cups to start with, which will give us the best result, and then also fingerprints."

"That's good, fingers crossed we get something" Mead replied, "Is there anything else to be fast tracked?"

Crofts thought for a moment "Not really at this time. If we try and put ourselves in the offenders place, there's not much he would have had to touch? We've swabbed the doorbell, and fingerprinted the door, but they hardly ever give a result, so they can go on the next submission. He has recovered all the empty cylinders, again showing us he knew what he was doing. We will focus on recovering as much DNA, fibres, shoeprints, and fingerprints from the areas of social interaction, and then the areas around the body. If we get someone in custody soon, they might all help."

Mead nodded and looked around the table "Any other ideas at this stage?" Everyone shook their heads. "Okay Simon, you get on with that, and get those cups off, asap. We could have this case cracked by tomorrow!"

Crofts smiled "It is never going to be that easy, Guv."

"I know" replied Mead "But we have to remain positive!"

"I know" Crofts replied, "But don't blame me if we don't get a result from them."

Bates smiled and said "You know we always do. It's part of the routine!"

Crofts smiled and shook his head before leaving the room.

Chapter 54

Having completed the submission and prepared the exhibits, he waited for the motorcyclist to arrive. When he did, he seemed quite happy with the prospect of a quick run up to the lab and back. Crofts guessed that he had had harder days at work. He then prepared a forensic strategy covering what had been decided so far. This would be a live document which could be added to whenever needed, depending on how the investigation was moving. It would also be dependent on results from earlier submissions, thus cutting down costs.

Every single exhibit submitted to the Lab, could end up costing a thousand pounds or more, depending what techniques were used. So the budgetary restraints had been put on lab work over the years, as some of the older enquiries had almost bankrupted some police forces.

He then headed out to the scene, grabbing some coffees for the team on the way. On arrival, and having donned his PPE, he was then logged in by the scene guard, a young female PCSO who looked a little scared. Crofts asked to have a look at the scene log, and she nearly jumped with fright.

"It's okay, there's not a problem" he told her "I always like to make sure that firstly it is being maintained, and secondly, that no-one has been into the scene that shouldn't have been while we weren't here" he continued, noticing the officer relaxing a little "Believe it or not, in the past I have found officers have been in the scene overnight who didn't need to."

"Really?" she asked.

"Yes, and some of the reasons have been pathetic" Crofts continued "Not only is it unprofessional, but it can also give the defence lawyers a way of questioning what that person was doing in there and why, leading to the jury believing that evidence has been altered."

"Oh no!" the PCSO replied, looking shocked.

"But there's nothing to worry about in this case" Crofts told her before entering and calling out to the rest of the team to join him.

Whilst they removed their masks and found somewhere to sit and drink their coffees, Crofts gave them a rundown of what had happened at the management team meeting and gave an outline of the forensic strategy. He finished it with "So, there's no pressure on us, but if we don't deliver, we might not solve this one!"

"Nothing changes there then" Leighton replied with more than a touch of sarcasm, which made Crofts smile.

Phil Jenkins then said "The problem with any contract shooting, is that the offender does know what they are doing. Whereas when a murder is committed following an assault, there is lots of chances of forensic materials being passed back and forth, whatever type of evidence we are looking for. In these type of cases, it is minimal" There were a few nods in agreement, before he continued "If you think about it, he has knocked at the door, been let in, had a conversation with the victims, even a cup of coffee, so minimal chances of cross transference. He has then shot Jimmy in the back, again no contact, and then gone and shot Natalie. It is only the fact that she then moved which has had any disruption, if she had died from the first bullet it would have been even cleaner." he paused again "However, he has then taken time to recover all the empty cylinders, which would have been a useful source of evidence. So, even less for us to deal with."

"Do you think he would have stolen anything?" Hannah asked.

"Not normally" Jenkins replied, "They have been paid to get rid of the target, and that's what they get paid for. They don't want to waste time searching for stuff, they want to get away as soon as possible. Also, anything stolen could easily be traced back to him later. He wants to be in, do the deed, and then out of there, as soon as."

There was a hush as they all took the information in. Crofts then told them "That is why this is such a hard scene to deal with. Minimal contact, and minimal time in the scene.

Obviously, the coffee cups are our best bet, but even if we get a DNA Hit, it doesn't prove a murder. We must go through everything with a fine-tooth comb and see if we can find that nugget that will unlock the case" They all nodded in unison.

"So I know this is going to be a slow process, but we need to recover every single bit of evidence we can, every swab for DNA, every fibre sample that we recover could be the most important exhibit later. Nobody knows where this enquiry will go, but we need to be happy that we have covered every eventuality in this scene. Everyone happy with that?"

They all nodded, and Leighton added a "Yes boss" knowing that Crofts didn't like being called that. Crofts just smiled and shook his head.

Chapter 55

They continued the scene examination for the rest of the day. Phil Jenkins decided that he had finished his work at the scene at about two in the afternoon, and said his goodbyes, and then Jo and Heather finished an hour later. Having thanked them all and seen them off, Crofts returned to the room where Jimmy had been shot, where Leighton and Hannah were still working away. "Just the A team left now then Boss?" said Leighton. "As usual we're the last ones left" added Hannah. "That's why you love your job so much" replied Crofts, getting ready to dodge anything that was thrown at him. There wasn't anything this time, as the two examiners were too busy. They had already amassed over two hundred exhibits from this small room alone. "I would suggest we call it a day when you have finished in this room. It's been a long couple of days, and then we can start afresh tomorrow morning?" both looked pleased, the end was in sight. "How much more is there to do?" Crofts asked "Just the final set of carpet tapings and then that should do it" replied Hannah.

"Okay" Crofts replied "I think tomorrow should start on the landing, and depending how well you get on, we'll leave the bedroom until the day after. Any objections?" Both shrugged, "In that case, whilst you two finish recovering those last items, I'll start taking the exhibits to the van." Leighton gave him a thumbs up as Crofts grabbed the first pile of brown bags. All exhibits had to be handed to the Exhibits Officer directly from the scene every evening. It was a slow process, but again enable them to dodge any questioning about the continuity of exhibits.

They finally left the scene around six pm and headed back to the office. They had both decided that a pizza was in order, as they had hardly eaten over the last couple of days, so Crofts ordered it while they handed the packages over to the exhibit officer.

They arrived back in the office the same time as the pizza delivery driver had called to say that he was outside the building. Crofts grabbed them and laid them out on the table, and the three of them tucked in. Nothing was said as they started on the first slices, but after a while Leighton asked, "What do you think?"

Crofts finished his mouthful before answering "About what?"

"About this job" Leighton replied, "You're an ex-military man, what do you think about this shooting?"

"Well, I can tell you that it was carried out very neatly" Crofts said, before adding, "Apart from when he didn't finish Natalie off with his first two shots. He would have been annoyed about that."

Leighton nodded, before adding "But the ballistics guy said that he would have shot them, and then got out of there quickly? But he obviously didn't, because she had time to move up the stairs, and into the bedroom, heading towards her phone. So he must've been in the house for a while?"

Crofts thought for a moment and then replied "Good thinking. Yes, the fact that he was still in the scene whilst Natalie did that shows that he was doing something else?"

"Also, doesn't that show he was doing something downstairs, or he would have seen her moving?" Hannah added.

"It surely does" replied Crofts, enjoying the moment, "I wonder what he was doing?"

"Something that was worthwhile, rather than making as quick a getaway as possible?" replied Leighton.

"I'll go and tell them in the room" said Crofts, finishing a slice of pizza.

He headed up to the incident room, he saw that the SIO's office door was closed, so there was obviously a meeting taking place, so he headed over to Kevin Bates who was deep in concentration reading yet another statement. He sensed someone stood by his desk and looked up. "Hello Crofty, what can I do for you?" he asked. Crofts explained the hypothesis that the SOCO's had produced. As with most members of the major crime team, no-one ever said no to an idea, sometimes the strangest thoughts turned out to be true.

"Yes, that's a thought" Bates replied at the end of the explanation "I wonder what it was he was looking for?"

"Whatever it is, it must've been good to hang around after he has finished the hit?" Crofts answered.

"Hmm" mused Bates, and then told Crofts "I will have a word with Louise Jacks, the FLO. See if she can get any ideas from mum and dad as to what there was worth stealing? You say there was no signs of a messy search, but if there was something targeted, and this man is obviously professional, there was something we haven't been told?"

"That sounds about right to me. Let us know if you find out?" Crofts asked.

"I will do, although I will tell Lou to call them in the morning. The last thing they want during their time of grief, is random questions at ten o'clock at night" the sergeant replied.

"I didn't realise it was that late" exclaimed Crofts, "I'd better get off before it's time to come back to work!"

"I know the feeling. See you tomorrow" Bates called as Crofts headed out of the door. He locked the now empty office and got ready for the cycle home, the sound of U2 with "The streets have no name" blasting through his headphones.

Chapter 56

The last couple of days had been worse than they could have imagined for the Goldsons.

Not only had they had to get used to the shock of what had happened to Natalie and Jimmy, and how. They had also had a barrage of calls, messages, and callers, including knocks on the door from the Press, at a time when the last thing they wanted to do was talk to anyone, let alone them.

They had also had to decide what they would do about the two events, on New Year's Eve and then New Year's Day at the restaurant. It hadn't taken them long. Neither of them had the energy or the motivation needed, and so they had decided to cancel both. It had caused a stir on the local social media, some of which was quite personal, and indeed nasty, but John didn't let Julie know.

There would be plenty of time for them to recover in the future, if they needed, but at this time, John didn't think he would ever want to return to the restaurant. He honestly felt like his stomach had been wrenched from him. He had heard of people talking about how deep grief could go but had not realised it would be as bad as this. He had experienced sadness before at the passing of both of his parents, but they had been elderly and ill, so it was expected. Natalie's death wasn't.

The only thing that stopped him completely from going under, was to show his care and support for Julie, who was still in a dazed state of shock. She had hardly spoken more than a few words over the last days. She just sat, staring out of the window and sobbing. She was inconsolable, but John tried his best to help her.

At about eight thirty his phone rang, and he saw it was Louise Jacks, so he answered. She said she wanted to come round and see them again. His first thought was to say no, but he also realised that she was just doing her job, and that it might help to have an update of how the investigation was proceeding. Louise had been in touch several times by phone the previous day, but it was a good thing for her to see them personally.

She said she would be about half an hour, so John told Julie to get a shower, and then took one himself, to pass the time, rather than just sitting staring at each other.

Lou arrived and John made coffee, whilst the FLO tried to engage his wife in small talk, without much luck.

Once they were all sat down, she asked them how they were coping, and explained about the support she could get them, with Bereavement Counsellors and anything else they required. John told her that he still felt it was too early at that moment, and she told them that they could take their time, but that all that support was there for them. She then gave them an update on what had happened in the enquiry in general, in the last couple of days. She explained about the coffee cups and the fact that they may get a result that day, and how the forensic teams were still working at the scene.

She then explained about the fact that they believed that the offender might have been looking for something in the house after the shooting. John and Julie looked at each other and shook their heads. They couldn't think of any valuable item off the top of their heads.

Lou told them to have a think about it, and if anything came to mind for them to call her. She was about to leave when John said, "Hold on a minute, there is something!"

Julie looked at him in amazement, Lou with surprise.

"Jimmy had a hidden safe!" John exclaimed.

"How do you know?" Lou asked.

"He was on about it one day at football. He'd had a few and was telling me about something to do with some cash he needed for a deal and said, "I'll look in my hidey hole.""

It was all coming back to John, now "When I asked him what he meant, he said he had a floor safe in the living room under the carpet for cash that didn't need to go through the books."

Lou had already pressed a number into her mobile, and it was answered straight away.

"Batesy, I'm with the Goldsons. John remembers Jimmy telling him he had a floor safe under the carpet in the living room. He told him one day when they had a few drinks."

"If he told one person after a few beers, he might've told others" Bates replied.

"Exactly" said Lou, trying not to sound too excited whilst still with the grieving parents.

"I'll get on to Crofts and his team to have a look around for it" Bates told her.

Lou turned to the Goldsons "That is a useful bit of information, and we will be searching for it straight away. I understand how hard it is for you at this time, but please try to think of anything else that may give us an idea of why they were targeted"?

John nodded "Looks like I'll have to think through some of our drunken conversations at the football!"

Lou replied, "It's looking like it."

She said her goodbyes and headed out to her car. Was this the tiny piece of information that would lead to this crime to be solved?

Chapter 57

The SOCO's were slowly working up the stairs and along the landing when they got the call. Painstakingly slow progress, photos, fibre taping, carpet samples, and DNA swabbing area by area.

So when Crofts phone rang, and he replied "Really? That's interesting, we will go and look at it" the two examiners had stopped and were waiting for Crofts to update them.

"Leighton, your theory may be true. There's a hidden safe underneath the carpet in the living room" he told them.

Leighton and Hannah high fived. "You can always rely on me" he replied with a grin.

They went back down to the living room. It had been photographed in detail, but no examination had taken place in there yet, as they had focused on the areas of interaction between the offender and the victims first.

Nothing looked out of place in the sumptuous room. The carpet was fitted, so they started to check the edges to find anything unusual. "This is it!" Hannah called in the far corner of the room. The other two rushed over to see what she had found. There was a small table with a lamp on it, but behind it when you looked closely, the carpet was not tacked completely to the floor like the rest of the room.

"Let's get that photographed and then we will recover the lamp and the table to send off to the Lab. They can use all the chemical treatments needed. If that is a safe under there, the offender must have touched both to move them out of the way" Crofts told them.

"He's then put it all back very neatly though" Leighton asked.

"I know, again showing his attention to detail" Crofts replied.

Hannah took several photos of the area, and they then recovered both the lamp and table. Crofts then reached over to the edge of the carpet which he then rolled back with ease to show a circular floor safe. It was red in colour with a digital number window, and a small number pad.

"Let's try his date of birth" Leighton said, which made them all laugh.

"It might be, although I wouldn't have thought he would make it that obvious" replied Crofts.

"Let's try Natalie's date of birth then!" Leighton continued.

"We won't be trying any dates of birth" Crofts stated "We could cause damage to the memory by doing that. I will get on to a locksmith, and he can not only open it, but he might also be able to tell us when it was last opened."

He got out his phone and scrolled through until he got the number for a locksmiths, he had used many times before. It also helped that he knew the owner well, so was able to ask for him directly and explain what was needed. He said he would attend personally within twenty minutes, so Crofts told the others to grab a quick drinks break while they waited.

When the locksmith arrived, Hannah helped him put his PPE on, something that he thought was quite funny, "Simon, I've met you at loads of crime scenes over the years, but you've never made me dress up like this!" he exclaimed.

"That's because they were usually burglary scenes, and so there wasn't a need to cover you up as much as this" Crofts replied, "No pressure, Pete, but we just need you to unlock the floor safe, and to see if you can tell us when it was last opened?"

"Sounds simple enough" he replied, "Although I'm likely to trip over wearing all this gear!"

The SOCO's all laughed, Hannah replied "I bet you thought our job was easy, didn't you?"

They took him over to the safe. He connected a small box to it, which bleeped.

"The code is 230773" he told them, Hannah grabbed her notebook "Hang on, yes, it's another one from the great Leighton Phillips. It's Jimmy's date of birth!"

Crofts groaned; Leighton punched the air with a "Yes!"

The locksmith continued "It was last opened at 10:45 on 27th December".

"That must've been after they were shot" Hannah added.

"Do you want me to open it" Pete asked.

"Yes please" replied Crofts.

It went quiet as they watched the locksmith key in the numbers, and then open the lid. Inside, the safe was lined with a black felt covering, but there was nothing else. The empty black hole looked like it was yawning at them.

"Well that tells a story" Leighton stated.

"It does" Crofts replied, before taking out his phone and calling the incident room to let them know what they had found.

Chapter 58

It was a busy briefing room at five o'clock that afternoon. It had been called at that time as it was now New Year's Eve, and the SIO was determined that as many of the team as possible would be able to have some time off that evening, as they all deserved it. Certain members of the enquiry team had been putting in the hours over the last few days, and they needed a break.

Mead gave a quick overview of what had happened at the scene that day, including the fact that they now had a much clearer idea of the time of the murders due to when the safe had been opened. He then asked Crofts if had anything to add?

"Not really Guv, just continuing to examine the principal areas of interaction, and recovering as much evidence as possible. Until we have any results or any names, we are recovering everything possible."

Mead thanked him and his team, before moving on to Lou, who gave an update on the Goldsons. She was halfway through when there was a knock at the door, so she stopped talking as everyone turned to see who it was. A very embarrassed looking Paula Shadwell, the Scientific Support Assistant was stood there beckoning to Crofts that she needed to speak to him. He knew it must be urgent, as there was no way she would have interrupted a briefing otherwise. Crofts excused himself and went outside. Paula had just taken a phone call from the Lab with the updates on the DNA work on the coffee cups, and she told Crofts the results. He sighed, and thanked her for the information, before heading back into the room. Lou was just finishing as he sat down.

Mead looked at Crofts with a quizzical look, and Crofts cleared his throat before telling them,

"The Lab have been on the phone with the DNA results from the coffee cups" he stated.

You could hear a pin drop such was the anticipation "The first cup had Jimmy's DNA and fingerprints on it. The second cup had Natalie's DNA and a smudged print on it." he paused before continuing "The third cup had no DNA or fingerprint detail, in fact the scientist commented that it appeared to have been cleaned." He looked around the room, noticing the disappointment on the faces looking at him "So our offender was savvy enough to have cleaned the cup after the shooting as well. One cool calm customer"

There were nods around the room, and a few murmurs of agreement.

Tom Mead recovered the moment by thanking Crofts and his team and wishing them luck on the rest of their examination, before reiterating to everyone that this was not going to be a simple case, and that it was appearing that the offender had been clever enough to cover his tracks so far. Not only with the cups, but also the fact that he had recovered all the empty bullet cases and had then not only managed to get into the safe, but then took the trouble to then put it all back tidily.

The room remained silent as the facts started to sink in.

Mead then asked Jill Maynard, the Financial Expert how her team were getting on with their enquiries. Jill told them that as it was over the festive period, they were making slow progress obtaining the accounts from various banks and building societies. It appeared that so far from what they could make out, Jimmy's business dealings appeared to be property orientated, and that there was quite a large amount of money involved in those transactions. All accounts had been frozen, and it didn't appear as though there had been any withdrawals since the murders took place.

Next it was the house-to-house team sergeant. He told the room that nothing untoward had been noticed by any of the neighbours in the days before Christmas, no strange callers, or unusual vehicles in the area. Some of the houses did have CCTV, but none of them had picked anything up, as most of their cameras were trained into their own properties, with most of them having high walls separating them from the road.

The supervisor of the telecoms unit told them that they had a lot of mobile numbers triangulated in the area over the period, and were checking through them, but he also added that no other phone had been picked up on the Wi-Fi in the house, so it was looking like the offender had not had a phone on him.

Mead then went round the room asking if anyone else had any other information, but there wasn't any.

"So, we have a complex job on our hands. It is not something that is going to be solved overnight, it's going to take a lot of time and energy from us all. However, tonight is New Year's Eve, and I want you all to go home and have a night off to celebrate, whether it's a big full-on party, or just a few drinks with your nearest and dearest, I want you to forget about this job and enjoy yourselves. Most of you are off tomorrow. Sadly the SOCO team will continue at the scene, as it's not something we can just halt like that. The rest of you have a wonderful time, and I'll see you at nine the following day for a briefing."

He was about to leave the room when he added "Oh, and by the way, Happy New Year to you all!"

There were a few replies, as everyone was in a hurry to get out and to try and take their minds off the case.

Crofts went up to the office and had a quick word with Hannah and Leighton. "Are you too sure you'll be OK to work tomorrow?"

"I'm on call tonight anyway, so I'm not even having a drink," said Hannah.

"Me too" replied Crofts.

"I might have a couple I'm not going out anywhere. Just thinking of all that double bubble overtime I'm going to earn tomorrow!" laughed Leighton.

"That's typical of you" said Crofts, and the three of them laughed together.

Chapter 59

As Crofts cycled in to work the following morning, it felt like he was the only person up.

The music of Fat Boy Slims 'Praise you' was pumping in his ears, and the roads were empty. He had sat up and watched the new year in with his wife, Deborah, and then watched the fireworks from London. He had then gone to bed, and had an uninterrupted sleep with no phone calls, which was unusual when on call, and especially on New Year's Eve.

Once in the office, he made the teas and Hannah and Leighton sat with him while they chatted about the job. It was slowly sinking into them all that this was going to be a long, slow enquiry. The thoughts that they would have an offenders name from the coffee cups had dissipated, they guessed that it wouldn't be that easy. Crofts then told them "These are the jobs where we earn our money. Somewhere in that scene, there will something that helps solve this crime. We might have already recovered it without knowing. But we mustn't get despondent. It's going to be a long haul, but we'll catch that bastard somehow."

Hannah and Leighton nodded in agreement.

"So let's get going" Crofts told them, as they headed out of the door to their vehicles.

On arrival at the scene Crofts chatted to the scene guard who told him that his colleagues had heard some loud parties going on overnight from the row of luxury houses, as well as numerous fireworks. It appeared that a murder a few doors away had not dampened some of their spirits.

Having finished the hallway the day before, it was now the main bedroom to be tackled. It looked strange to them now, as the body had been removed, and there were just several pools of blood on the carpet, which could have just been stains of anything if it hadn't been at a murder scene.

Crofts decided that they would move the double bed to one side to give them more room in the area that Natalie had died, and then they could move it again once they had finished. They recovered the bedding first, and then took the largest brown exhibit bag available, and packaged the mattress. Nobody knew at this stage what the motive for the murder was, so an item such as this would be recovered now and stored. Later it might be needed for examination, to prove or dis-prove allegations. They then moved the frame out of the way.

"Holy shit!" Leighton shouted.

Crofts and Hannah both looked at him.

"Look at that!" he replied, pointing down.

Crofts looked, as Hannah shouted "Yes."

Laying on the floor was a tiny piece of brass. It was a cylinder casing from a bullet.

"He obviously didn't see that when he recovered the others" Crofts said, "It must've rolled under the bed, and he didn't notice" He smiled to himself before saying "We need to get this up to the Lab as soon as."

Hannah was already photographing it as Leighton was rummaging about amongst the exhibit packaging for a box and some polythene to recover it with. It had to be packaged in that way as other materials could potentially damage the surface of the shell.

There was so much potential evidence on this one small item.

On the ballistic side, the striation marks could be used to match it back to the weapon it was fired from, later.

It was also a useful source of fingerprints as the bullets were produced in factory conditions, untouched by human hands. When they were removed from the box for the first time for loading into a magazine, it would sometimes leave fingerprints, almost burning into the smooth brass surface.

If the offender had used gloves whilst loading, that wasn't a problem as it was likely that some DNA material would have been caught in the tiny numbers on the base of the shell.

It really was a brilliant piece of evidence, and they all knew it.

"Happy New Year!" exclaimed Leighton

Crofts and Hannah just looked at each other and burst into laughter.

Having packaged it, Crofts decided to call Tom Mead. Even though it was New Year's Day, he knew the SIO well enough to know that this was something he would want to be informed of.

Having got through the pleasantries of the new year, Crofts went straight in to telling Mead what they had found.

"That is brilliant news!" exclaimed Mead "You and your team may have saved the day once again!"

"I wouldn't say that yet, Guv" Crofts reminded him "Let's see what evidence it actually yields before we celebrate too much"?

"I know mate, but after yesterday's disappointment, this is just what we needed" said the SIO, before continuing "There will be no-one at the Lab today, but I'll arrange for someone to get on the road early tomorrow, and we'll get it up there during the morning. We can ask for a Premium Service and get the result the next day. I know that costs a lot, but in a case like this, with no other evidence, it's worth it."

"I agree" said Crofts "It is packaged, and I will deposit it in the exhibits store tonight, so that it is ready whenever your driver is."

"Great stuff, and well done to your team" Mead said, "That's made my new year already!"

Chapter 60

Crofts found himself happily whistling the following morning as he made the drinks for his staff. He had enjoyed a lovely evening at home. Deborah had made a lasagne for their dinner, and as it was one of their favourites, he and Oscar had polished it off. The conversation was all about football, as Oscar updated his dad with all the happenings from the previous day, which Crofts had missed. He had scanned the scores quickly, but now the youngster was filling in every detail.

As he wasn't on call, he had been able to have a few glasses of red wine, and had slept soundly, waking up feeling good. He sometimes dreaded going back to a scene when they had been there several days, as the task could sometimes seem never-ending, but the discovery of the shell casing had really lifted him. He could see it had also boosted the rest of his team, as they arrived in the office with big smiles and were telling the other members of staff about what had happened. Leighton dramatically replaying how he had moved the bed and found the cylinder.

Crofts smiled and headed up to the briefing room, which was also alive with excitement. There were a few "well done" calls shouted over to him as he took his seat before Kevin Bates came over to tell him "Your exhibit left here at seven o'clock this morning."

"That's impressive, I wouldn't have thought it would get away until about ten?" Crofts replied.

"Come on Crofty, you should know we're more professional than that" Bates beamed.

"Never in doubt" Crofts responded.

Mead entered the room and there was a slight hush. As he sat down and looked around the room at all the happy faces he said, "I don't need to ask if the word's got around, do I?"

There was laughter, and Croft thought that it felt like it was an end of course dinner.

"Anyway" Mead continued "As good a find as it was, as Mr Crofts said yesterday, it isn't any good until we get results" he paused, letting his words sink in, "We still must continue with all our enquiries as if we haven't had this lucky break. We can't just rely on one exhibit."

He handed over to Alison Williams who started going round the room, asking for updates from all departments. There wasn't much, as most people had been off the previous day. There was nothing new from the house-to-house teams or the major crime teams. The only update was from the financial team, who were slowly unravelling the business accounts of Jimmy. The safe had been found empty, so there was no way of knowing what might have been in there. Hopefully, over the next few days, they might be able to work out how much money Jimmy was putting to one side, although the world of cash transactions would mean that they wouldn't ever get a true figure.

The telecoms supervisor said that all numbers that had been in the triangulation area on the day in question had now been traced and spoken to, and none of them seemed untoward.

They were about to finish when Kevin Bates picked up his phone and said, "Just got a text from Simmo, and he's just arrived at the Lab" There was a small cheer.

"What time do we get the result Crofty?" one of the detectives asked.

"Some time tomorrow" Crofts replied, receiving a groan.

"I thought we were paying premium service" the detective responded.

"Yes, we are" Crofts replied, "But the process still takes some time, and that is the earliest they can get the results" he could see the disappointment around the room, so added "You lot are never happy, are you? It was only a few years ago, DNA results would be a fortnight!"

There were a few smiles, and then Alison added "Yes, and don't forget all the other lines of enquiry, as the SIO told you earlier. Now off you go."

There was still an enthusiastic sense of bravado, as everyone left the room. Crofts stopped to have a quick chat with Mead and Williams.

"Can I just say that I am not coming to another briefing until I get that result!" he said.

They both smiled before Mead replied "It's because we have absolutely no clues to help us in this case. It's not the first time we will be relying on the forensics to solve it."

"I know" replied Crofts "But all this expectation could end up with nothing."

"I know, but until then, it really is all we have" the SIO answered, before adding "Is there any way you can get the result speeded up I know you have contacts up at the Lab?"

Crofts smiled, "Seriously, no. It is the process that takes the time. I will contact Jo Whatmore in a minute, and she will get it ready as soon as she can, but it won't be until tomorrow."

"Any idea what time tomorrow?" Williams asked.

"When it's ready" Crofts replied, and they all laughed together.

## Chapter 61

Crofts went back to his office to call Jo Whatmore, the forensic scientist. She answered the phone with "Yes, Simon, I know it is here, and I have already got it prepared to be loaded on to the system!"

"Thanks for that" Crofts replied, "I didn't realise you would know so quickly?"

"I put a word in with reception that it would be arriving today, so they called me when it got here, that was early, by the way!" she replied.

"I know" said Crofts "Everyone is so excited about this exhibit. I couldn't believe it when we moved the bed."

"I know, it's funny that it was there while we were all in there, without us knowing" Whatmore answered.

"I know, but we must deal with the scenes methodically. If we went in and turned the place upside down at the start, we would cause more damage than good" Crofts said.

"Of course, that's the right way to do it. Anyway, it is on the system, and I can honestly say that your exhibit has just gone straight to the front of the queue, in front of all submissions for the last couple of days" the scientist told him.

"Thanks for that. I look forward to hearing from you tomorrow" Crofts replied.

"I will keep an eye out for it and call you personally as soon as I get it" Whatmore replied.

"Thanks Jo" said Crofts before finishing the call.

Crofts spent the next hour quickly catching up on his emails and leave requests that were part of his job that still had to be done even though he was working long hours on Op Durham. It came with the role and as boring as it felt at times such as this, it needed to be done.

He then drove over to the scene, stopping for some coffees on the way. On arrival he called up to Leighton and Hannah, and they all sat in his car with their drinks. "I know it's all going to be a bit of a come down after yesterday's excitement, but we still must recover every single piece of evidence that we can. There's no way of knowing what will be needed to prove or disprove later, so we still must get it all. We mustn't think that we've solved the case with just one exhibit."

"I know that" Hannah said, "But it was a good one, wasn't it? Do you reckon we'll get a profile?"

Crofts could see them both watching him intently, "I don't know. We've had some reliable results from empty cases in the past, but not always" he replied.

He saw their disappointment "Who knows? The killer has been careful in a lot of what he has done, but there's no way of knowing what this item will yield.

They all thought about it for a moment.

Leighton replied, "When you say it like that, it does seem as though there will be some material on it, although I've had a couple of exhibits recently that I had sent off for profiling knowing that the offender had brought it to the scene, and they came back as negative."

"I know" Crofts answered, "It really is luck in those situations. Dependant on what the object is made of, and how much it was handled by the villain, we just must hope in this case, that luck is on our side."

Hannah sighed before adding "He's been lucky so far, though, hasn't he?"

Crofts pondered for a while before replying, "He has, but everyone's luck runs out sometime. He was careful at the scene except for this one item, but it is down to what he did with it prior to attending this house. Where he got the ammo, where he loaded the magazine, where he put the gun prior to attending, all come into play. You'd like to think that at some point, some of his DNA has been transferred to that casing?"

"I bloody hope so" Leighton replied, "If he hasn't, we haven't got much else from the scene, so far, have we?"

"No, we haven't" Crofts agreed "But don't forget, there are always other parts to the enquiry, something will come from there, eventually. It just might take a lot longer if we don't get a breakthrough with this."

Hannah smiled and said, "Before you say it, there are lots of pieces to the jigsaw of an enquiry, and forensics is just one of those pieces!"

All three laughed, it was indeed one of Crofts favourite sayings.

"Right, let's get cracking then" Crofts said, getting out of the car, "We've work to do. Lots of it!"

Chapter 62

Louise Jacks had left the briefing and headed over to the Goldsons to update them with the latest news. She noticed that when John answered the door, he seemed a little more upbeat, and the same with Julie, as they busied themselves making coffees. This was to be expected. It was now five days after the bodies had been found.

The range of emotions when something as catastrophic as this happened to people was like a rollercoaster. Lows followed by highs, followed by lows, interspersed with anger at various times.

The Goldson's lows had lasted for a few days, but now that they had got used to the situation, they would be able get their minds around it, hence the slight upturn for them both. Lou knew that it wouldn't last and that there would still be lows for them to cope with, but also knew that she had to try and keep them in this frame of mind for the time being.

They went through to the lounge, which was full of flowers and cards of condolence. She sat down and started to go through what had happened over the previous days. She told them they had found the safe, and that it was empty, to which they both looked shocked before John said "We don't know if there had been anything in it though, do we. Jimmy only mentioned it the once, and that was after he had had a few?"

"We don't" Lou replied "However, when the locksmith downloaded the data to get into it, he told us that it had last been opened at 10:45 the morning that the bodies were found."

"Bastard!" John said aloud, before apologising to Lou.

"Don't worry, I'm used to worse than that. Anyway, I agree" she replied, "It does show a motive though, rather than just being shot as a contract killing."

"I suppose so, but what did he have in there, that was valuable enough to kill two people?" he replied, making Julie sob.

"I don't know," Lou replied, "We will hopefully find out in the fullness of time. I do have a better piece of news though."

"Go on" John replied, looking eager.

The FLO explained about the finding of the shell, and the possibilities of a DNA result from it.

"So if it has got DNA on it, it will give us a name?" John asked.

"Hopefully" Lou replied "The crime scene manager has stressed that it might not have. Remember the lack of DNA on the cup? However, this is something that the killer didn't realise he had left behind, so he may not have been as careful."

"Oh God, I bloody hope so" John replied, looking at Julie who added "Me too, the bastard."

John then asked about when they would be able to start organising the funerals. Julie explained to them that she was unable to give an exact date as the bodies were still under the authority of The Coroner.

In cases such as this, the bodies were kept in the mortuary until a defence postmortem had been carried out. This would happen when someone was arrested for the crime. The defence solicitor would require another postmortem to be carried out by a different, independent pathologist to make sure that the original examination hadn't been biased. If no-one was in custody in a certain amount of time, The Coroner would organise another postmortem, to be used later by a defence team. That was when he would then agree to release the body back to the family.

The Goldsons took it all in.

"Not sure if you've thought that far ahead" Lou added "But are you going to have a joint funeral, or two separate services?"

"Natalie will have her own funeral, surrounded by her friends and family" Julie stated.

Lou knew that she also meant that she did not want Jimmy's family involved in it. She knew that both Goldsons would always blame him for the death of their daughter.

"There is one other question I need to ask you? Lou told them
"What is that?" Julie asked.

"Would either of you like to take part in a Press Conference, requesting the public for information?"

They looked at each other as Lou added "You are both well known in the town, and Natalie was too. These appeals help jog people's memories. They might have seen something suspicious happening without realising it. It might have been a car in the area, a person in the vicinity, all in the run up to the day in question. They can be so useful."

"I'll say yes" John replied, "Anything that helps to bring Natalie's killer to justice, I will do it."

He looked at Julie, "How about you, love?"

"I'm not sure I could cope with it" Julie replied.

"It's not a problem, you've got to be happy with it. John would be fine on his own anyway. Have a think about it after I've gone? It will be the day after tomorrow, which is a week after the event. There will be a lot of police activity in the area around Cooden Beach that day, as they try to get people to remember what they were doing on that day, again to jog their memory."

Lou then went on to explain that it would be held at the Major Crime Base in Eastbourne, and she would show them around the Incident

Room and introduce them to some of the team members while they were there, if they wanted.

They both said that they would like that, and that they would think about the press conference.

Lou said her goodbyes and headed off. She now had even more to organise.

## Chapter 63

After a busy day at the scene, where another two hundred exhibits had been recovered, Crofts had finished early, enabling the three of them to get home for an evening off with their families. They certainly deserved it. The hours they had put in over the last few days was enough anyway but coupled with the stress of the scenes they had dealt with, and the concentration levels always needed, meant that they all needed a restful evening. He had made sure that none of them were on call that evening to enable them all to chill for the night.

He spent his at home, with Deborah and Oscar, just what he wanted. They had a lovely Mexican meal, with a few beers, and then watched a game of football, before Oscar went to bed, and he and Deborah watched a film. It was a romcom, not one of Crofts favourites, but something easy to watch. He always avoided police dramas and films. One, because he would spend the whole film finding fault in the technicalities, especially with the crime scene side of things, but also that they were usually so far-fetched that he couldn't take them seriously. Deborah had enjoyed it, which was the main thing.

It had taken his mind of the job a little, but not entirely. So by the time he started up his computer the next morning in the office, he was fully focused.

As if from nowhere, Leighton appeared with a cup of tea for him.

"Morning boss, did you have a great evening?" he asked.

"Yes, thanks mate" Crofts replied, "Nice and relaxing. You?"

"Me and Josie had a curry and a few beers" Leighton said, and then stood looking between Crofts and his computer.

"What?" Crofts asked.

"Is the result in yet?" the Welshman replied.

"Bloody hell, give me time to actually log on!" Crofts said, shaking his head, but smiling.

They both waited for Crofts to open all the different computer systems needed for his work. Finally the email system updated, and showed he had seventeen new emails. He scanned down them.

He looked up at the expectant face of Leighton, who had also now been joined by Hannah, and he could tell that the four other members of staff in the office had also stopped talking and were listening in. "Sorry folks, nothing so far!" There was a deep sigh of disappointment.

"I wasn't expecting it overnight anyway. By the time it is taken off the system and checked, it will be lunchtime."

They all carried on with their own work as Crofts headed along to the briefing room. Everyone stopped talking as he entered and looked up at him. "The answer is no, not yet" he said as he walked in, which was met with a few friendly boos.

Crofts just shook his head and took his seat. Tom Mead and his deputy entered the room, and both looked at Crofts. "Not you two as well? The answer is not yet!" he said.

"No need to get tetchy" Mead said with a smile "It's not as if everything is relying on this result, is it?"

There were a few laughs around the room.

Crofts smiled back "It's not as if I wouldn't have told you immediately Guv. I imagine that by the time the samples are taken off the system and results are analysed it will be about lunchtime" he told them.

"That's technically more than 24 hours" one of the detectives remarked "I thought we paid good money for this?"

There were a few smiles around the table and Crofts replied, "I'm not even going to bother answering that one!"

More laughter ensued.

Mead let it continue for a while before interrupting and calling them to order to start the briefing. Slowly going around the table with each group updating what had happened over the past twenty-four hours. There was plenty of information coming in. It would all be fed into the HOLMES system, which would lead to more enquiries for the team.

It was while Kevin Bates was giving his update about how the incident room was coping with the information so far, that Crofts felt his phone vibrating in his pocket. He always turned the ringer off whilst in briefings. He quickly checked the screen, and saw it was from Jo Whatmore's personal phone. He got up and headed out of the room, causing Bates to stop talking. The phone had only vibrated, but in the quiet of the room, most had heard it, and the fact that Crofts had got up to answer it straight away meant that they knew it was important.

The room fell silent after Crofts closed the door.

"Anyway Kev, please continue" Alison Williams said.

"Yes" said the sergeant and tried to concentrate on what he had to say.

# Chapter 64

Crofts left the room and let himself into an empty office along the corridor before answering.

"Hi Simon, I knew you were waiting for this result, so I got in early this morning, and took it off the system personally" the scientist told him.

"Thanks for that, Jo, so what have we got?" Crofts asked.

"I've got some good news, and some bad news" she replied.

"Really? Go ahead" Crofts asked.

"The good news is that there was enough DNA material recovered to get a DNA profile" Jo paused before continuing "The bad news is that the profile is not on the Database."

"Blimey, I wasn't expecting that" Crofts exclaimed.

When the National DNA Database had been set up in the early nineties, the law was changed so that anyone taken into custody would have their DNA taken and added to the fledgling database. This meant that over the coming years, more offenders were added until there were now over six million people on the system. This was added to daily as more offenders were sampled.

Whenever a crime scene sample was sent to the Lab, it could be checked against all the database in seconds. Over the years there were very few crimes that weren't solved using this system, as most offenders were on it. However, there would always be a few that had not been in custody at all, and so were not on the database.

"I know, it's disappointing" Jo replied, "It's hard to believe that someone carrying out a crime of this magnitude would have never been caught in the past?"

"It is. They have either been very clever, or incredibly lucky" Crofts answered, thinking aloud, "What do we do now?"

"I will look into it for you" Jo answered, "There are always new techniques being developed that might enable to have us look at this sample more closely."

"Such as?" Crofts asked.

"We can investigate it to find gender, which I know isn't much use in this case, but we might be able to find ethnicity, or some features such as hair colour, or eye colour. They might all help eliminate, or include people in your enquiry at some stage?" Jo told him.

"That could help" Crofts replied.

"I haven't had chance to look at it properly yet, as I just wanted to get it loaded on the system. Once we start breaking it down, who knows what we will find?"

"That sounds good, although I've got to tell a full briefing of the team this result. They all thought it would be over today!" Crofts laughed.

"I knew they would, but it's not a complete negative yet, and we will continue to work on it. One thing to consider for the enquiry team?" she added.

"Go on" Crofts replied.

"It might be a clever idea for the SIO to add to the policy that all witnesses and acquaintances of the victims have an elimination DNA swab taken, if they are not on the database?" she said.

"Right" Crofts said.

"It will ensure we know it's nothing to do with those people to start with, and then may also help out later if we need to do a mass screening of some description?" Jo stated.

Mass screening was when a specific area of the population was asked to give voluntary DNA samples to help solve a case. It would be defined by what was known about a suspect in each case. It was terribly slow, and very costly, but it was something that could be used as a last resort.

"OK, Thanks" Croft replied.

"Also, do you and the SIO want to come up here for a meeting sometime next week we can go through the possibilities with you? We would have had a chance to look at the sample fully" the scientist asked.

"Of course we can, I'll speak to you later" Crofts ended the call.

He went to the briefing room door and took a deep breath before entering.

Chapter 65

Louise Jacks knocked on the door of the SIO's office. She could hear what sounded like serious voices inside, which stopped on hearing her. The door opened and Kevin Bates looked out. "Hello Lou, come on in" he said.

There was only the SIO, and his deputy together with Bates in the room. Lou called feel the tension in the room.

"I take it you are aware of Simon Crofts' update?" Mead asked her.

"Yes, I am, I'm just wondering how I am going to break it to the Goldsons" she replied, "They were so expectant when I told them yesterday."

"Yes, we all were, weren't we?" He raised his eyes to the others who both nodded in agreement.

"Poor Simon, he acted as though it was his fault when he gave us the update" Alison Williams added.

"Yes, he did" Mead replied, "I'll have a chat with him later, it's not their fault at all. They just think it is. The enquiry continues all avenues, forensics isn't always the be-all and end-all that we sometimes believe it is. Anyway Lou, I saw your message about the press conference tomorrow. How are the Goldsons holding up now?"

Lou repeated the conversation from the day before, telling the senior investigators that she felt that the couple had slowly come to terms with the situation. "The time is right for them to take part in this. I'll finalise whether Julie wants to be a part of it later today."

Bates then told her "We've got quite a lot going on tomorrow morning, trying to get people to remember what they saw last Tuesday. The offender would have been seen somewhere during that morning; the public just don't realise what they have seen. We can't do a reconstruction like we normally do, as we don't think either of them left the house that morning. We just need to find the members of the public who were going about their normal business that morning oblivious to the fact that a killer was among them" he finished.

Williams added "We're also targeting those on the trains that would have stopped at Cooden Beach station, which of course is only a few hundred metres from the scene, but those passengers who went past the scene that morning. Again, people have seen things that they haven't realised are important."

They all nodded.

Mead continued "I've been onto Trevor Innes from the Media Department, and he's arranging invites for the actual conference. As you are aware, it has hit the national news and the papers, so it will be well attended."

"We need to make sure we have the correct security in the building, Kev" Williams added "We don't want reporters or photographers from the tabloids wandering around the building on their own. God knows what they would photograph!"

Bates smiled "All received. They will be under strict control" He looked at Lou and asked, "How do you think the Goldsons will react?"

Lou thought for a moment before answering "I think John will be okay, but not sure about Julie, if she agrees to do it. I would also worry about the questions from the reporters? If any of them saying anything negative about Natalie, they could blow."

"Yes, I realise that" Mead replied, "I take it they blame Jimmy for her death?"

"Without a doubt" Louise said.

"As long as we all know that, at least we will be able to change the angle of questioning from them" Williams added.

"I don't believe they will take that angle, anyway" Mead said "Natalie has been portrayed in the press as such a nice person, which, of course she was. I think the red tops will be trying to get the dirty on Jimmy. They've already started to portray him as some kind of gangster!"

They all shook their heads.

"Guv, are you still okay to meet the Goldsons privately?" Lou asked.

"Of course I am, it will be a pleasure. Sadly, the last time I met them; the circumstances weren't good," said Mead.

"Can we also give them a tour of the Incident Room?" Lou asked Bates.

"No problem" he replied, "Although I will have a look through the information that is on the boards in the room. I don't want them to see anything that will upset them, but at the same time I want to show them that we are doing our utmost in the pursuit of the killer."

"Thank you all for that" Lou told them.

"Thank you for your efforts, Lou" Mead said "I know you are experienced in the role, and we couldn't have asked for anyone better, but we are all aware of how hard your job is, and how much it takes out of you. Let me know if you need a break at all. You can't go on forever."

Bates and Williams both nodded.

"I'm fine now. They are such a lovely couple, and I just want to help get them through these next few days. I desperately want them to get justice for Natalie."

"So do we all, Lou" Mead replied, before adding "See you tomorrow. It's going to be a good one."

Chapter 66

Crofts and his team were sat in the car, drinking their coffees. He had just told them about the news from the lab, so they were all quiet.

Leighton was the first to speak, "Surely, someone who can go out and kill two people in cold blood must have committed a crime at some time in their life?"

"It doesn't mean he hasn't ever committed a crime" replied Crofts, "It just means that he hasn't been caught. He is either very switched on, or incredibly lucky."

The two others nodded. Hannah then ventured "Maybe it was a contract killing after all. I imagine the best hitmen wouldn't be on the database?"

Crofts thought for a moment before replying "It might be, although it doesn't add up with him searching for, and finding the safe. A professional hitman wouldn't normally have wanted to stay around for that. They will make the hit and go."

"What about ex-soldiers?" Leighton said, "They would be prepared to kill, and maybe cool enough to search around?"

"The thing is whoever did it knew about the safe. So it must have been someone who knew Jimmy." Hannah added.

"Also had a coffee with the victims, so obviously knew him." Crofts reminded them.

Just then his phone rang, Crofts saw that it was Tom Mead.

"Hello Guv" he said.

"Hello Simon" replied the SIO, "Are you with your team?"

"Yes, we're just having a coffee break" Crofts replied.

"Can you put your phone onto speaker? I just wanted to have a quick word with you all" Mead told him.

Crofts pressed the button and then told him they were all listening.

"I thought I'd just give you a call to thank you for all your work so far on the case." Mead said "It's been long hours, and gruesome sights, but you have all done so well. I know you'll all be disappointed about the latest update from the lab, but I'm sure that somewhere in the hundreds of exhibits that you have recovered, there will be that little piece of evidence that will eventually help solve this case."

"Thanks for that Guv" replied Crofts, with the others agreeing.

"No problem" Mead continued "We really do appreciate your hard work." Before ending the call.

"Well, that was a turn up for the books!" Leighton said.

"He's a good egg" Crofts replied "He's also a great fan of forensics, unlike some of the older SIO's. We've got him some impressive results over the years, and he's thankful for that. He's as disappointed as we are about the results so far, but as he said, we'll get something soon."

"Indeed" Leighton replied.

"So let's get in there and carry on doing our job" Crofts said.

"Ever the task master" Hannah said with a grin.

Chapter 67

The following morning, the residents of Cooden Beach had never seen so much police activity.

There were officers on each of the roads into the village, stopping traffic and asking the drivers what they had been doing the same time the week before. If it was deemed that they had been driving in the area that morning, they were asked some previously prepared questions. Even though the case had been plastered all over the media, there may have been instances where someone had seen something, whether a person or car, without realising that it was something to do with the crime.

There were also officers getting on to the trains and questioning passengers who had been on the previous week. The line ran along opposite the houses, and again, people may have seen something that they didn't realise were important.

It was a massive commitment from the force, using many officers, but it was a one-off chance to jog memories a week to the day after the incident.

Tom Mead and Alison Williams had both got in early to be around for the occasion. Mead liked to show his face at this type of event. Firstly to let the officers involved know that he was interested in their work, but also with talking to the press. It was an area of his role that he knew was important and had helped to solve many crimes in the past. They did sometimes get on his nerves, especially if they started accusing the police of failing to do their job, but those times were few. Mostly, the press were on the same side, and their reporting helped give the publicity needed.

Over the years he had got to know a lot of the reporters, and so found it easy to talk to them. So he moved from camera to camera, answering their questions. Alison was by his side but didn't get interviewed at all. As the deputy, the members of the press didn't want to speak to her while Mead was around. She did sometimes speak on some of the lesser jobs, or if the SIO was unavailable for some reason, but her time would come.

Having spoken to all the press reporters and the TV stations, Mead looked around at the amount of police activity going on in every direction. He walked over to where one of the roadblocks was taking place.

The police officer recognised him and stopped talking to the driver of the car was questioning, "Morning Sir" the officer said.

"Morning, don't let me stop your work" Mead replied, nodding at the driver of the car.

"Oh yes, of course" the officer replied, and then continued to go through the questionnaire. On completion he thanked the driver, who then moved off.

"How's it going?" Mead asked.

"Nothing special" the officer replied, "Nearly all the people I have spoken to didn't see anything untoward last week. They are mainly older folks with the same routine each day, so would notice anything unusual."

"I know, it's a tough one" Mead replied, "Quite often when we do this sort of thing, we will have an actor playing the part of the victim walking where they were last seen or similar. In this case we can't do that, as it doesn't fit the scenario. Keep going, we'll find something."

"Yes, will do sir" the officer replied, turning to wave at an approaching car signalling for it to slow down. It didn't look as though it would stop, and the officer had to jump out of the way before it eventually came to a halt.

Mead watched as the occupant of the car lowered the passenger window, revealing a little old lady aged about ninety.

Mead and Williams looked at each other. "I don't believe she would have seen anything." He said, at which they both had to try and keep a straight face as they walked back to their car.

"Come on" said Mead, "We've got a press conference to attend."

Chapter 68

Louise Jacks picked the Goldsons up at nine thirty. John had texted first thing to say that Julie wanted to be part of the conference, so she was ready for them both.

"I'm glad you agreed to come" she told Julie, "I know it's not going to be nice for you, but if you hadn't come today, you would have regretted it later."

"I know, that's what I thought" Julie replied, adding "I'd hate to think that I'd let Natalie down."

"No-one would have thought that" Lou answered.

"I know, but I would have" Julie replied.

"You mustn't think like that" John added.

"It's just the way I feel at the moment" his wife answered.

"That's understandable" Lou told her, "Hopefully today will help you feel better."

They then drove in silence for the next couple of minutes until they arrived outside the Major Crime Base.

Lou swiped herself in and took the Goldsons up the stairs to the Incident Room. As she entered the room, there was a lull in the conversations. To cover the silence, Lou then introduced the Goldsons.

She then took them around the room telling them who all the individual officers were, and what their roles consisted of. They both took all the information in, impressed with everything that was being done, and the depth of the investigations.

Julie couldn't help herself and was thanking every single officer for their help in the investigation.

The individual officers appeared embarrassed, as they all felt that they were 'just doing their job' and it wasn't often that they were personally thanked by someone from outside the organisation.

Having met everyone and heard everything that was happening, Lou then took them through to Tom Mead's office where they were offered coffees. Whilst someone went off to make them, Mead asked them how they were feeling.

"I think we are still both in a dreamworld, not really believing what has happened." John answered, "However, having just been around the incident room, and seeing how much work is being put into finding the killer, it has given me a different outlook completely."

"I told you on the first night that we would find the killer, and nothing has changed. We will." Mead told them.

"I know" John replied, "I never doubted that. It's not until we have seen the whole enquiry up and running that we realise how much there is to it."

Mead nodded, "I know. It is complicated, but it is something that we are good at, so it is a pleasure to lead a team like this."

Lou then asked whether he could let the Goldsons know what would be happening in the press conference.

"Of course" the SIO replied, "We will shortly head down to the conference room. There is a table laid out at one end of the room. We will sit behind that. There will be the two of you, with Lou and I either side of you. Okay so far?"

The Goldsons nodded.

"As soon as we get into the room, the cameras will be running, and there will be flashes from cameras, so prepare yourself for that,"

They looked at each other before nodding again.

Mead continued "I will then give a short statement about the circumstances of the crime, and then ask if there are any questions. I will then introduce you both. Have you thought about what you would like to say?"

There was a pause before John answered "I did think about writing a speech, but then decided against it. I would rather say it from my heart at the time."

"That's absolutely fine," Mead told them, "It's better to do that. A pre-prepared statement can sometimes seem a bit too plain. Once you have both spoken, I will allow the press to ask you questions. Now, I'd better warn you. The members of the press can sometimes produce some weird and wonderful questions. Sometimes on a tangent that you wouldn't have thought of. Don't worry. If there is anything you do not want to answer, just say. We can soon move them on to another question."

They looked at each other again, before John replied, "That's good."

"Right" Mead said, "Let's get down there."

Chapter 69

There was a general hub bub of conversation in the conference room, which stopped abruptly as the four of them walked in.

The room was decked out in pale blue Sussex Police signage behind the table they were to sit at, and then there was a gap of only a couple of metres before the chairs started. The room was full. Those that hadn't been able to get a seat were stood at the back. There were camera flashes going off from all directions as they sat down.

The Goldsons just stared at the scenario in front of them. Although they had been briefed, nothing could have prepared them for the reality.

Mead waited until the camera flashes had calmed down before speaking. He introduced the panel and then went through what had been found at the scene. Most of this had previously been released to the press, so was in the public domain already. He then went on to ask for sightings of unusual behaviour in and around the scene location, and in the days before the murders. He then asked for questions.

The first was from a reporter for one of the national newspapers who asked whether it was a contract killing?

Mead said that they were keeping an open mind at this stage. Which caused several of the hacks to look knowingly at each other.

Another question was whether Jimmy was known to have been involved in any criminal activity that would have been the reason for his murder?

Mead replied that as far as they could tell at this time, Jimmy was a successful businessman, and there was nothing to make them feel that his involvement in his companies had anything to do with his murder.

The next question was whether the victims had known their killer?

Mead told them that there were signs at the scene which appeared to show that there had been social interaction between them. This caused a few murmurs, and someone called out "What exactly do you mean by that?"

Mead responded, "We're not able to tell you that at this stage of the enquiry." Which caused a few more whispers.

Mead and Louise Jacks glanced at each other. They didn't know what was being inferred, but whatever it was, they weren't too happy about.

There was a brief lull, so Mead asked for any other questions.

A small, diminutive reporter with glasses that appeared too big for him asked "Yes, I would like to ask if this is going to be another case that Sussex Police failed to solve?"

Mead stared at the man before asking "What do you mean by that?"

"Well" he replied "It is well known that over the last ten years, you have failed to solve three murders. Is this going to be another one, and is it something that you should be handing over to a proper force like the Met Police, to solve properly?"

The room went silent.

Mead paused to summon his thoughts. He recognised the reporter, and he knew that he obviously had a problem with Sussex Police, as he spent most of his time covering those cases, producing all kinds of conspiracy theories. None of which were correct.

"The cases the gentleman is talking about, are indeed all unsolved. They have however been reviewed both internally and externally, by other forces, and seen to have been always investigated thoroughly. They remain open cases and are still under investigation." He paused before adding "Are there any further, sensible, questions about this particular case?"

It was silent in the room, so Mead introduced John Goldson to say a few words.

"As you can guess. This has come as a devastating shock to Julie and me. It is the worst living nightmare. Hearing that your lovely daughter is dead was bad enough, but then finding out how she and her husband Jimmy died made it even worse." He paused, "I would like to say a thank you to Mr Mead and his officers for the professional way they have dealt with this from the outset."

Mead asked if there were any questions.

A reporter from ITV news asked him to describe Natalie for them? "She was the prettiest, loveliest girl ever." John replied, "I know I would say that as she was our daughter, but she really was." He paused, as his bottom lip started to quiver, and then composed himself before continuing "From the minute she was born she was beautiful. As she grew up, she became a popular, caring young girl. She then blossomed into the lovely young woman that she was before cruelly having her life taken away." He stopped as a tear ran down his cheek.

He didn't need to say anything else.

Julie put her arm around him and pulled him to her before sobbing "Please. Anyone who knows anything about who killed our lovely Natalie, please tell the police. This evil monster needs to be caught."

The Goldsons sat hugging each other, sobbing together.

Mead stood up and said "Thank you all for attending. Now, if you'll excuse us, we will be taking Mr and Mrs Goldson home" as he led them both out of the room.

Chapter 70

It had been a good journey up to Oxfordshire, having left at seven o'clock. Kevin Bates drove into the car park of the Forensic Lab with his passengers, Crofts, Tom Mead, and Alison Williams.

It was a couple of days after the press conference, and it had been the main topic of discussion throughout the journey. They had all agreed that Mead had kept his cool with the annoying reporter. Mead admitted that he found it hard, but at the same time knowing that he had to concentrate on the Goldsons rather than get into arguments.

"You did" Williams told him "He shouldn't have even broached that subject, especially when we were dealing with such an important job."

Mead told them that he had contacted the Editor of his newspaper and informed him that he was not welcome at any further interviews.

"Wow, what did he say?" Crofts asked.

"He was exceptionally good about it. I told him that I agreed with the freedom of speech etcetera, etcetera, but that in this instance he had overstepped the mark, and that I didn't want to deal with him again. He apologised on his behalf and said that he would have a word with him, and make sure he wouldn't be attending any of our interviews in the future."

"Too right, I'm all for investigative journalism in the right context, but he just harps on about the same issues over again, with no new evidence." Bates replied before adding "I wonder what happened to him which gave him such a hatred of Sussex Police?"

They all agreed, but none of them knew the answer.

On arrival at the reception, Crofts gave their names and said that they had a meeting with Jo Whatmore. Having made a phone call, the receptionist asked them to sit while they waited. The scientist arrived within a couple of minutes and led them to a meeting room. It was a nicely decorated room, with all modern facilities, including the obligatory coffee and biscuits.

"This is all very nice" Mead said, "I suppose this is where all our money goes!"

Jo laughed, she was used to this type of comment from visiting officers "I'll have you know, that this is the only room like this in the building. The rest is just loads of laboratories helping you solve crime!"

"Touchez" Mead replied, "We do appreciate the work you do for us, of course, and anything you can help us with on this case, the better."

The scientist then ran through all the results so far. They had seen the reports already, but Jo explained them further.

"So, realistically, we will have to wait until the offender goes on to the database?" Bates asked.

"As it stands, yes" Jo answered, "But there is something else we could try?"

"Go on" said Crofts, becoming more interested having listened to all the previous negative results.

"Have you heard of Familial Searching?" Jo asked.

"Yes, I have, but I thought it was only used in specific cases with strict criteria" Crofts answered.

"It is, but I think we might be able to try on this case" the scientist replied.

Bates interrupted "Sorry, am I the only one who doesn't know what you are talking about?"

Mead and Williams both smiled, "I had heard of it, but same as Simon, I thought it was only unusual cases?" the SIO asked.

"To explain to Kevin, Familial DNA analysis is the strategy in which biological family members' DNA is used to provide investigative leads for identification of the unknown individual. As they share genetic information close to other family members" Jo replied

"Go on" Bates said.

"So parents and children, and siblings will have similar DNA to each other. We load the offenders DNA profile on to the national database and ask the system to produce similar profiles using a special computer programme." Jo explained.

"Right" Bates replied, adding "but how many will that be?"

Jo answered "That can depend on how we deal with this. For instance, we can target certain areas of the database, such as location."

"How is that?" Williams asked.

Jo smiled "When someone is taken into custody and have their DNA saliva sample taken, the postcode is added. In this case we know that the offender was known to the victims in some way, so may be local. We will set it up to only check samples from this area to start. We can widen the search later."

Mead nodded his head before asking "So, what are the drawbacks?"

"Money and manpower." Jo answered.

"Really? I could have guessed the money side of things, there is always an extra cost" he smiled before continuing, "But how does manpower come into it?"

"Well, we will produce a list of people, usually around the hundred mark, who 'could' be related to the offender." Jo replied, "You will then need officers to visit all those people and ask if they have any male relatives? If they have, those people must then be visited, and a DNA sample taken from them. It is quite a slow process and may not even give you a result." She finished.

"But this has worked in the past, hasn't it?" Crofts asked.

"Yes, it has" Jo replied, "But not that often. It has been attempted on over a hundred cases, but only worked in a quarter of them."

"Oh" Bates said aloud.

"We don't have a lot of other evidence so far," Crofts replied, "And either by skill, or by luck, this offender has not been in custody until now, so is not likely to be anytime soon." He looked at the others "We have a great piece of evidence that would prove this crime. I think we should give it a go."

Tom Mead thought for a second and then said "Simon's right. If this works, it will give us a result. How long does it take?"

Jo smiled, "Once it is set up, we can do it over a forty-eight-hour period."

"So if we gave you the go ahead. We can expect a result at the beginning of next week?" Bates asked.

"Yes" Jo replied.

"Who do I see about costs?" Mead asked.

"I can arrange for you to go and have a chat with our Finance Director, whilst you are here" the scientist.

"Let's go" Mead replied, rising from his chair.

Chapter 71

Having finished his meeting, Mead returned to the room and thanked Jo for her work and told her to get it ready to go on Monday morning.

"That's great news," she replied, "I take it all sorted out on the finance front?"

"Yes, indeed" Mead said, "Not as bad as I thought."

"We do try hard" Jo answered, "Although not according to some SIO's."

The others all laughed, they all knew that in the past there had been quite a few 'indifferences' between labs and investigating officers.

After saying goodbye, they all returned to the car for the journey home. Once on the road Mead said "Right, I'm famished. We deserve some food paid for by the job for a change. Everyone agree?"

"Too right" said Bates, I feel like I've lived on sandwiches and pizzas for the past week."

"If you head into Abingdon, there's a lovely pub by the river that does decent food" Alison told them, "I was up on a course at the lab last year, and we managed to find it every evening!"

Bates followed her instructions, and then parked up outside The Kings Head, overlooking the Thames. The winter sun was out, and it looked glorious, but they decided to take a table inside.

Having ordered their food and been given their drinks, as the waitress left, they all started to talk at once, making them all laugh aloud. The few others in the pub all stopped to look at them. Mead cleared his throat and said to the others "It's not the place to talk about the job. Let's just enjoy the moment and savour the food. We've all deserved it."

The others nodded, and they had a conversation about pubs they had visited. The food was served, and it was delicious.

While they were waiting for the bill, Bates remarked "The only shame about this is the lack of alcohol."

"I know" said Mead, "It wouldn't have been like this when I first got on to CID. We would have all had a couple of pints by now. How times have changed."

"You wouldn't have been thinking of Familial DNA either" Crofts replied, "When I started in the early nineties, we couldn't even get DNA from blood found at a scene. We didn't even send it off, as it would've only given us a blood grouping which was no good whatsoever. Could have been one in five of the population. We now get DNA reports saying it is one in a billion people."

"It is amazing how much things have changed" Mead responded, "Shows how old we are all getting!"

The others agreed and headed out to the car. "I hope you're not all going to sleep on the way home" Bates said.

"I'm too excited" Crofts answered.

"Me too" Alison added.

"So, Simon, what do reckon our chances really are with this?" Mead asked him.

"As Jo said, it can be an element of luck, and hasn't worked every time but that's always the case when we submit evidence. We think we know what the best evidence is, but we all know that it's often not the case."

"Yes" Bates continued, "I can think of loads of jobs where we thought we knew the outcome, only to be shot down in flames by the evidence. It's what makes investigations the best part of policing."

Mead nodded in agreement and then added "It really does sound like a promising idea. However, we can't just rely on this piece of work. We still need to follow all the other avenues of enquiry."

"Definitely, Guv" Bates responded, "We still have plenty of actions outstanding that need to be investigated."
"I want as many done as possible over the weekend" Mead replied, "That way, when we get our list of names next week, we will have as many officers as possible to respond."

The others all agreed.

"I'll make sure we order more DNA sample kits and make sure they're all in date," Crofts told them, "I'd hate to get a result on this and then find out later that some smart arsed defence barrister tries to get the evidence thrown out due to an out-of-date swab."

"I know, and they would" Bates replied.

"We also need you to brief all of the officers who will be going out to take the samples" Alison told Crofts, "It's not something that they do on a daily basis, and we want to make sure it is done correctly."

"No probs, I will organise a briefing video for them, and then personally talk to as many as possible" Crofts answered.

"All sounds good to me" Tom Mead said, before slowly closing his eyes for a nap.

## Chapter 72

It had been a busy Monday morning for Crofts. It had started with the briefing, with nothing much to report on over the weekend, as most departments had allowed plenty of their staff to have some time off.

After the meeting, he had driven out with Tom Mead to formally close the scene. His team had been there for a total of thirteen days, during which time they had recovered over three thousand exhibits. Most of them would go straight into the exhibits room, never to see the light of day again, but many would be sent off to the lab, and somewhere in amongst them could be the item that solved this case.

Crofts showed Mead around the scene, explaining what they had found, and the SIO then signed his notebook to say that he was happy to record that.

There was still one other process to be carried out when they had finished, and that was to paint the walls with chemicals for fingerprints. As the examiners had been processing the scene, they would have been using their normal powders to dust any smooth surfaces for prints and recovering any movable items to be sent to the lab for various treatments.

The house was now completely empty, and the walls would be painted with Ninhydrin. This was a chemical used for developing fingerprints from paper, where the solution reacted to the amino acid in the sweat of the prints. It was, however, very toxic. The experts from the lab would enter wearing full hazardous clothing and breathing equipment and paint it on all walls.

The chemicals took about a fortnight to develop, so the scene would be locked and sealed, with a team returning with light sources to see what had been found. They would find hundreds of prints, and all would be recovered. The elimination of the householders would take place first, and then a search through the remainder of the outstanding marks. Somewhere in amongst them could be the offenders fingerprints.

However, that was weeks in advance, and Crofts had something more important on his mind, the call from the lab. He was sat in his office, trying to concentrate on the extensive list of emails that he needed to deal with.

The call he was waiting for came at about two o'clock, and again, Jo Whatmore was calling on her personal mobile. After the normal pleasantries she said "All good news! We've got a list of forty-three people from the national database who have similar markers in their DNA to the outstanding sample from the scene."

"Sounds good to me" Crofts replied.

"It might be" the scientist replied "Remember, this is only using data from a computer programme. It does mean that the names we will give you 'could' be related to the offender. Remember that, could be related."

"Yes, I realise that, but it is something that is definitely worth trying in this particular job, isn't it?" Crofts asked.

"Oh yes" Jo answered, "I just hope everyone realises that it is not given that it will get you a result."

"I'll reiterate that when I brief the officers" Crofts told her, "So what happens now?"

"I will send the list over to Kevin Bates in a minute, and he can organise how they are going to start the investigation."

Crofts thanked her and headed up to the incident room. Bates was on the phone, but when he saw who it was waiting to talk to him, he cut off the call sharply, "Anyway, I must go, I've got someone more important than you waiting to speak to me!" he said before clicking the end call button.

Crofts smiled, "Who was that?"

"Only the Chief Constable" Bates replied.

"No it wasn't" Crofts said.

"I know, it was one of the enquiry team, but I would have said the same to the Chief in these circumstances!" Bates answered, "So what have we got?"

Crofts explained what Jo Whatmore had told him.

"I think we should go and see the boss and let him know." Bates said, logging off from his computer and walking round to the SIO's office.

Mead and Williams looked up as they entered, "Is this the news we have been waiting for?" Mead asked.

Crofts explained again what the scientist had told him, he also reminded everyone that it was only a 'could' be.

"Forty-three is ok, for us" Bates said when Crofts had finished, "I have earmarked six DC's to carry this out, so that's only seven each really."

"I imagine some of them will be straight forward, won't they?" Williams asked Crofts.

"Yes, if they contact the person and find they have no male relatives, that's the end of that enquiry. I expect there will be some that are much more complicated to track down though" Crofts told them.

"Sods Law there will be" Bates replied, "Investigating is never that simple."

They all smiled, then Williams said, "Are you able to brief the officers tomorrow morning then Simon?"

"Yes, no problem" Crofts replied.

"Great I will contact them all now, and make sure they finish off whatever enquiries they are dealing with today so that they are ready for this tomorrow morning." She replied.

Chapter 73

The following morning Crofts and Bates met in the briefing room with the six detectives allocated the task of researching the results from the lab.

Crofts started by explaining what Familial DNA was, and how it worked. He knew that he would have covered this in his input to the CID courses over the years, but also knew that it was something that they needed to be reminded of. He could see that all the officers were looking as keen as mustard today with plenty of questions. They all knew how important this process could potentially be.

Crofts then showed them the correct way to take a buccal swab. He knew they all did it at some stage of their career, but it didn't hurt to remind them how to do it properly.

He then explained what the procedure would be for them, "So, the first thing you need to do is get the first name on your list and find out their contact details. Once you have them, give them a call. You need to explain why you are contacting them. You can say it is for an enquiry. You don't have to say which one it is. You need to then arrange to visit them.

When you meet them, you need to ask if they have any male relatives?" He paused and looked around the faces of the officers, "If they say no, then that is it for now. If they say yes, we then need contact details of those relatives. You will then need to contact those men and arrange to meet them. Once with them, you will then carry out the buccal swab and send it to the lab. Any questions"

"Yes" said a young detective with brown hair and designer stubble, "What if they lie about having a male relative?"

"At the moment we will just take it as read" Crofts replied "However, at a later date, all of the negatives will be researched further, if we need to."

"What about if they refuse to cooperate?" asked a blonde-haired female officer.

"Again, it will be noted, and then looked at later" Crofts answered "You can, when talking to them explain that is for elimination purposes only, and that they won't be added to the DNA database. Hopefully, most members of the public will be happy to do that."

"What about if it is the actual offender? If I was him, I would just refuse point blank and I doubt if there is anything you could do?" the blonde girl added.

Bates interjected "If it is a flat refusal at that point, that man then becomes a person of interest, and we will make further enquiries. A sample can also be taken by force if needed."

A couple of officers smiled. They had been previously involved with attempting to take samples from prisoners when they didn't want to give them, and it wasn't simple. Crofts saw them and added "I know what you're thinking, it's not easy, but we will get it somehow."

Crofts then went on to explain that once they had the swabs, they had to put them in the fridge in the exhibits store, and they would be sent off daily on the lab run. He finished by saying "I know you're all experienced officers, and I'm not trying to teach you to suck eggs, but you must make sure everything is in order" he paused as they all looked at him intently, "That means making sure all the paperwork is correct, and that all the information on the exhibit bag are correct before you leave that person. We don't want to get a positive result further down the line and then find that the evidence is thrown out because of a mistake in the details written on the bag."

They all nodded in agreement.

Bates then told them "Right let's get cracking. I want this procedure done as swiftly as possible."

There was a scraping of chairs as the detectives all got up and left the room.

Bates looked at Crofts and said, "Let's hope we get a result from this."

"I hope so too" Crofts replied.

Chapter 74

Jenny Simpson had worked at the estate agents in a small row of shops in the Langney Point area of Eastbourne for ten years, and she absolutely loved the job.

She enjoyed meeting different people every day. She met the sellers first, and quite often got to know them well. Then she would meet all the countless buyers she showed around the properties. Again she would get to know some families well through the ups and downs of the housing market.

She was there when the chain broke and she had to inform several people that their dream home wasn't going to be, but that was also there when she handed over the keys, and everyone was all smiles. She had always admitted that she was also a bit nosy and enjoyed looking around other people's homes.

That was why one of the reasons the job suited her so well.

Having started in the business in her twenties, she was working on the sales team at the newly built Sovereign Harbour, when she met Barry, an electrician working on the site. They had fallen in love and then married a couple of years later. Having had two girls, Demi and Lauren, Jenny had given up work to become a full-time mum.

It was then an ideal job to return to after the girls had become teenagers and were able to fend for themselves a bit more. It had been a struggle on the one wage, but Barry had worked hard for them over the years. She was now able to add to the coffers with the money she earned, enabling them to enjoy the luxury foreign holidays they enjoyed so much.

It was one of those that Jenny was thinking of this morning. The freezing rain and drizzle on the drive into work had made her think of their upcoming visit to Jamaica in three weeks' time. She could almost smell the coconut oil as she lazed on her sun bed sipping a cocktail.

Instead, it was the kettle boiling for the first coffee of the morning which brought her attention back to the day. As she poured a coffee for her and her best friend and colleague, Wendy, she heard her mobile phone ring in her handbag. She took it out and saw that it was a withheld number. She nearly didn't answer but thought better of it and clicked on the green button.

"Hello?" she replied.

"Is that Mrs Jenny Simpson?" a male voice asked.

"Yes, it is" she replied expecting it be a cold caller.

"Hello, let me introduce myself. I am Detective Constable Graham Johnson from the Sussex and Surrey Major Crime team" the male caller said.

"Oh" Jenny replied, feeling a sinking feeling in her stomach. She was apprehensive about talking to the police.

"Nothing to worry about" the detective continued "We are currently investigating a case, and I believe that you may be able to help us with our enquiries. Would it be possible for me to see you and have a chat?"

"Er, yes of course" Jenny answered, "When would you like to see me?"

"Whatever time suits you?" Johnson replied, "The sooner the better really, it won't take long."

"I'm an estate agent, so I'm around and about all day, but I could pop home and meet you at eleven this morning?" Jenny asked.

"That'll be perfect, what is your address?"

Jenny gave him the details and put the phone down, just as Wendy walked in, shaking her umbrella at the door. She turned and looked at Jenny "What's the matter? You look like you've seen a ghost?"

Jenny shook herself and replied, "Just had an odd phone call from the police."

"What have you been getting up to?" Wendy asked.

"Nothing!" Jenny laughed "They said I might be able to help with their enquiries."

"That sounds intriguing" Wendy replied.

"I know, but I can't think what with?"

Wendy thought for a moment before replying "It'll be about one of the houses you have visited recently. I had it a couple of times. If there's been a break-in or something and we've got the keys?"

Jenny gave a sigh of relief "Of course it will be."

## Chapter 75

The outside enquiry team office was buzzing this morning. The six detectives were searching through the different computer systems available to them to find contact details for the names they had been allocated. Every now and then one of them would be picking up one of the phones and arranging to meet those people.

Bates entered the room and asked them how they were getting on. Two of the detectives were still looking for their first name. "If you don't find it quickly, move on to another name. You can always go back to the more difficult ones later. I just want to get some samples taken and sent off, the sooner the better."

The two detectives nodded and diverted their searches.

"How are you getting on Johnno?" he asked.

"I'm off out at eleven to meet one of the names." He replied.

"Is it local?" Bates asked.

"Yes, it's just down near the harbour" Johnson replied.

"What was he done for?" Bates asked.

"It's not a 'he.' It's a middle-aged female, she's an estate agent. Back in ninety-five she had it taken when arrested for drink driving" the detective replied.

"Blimey, that was only just after they started taking DNA in Custody" Bates said "And for drink driving? That's not exactly a seasoned criminal, is it?" he chuckled "You're not doing too well on this enquiry, are you?" The others laughed, joining in the joke.

"It's not my fault. I can only deal with what I am given!" Johnno replied with a hurt look on his face.

"She doesn't go by the name of Hit girl on fakebook does she?" one of the other detectives called over.

As the laughter started, Johnno continued to shake his head "It's hard to soar with eagles when you work with turkeys!" was his response.

Bates smiled before saying "Right that's enough of the frivolity. Let's get back to work and let Columbo get on with his job!" nodding towards Johnson. There were a couple of more sniggers before they all continued with their work.

Chapter 76

Jenny had arrived home fifteen minutes early. She always liked to be punctual with her job anyway but thought it would be better if she had time to compose herself before the police attended. She put the kettle on and waited.

She knew it was him as soon as he parked outside. She lived in a quiet street where hardly any cars moved at this time of day anyway. As he got out of the car, she could tell he was a police officer even though he was in plain clothes.

She let him ring the bell before going to the door, even though she was aware he was there, it seemed the right thing to do.

Having shown her his ID, Johnno entered the living room and accepted the coffee he was offered. Jenny went into the kitchen as the detective surveyed the room. A nice cosy lounge, with a large TV screen on the wall and brown leather sofas to watch it from. Jenny entered and gave him the coffee.

"Lovely home you've got here" Johnno said.

"Thank you" Jenny said, her voice sounding nervous.

Johnson noticed that and continued in his light Geordie accent "As I said on the phone, it's nothing to worry about. We are carrying out an investigation and something has come up that you might be able to help us with?"

"Okay, so what exactly is it?" Jenny asked.

"We are on an enquiry where the offender has left a sample of DNA at the scene, but we don't know who he is as he is not on record."

"Right," said Jenny "So how can I help?"

"When this happens, we use a system to look through the DNA database to find similar samples to the one we have."

"Okay" Jenny replied, feeling herself reddening.

Johnson noticed it but continued "I'm aware that your DNA is on the database."

Jenny started to cry.

"I didn't mean to upset you, but I know it is there, I was just stating a fact."

"I know, but it was such a long time ago, and I've never been in trouble with the police since." Jenny sobbed.

"I know" Johnno replied, "It was only a drink drive offence, but you had your DNA taken whilst in custody, do you remember?"

"I do, I have always been so ashamed about it. It was during one of the Christmas period vehicle checks that they did. I had been out for a festive lunch at one of the seafront hotels. I only had a couple of glasses of wine, and I thought I would be fine as I was eating" Jenny paused as she composed herself again, "But the officer said he could smell alcohol on my breath at the vehicle stop, and asked me to take a breath test, which I was happy to do. It showed positive, and I was arrested, fingerprinted, and gave a DNA sample. I felt like a real criminal."

Johnno nodded sympathetically as she continued, "I was only just over the limit, but rules are rules, and I got fined. It has always haunted me, as I have never been in trouble with the police before or after that day."

Johnno paused a while, letting Jenny get her composure back before saying "The thing is, when it was run through the system, there were parts of it that showed it could be a male family member of yours that we are after" He waited to see if Jenny had understood what he had said, before continuing "So is your father still around?"

"No, he died five years ago" Jenny replied.

"Do you have any sons?" the detective asked.

"No, just two daughters" she said, feeling relieved.

"That's okay then. How about any brothers?"

Jenny laughed "Yes, I do have a brother, he's an accountant. I can't imagine he's the sort of person you would be looking for, the worst crime he has ever committed would have been stealing sweets off me when we were kids!"

Johnno smiled, "I'm sure that's true, but I will need to visit him to get an elimination sample. That way we can rule him out of our enquiries."

"Not a problem, let me just get my phone, and I will get you his details" Jenny said heading into the kitchen.

She returned and gave the detective the contact details she had for brother, who was working over in Hastings.

Johnno noted the address and phone number and then said, "I know it seems a bit over the top, but can I ask you not to contact him about this before I get over to see him?"

Jenny smiled and replied "Don't worry about that, even if I did call him, Bob is very conscientious, and turns his phone off while with clients. If I ever leave him a message, he only calls back at the end of the day when he has finished work."

"That's great then" Johnno replied, "I will head over to see him now, and get this cleared up."

"That's good" Jenny answered, "At least that will help your enquiries, won't it?"

"It will" said Johnno smiling, "And sorry for upsetting you earlier, I'm afraid I had to do it."

"I understand" Jenny said, feeling much better, "I hope you get your man, whoever it is."

"I'm sure we will" replied Johnson.

Chapter 77

It had only taken forty minutes for Johnson to drive over to Hastings. He found the address that he had been given for Bob Pearson just off the seafront in Warrior Square. He parked outside and took in the view. It was in a row of four storey Victorian terraced buildings. Originally, they would have been private homes but were now used by firms of solicitors and accountants.

The individual building that Johnno was heading to was very smartly decorated outside, newly painted white with black railings on the street level. As he approached the door, he noticed on the brass plaque that Pearson was a partner in the business.

Having entered the front door he found himself in the very plush reception area. The furniture was all polished deep oak, with lime green upholstery, smart beige rugs were scattered around the room on the marble flooring.

The reception desk was also deep oak, and behind it sat two receptionists. One was on the phone, but the other had efficiently already spotted the detective.

"Good morning, sir, how can I help you?"

"Hello, I am Detective Constable Graham Johnson from Sussex Major Crime Branch. I would like to speak to Bob Pearson?"

"Do you have an appointment, detective?" she enquired.

"No I don't Johnno replied.

"I'm afraid Mr Pearson doesn't see anyone without an appointment. It is one of his stipulations." The receptionist told him.

"I'm not here for accountancy reasons, I am here for police investigations. I need to speak to him as soon as possible. It is only a quick enquiry and will only take a couple of minutes. I can see him in between his appointments." Johnno told her firmly.

"Okay, I will go and speak to him" she replied rising, "Please take a seat over there" she said, pointing to the expensive furniture in the bay window area.

Johnson sat down and looked out of the window as he waited. The receptionist returned after a few minutes "Mr Pearson will see you shortly" she told him.

"Thank you" Johnno replied.

The phone rang and the receptionist picked it up, answering "Okay" before rising and indicating for Johnson to follow her. They walked along a corridor, all painted white, with landscape paintings hanging either side. There were deep oak doors either side and she stopped at one and knocked.

"Come" was the reply.

Johnno was ushered into the room where he was introduced to Bob Pearson, a fifty-year old man with greying hair, slim and dressed immaculately with blue suit, white shirt, and a plain dark blue tie. Johnno also spotted he was wearing shiny black leather brogues as he came round from the other side of his desk.

Having shook hands, the accountant asked Johnno if he wanted a coffee, and on confirmation, he asked the receptionist to make them a pot.

As she left the room, he asked "What can I do for you officer?"

Johnno explained about the DNA and the familial search which had brought up Jenny's profile.

"Wow, that's amazing" he said "Poor Jenny has always regretted that lunchtime drink" he continued, "It was so out of character for her, and really upset her at the time. She became tee-total after that you know."

"I saw how it affected her when I mentioned it" Johnno agreed.

There was a knock on the door, and the tray of coffee and some French biscuits was brought in. Johnno thought to himself that the place reeked of class and of money.

Once it had been poured, and they had both sipped on their drinks, Johnno continued to explain that he needed to take a DNA buccal swab from the accountant to eliminate him.

"I take it I don't have any choice?" he said, smiling.

"It is within your rights to refuse, but that would make you a suspect, and it could be taken by force if necessary" the detective told him.

"I don't think I would want to do that!" Pearson laughed.

Johnson took out the swab kit and took the saliva sample from Pearson's mouth and then sealed the bag.

"That's all there is to it" Johnno told him.

"That was simple" Pearson said, "How long does it take for you to get the results?"

"We will be sending it off daily as we have quite a few in this enquiry. It takes about forty-eight hours for the result." Johnno told him.

Having finished the formal work, Pearson then chatted to Johnson about some of the police officers he knew from the golf club he belonged to in the town of Battle, a few miles north of Hastings. Johnno noticed that they were all high-ranking officers, something that didn't surprise him.

Having finished the pot of coffee, they said their goodbyes and Johnson headed out to the car ready to drive to his next appointment.

Chapter 78

At the briefing the following morning, the six-man team updated the rest of the room on how they were getting on with their investigations.

It was starting to become obvious that it wasn't as simple a task as most of them thought. Although there were only forty-three names for them to follow, those names were just names from the database of people who had been in custody at some time in the past twenty years or so. When it came to finding those people and locating them, it was proving difficult.

There were one or two who had committed other crimes over the years, so it was easy to track them down to a current address, and detectives were able to see them straight away. In those cases there had been a couple who had originally refused to talk to the officers, as they 'didn't want to grass' on their relatives, but after having things explained to them about how their relatives could become murder suspects, they were co-operative.

Some, like Jenny had not committed another offence and had not moved from their local town. They were easy to locate using some of the intelligence systems available to the police and most had been visited within the preceding forty-eight hours. The detectives were all surprised how helpful most of those they had visited had been. There appeared to be no resistance to what they were being asked, and then the swabbing of their relatives had been straight forward.

However there were others who had almost vanished from the system. There were six that at this stage, where they had no idea where those people were. It could be for several reasons.

That person may have died, in which case the database might not have been updated.

It may have been that those people had changed their name for one reason or another and had not been caught for any other crime since, so their records hadn't been updated.

It could even have been an administrative mistake when the original swab was submitted. At the time it was a new system that was being introduced, so any errors may have been missed.

All these reasons meant that the team had to delve deeper into the system to investigate, and that then meant that they would take even longer for them to find, which wasn't good when time wasn't on their side, and a result was needed as soon as possible.

The good thing was that twelve samples had been sent off already. Even if they all turned out to be negative, it then cut down the number of suspects in the case, which meant that they were getting closer to the offender.

If this process worked.

Chapter 79

Crofts was at his desk the following morning, working through the piles of admin that had built up while he had been working on Op Durham.

His favourite part of his job was working at scenes. He enjoyed the investigation, enjoyed working with his team and the excitement of a major crime enquiry. However he also had a busy office to run with twenty staff.

Their leave requests, development reviews, and daily personal issues meant that he and his opposite number, Maria Milligan were always busy. The fact that she was currently up in Scotland visiting her parents meant that Crofts had even more work. He smiled to himself as he thought of the amount of ribbing, he would be able to give her for missing such a decent job. It had been the first Christmas she had not worked for three years, which was why she had headed up north for the festivities. He knew she would have been watching it unfurl on the news, and he knew she would secretly be disappointed that she had missed such an excellent job.

His phone started ringing. It was plugged in on charge the other side of the room, so he got up and walked over to it. He notice that it was Jo Whatmore calling on her personal phone.

"Hi Jo" he answered.

"Hello Simon, I've got an update for you" the scientist said.

"Go ahead"

"Well, as you know, in the first submission there were twelve samples sent in from relatives" she said.

"Yes, and we've got a few more heading over to you today" Crofts replied.

"That's good" Jo replied, before adding "We have actually got a hit from one of the first batch you sent."

"What?" Crofts shouted, making the other three examiners in the office stop what they were doing and look up.

"You did hear me correctly. We have a hit!" Jo answered happily.

"Oh my god! Who is it?" he said excitedly.

"It is a man by the name of Bob Pearson, and he is from Battle in East Sussex" she replied.

"Okay" said Crofts writing the name down quickly, "Obviously, I have no idea who he is, or what the connection to one of our names is, as I need to go up to the incident room to find out."

"That's okay" the scientist said, "Just keep me updated when you find out?"

"Of course I will" Crofts said, already heading out of his office, past the bemused members of his staff, and heading up the stairs to the MIR.

Chapter 80

In the incident room he walked over to Kevin Bates and flashed the yellow post-it note at him and said "Batesy, we need to go and see the SIO now!"

The detective sergeant looked at him quizzically but followed him anyway. Crofts knocked on the door of the SIO's office, Williams, and Mead both looked up, having been engrossed in their work.

"What is it?" Mead asked.

"We've only gone and got a hit" Crofts said simply, trying hard not to smile.

"I don't believe it!" Williams exclaimed.

"Close the door and tell us about it" Mead told them.

Bates did that and they all sat around the table, and Crofts recalled the phone call from the lab.

"Let me check who took the swab" Williams said, moving back to her computer. It only took a few clicks for her to find out, "It was Johnno."

Bates rose from his seat, "I'll go and see what he is up to." He told them on his way out of the door.

Mead, Williams, and Crofts sat waiting, all with big smiles on their faces, "I can't believe it" Mead said, "I must admit, the odds were so low, I didn't think we would get a result."

"Come off it Guv, you know forensics always gets you a result!" Crofts replied, and the two senior detectives both laughed, just as Bates arrived back with Johnson in tow.

"Oh no. What have I done wrong now?" Johnno said.

"Nothing this time" Williams replied, "However, you have done something very right for a change. Do you remember taking a swab from a chap named Bob Pearson?"

"Yes," he replied.

"What was he like and where does he live?" Williams asked.

"He's an accountant in Hastings but lives up in Battle" Johnno answered.

The other four looked at each other quizzically.

"Why, what's up?" Johnno asked.

Crofts told him about the DNA result.

"Is that a definite? Can it be checked?" the detective asked him.

"It will have been" Crofts replied, "They wouldn't have reported it if it wasn't definite."

"I must admit, I wouldn't have had him down as the offender" Johnno stated, "Nice chap, friends with several of our high-ranking officers at the golf club."

"Really?" Mead asked.

"Yes, and we only got his name because his sister was on the database from a drink drive twenty years ago!" he told them.

"That shows that he would never have been caught without familial searching then, doesn't it?" Crofts asked.

"It certainly does" Mead replied, "I have to say Simon, that forensics have certainly solved this one."

"Seriously though" Johnno said, "Weren't there some mistakes in the past with regards to DNA hits, where wrong people were accused?"

"There have been" Crofts replied, "But that was in the early years, and down to mistakes in the recording of the data. This, however, is the result of a sample that was only taken this week. There won't be an issue. This is your man."

"It looks like we need to organise an arrest strategy then Alison" Mead told his deputy.

"I'm on it straight away" she replied.

Crofts noticed the smiles on everyone's faces in the room, glad that he had been the bringer of the good news.

Chapter 81

It hadn't taken long for them to arrange the strategies and for them to obtain search warrants for Pearson's office and for his home address. Johnson was going to the accountants' office with a search team, and Martin Buller was going to the house with a team. Luckily, there were plenty of search trained officers already on duty, so at twelve o'clock, two vans headed out of the back of Hastings police station, one turning left to the town centre, and one turning right and heading out to the town of Battle, six miles away.

Johnno was sat in the front seat of the van. He'd already had some banter from the officers in the back, as it wasn't often that a detective from major crime would be joining them for a search. He loved it and was enjoying giving them some stick back.

The driver had asked whether to travel on blues and twos, but Johnno had replied "The bloke's got away with it for a couple of weeks, so another few minutes wouldn't hurt" which had caused amusement in the back.

On arrival at the office, Johnno told the officers to wait while he went in alone. He decided that he would be able to cope with Pearson on his own better than making a scene. He entered the door the same as he had only two days before, but for a different purpose this time. The same receptionist recognised him and called him by his name, asking what he wanted.

"I'd like to speak to Mr Pearson as soon as possible." He replied.

"I'm sorry, he's not in the office today" she answered.

"Oh" Johnno said, not expecting that reply, "Do you know where he is?"

"I'd rather not say" she replied, protectively.

"It is imperative that I speak to him straight away. It is a matter of most importance." Johnno stated formally.

"Oh, I see" the receptionist said, looking around the room before adding "I imagine he is at home. He sent us an email yesterday saying that he was feeling under the weather and was going to work from home. As he didn't come in today, it means he is still unwell."

"Okay, I will contact him there. Thank you" Johnno said, exiting through the door.

He jumped in the van and said "Move off" to the driver.

"Where are we going?" he asked.

"Anywhere" Johnno replied.

He waited until they were at the corner of the street before turning round and telling the other officers "Right, the suspect's not there, he's told them he's working from home" He waited while the others exchanged knowing glances, "I know we've got a warrant for his offices, but I'll wait until we get an update from his house before we go back for that, just in case one of his employees tips him off. It'll only be about twenty minutes. Who's getting the coffees in?"

He was treated to a barrage of abuse about how much extra money he was on as a detective on major crime and told in no uncertain terms who was going to pay for the coffees. Johnno just chuckled.

Chapter 82

Martin Buller was in the front seat of the other van, having the same sort of banter with the search team as was happening in the other van, when his phone rang.

"Hello mate, have you got him?" he asked.

"No, he's not here" Johnno replied, "He's not well, and working from home, allegedly."

"Really?" Buller asked.

"That's what I thought. It does now mean that you are likely to be the arresting officer. So I thought I'd better warn you" Johnno told him.

"No problem, I'll let you know how we get on" Buller replied, before telling the team in his van.

They continued their journey, soon reaching the outskirts of the small town of Battle. The driver then headed left along a road which led them back out to the countryside, before turning into a gateway which was the start of a long driveway, eventually arriving at a large, detached house.

"Very nice" one of the officers said from the back of the van.

"Indeed" said Buller before telling them to wait in the van whilst he went in to speak to Pearson.

He pressed the brass button inset into the wall, and heard the bell ring some distance away in the house. He waited for a while and was about to ring when he heard approaching footsteps. The door opened and he was confronted by a tall, slim, blond woman in her forties.

"Can I help you?" she asked.

"I am after Mr Bob Pearson" Buller stated.

"Can I ask who you are?" the blond asked, eyeing him suspiciously.

Buller showed her his warrant card and told her his name.

"Okay, detective, that's fine, but he's not here." She replied.

"Oh, can you tell me where he is?" Buller asked.

"Yes, he's up in London at a meeting" she replied.

"Really?" Buller replied, "His office have just told me he is unwell and working from home."

As an experienced interviewer, he could tell that this wasn't what she was expecting to hear.

"There must be some mistake" she said, recovering her composure "He called me from his hotel last night."

"There obviously is some mistake, as he told his office that he was working from home yesterday, as well" Buller replied.

"Oh" she replied, looking at Buller with a worried expression.

"Whatever has happened to him, I have here a search warrant signed by a magistrate instructing that I search this property. So I would like to instruct our officers to commence that search." Buller told her.

She looked up and over his shoulder, seeing the police van containing the officers for the first time, "Do I have to let you? Can I speak to my solicitor first?" she asked.

"Yes, you do, and you can speak to your solicitor, but he can't change anything. I also suggest you contact your husband and find out exactly what is going on and where he is. We need to speak to him as soon as" Buller told her.

"Okay, yes, and I will" she replied, taking her phone out of her pocket, and calling a number.

While she waited for whoever to answer, Buller motioned the search team over and gave them a quick update, adding "As well as looking for the items on your strategy, I will now also add that you look for any clues in to where he currently is, travel plans, etcetera. It looks like he may have done a runner." The officers nodded and started unloading their equipment out of the van.

He turned back to Wendy Pearson who was looking perplexed "His number is now showing as unattainable" she said.

"Now that doesn't surprise me" Buller replied, trying to keep a sarcastic tone out of his voice. He believed that this poor woman really was telling him the truth and didn't know anything about her husband's whereabouts.

"What is he up to?" she asked.

"I really don't know" the detective replied, as he took his phone out and made a call himself.

"Hello Johnno. He's not here either."

There was silence at the other end of the line.

"Are you there mate?" Buller asked.

"Yes, I am" Johnno replied, "It's just sunk in that this is not going to be as simple as we thought."

"That's exactly what I thought, his missus obviously doesn't know. She thought he was at a meeting in London. He called her last night, allegedly from a hotel up there." Buller told him.

"Why did we think that someone who has carried out this type of job would just sit there and wait for us to find him? We must be mad. He's had two full days to get away now, as well."

"Of course he has. I'll head back and meet you back at the office. I'll let you tell the SIO!" Buller replied.

"Thanks" said Johnson.

Chapter 83

Johnson walked back into the SIO's office, noticing the occupants were all looking crestfallen.

"Before anyone says it, it's not my fault!" he stated.

It raised a smile on their faces.

"I know it isn't" Williams told him, "We were just discussing what went wrong."

Bates continued "Yes, we've talked it over and decided that there wasn't much else we could have done, we are victims of our own success. If we hadn't had such a quick result, he would have still gone. He would have realised the minute he had to give that sample that it was only a matter of time before he would be caught."

"Exactly" said Mead, "We have discussed whether we should have kept an eye on him after he gave his sample, but that wouldn't have been feasible. We couldn't have watched all forty odd suspects until we got negative results, just in case. We know he's our man, but there was nothing to indicate him previously was there?"

"Nope" Johnson replied, "As I said before, when I went to take the sample, he was polite, and didn't look worried about giving the sample."

"When you think how cool he was at the scene, and carrying out the shootings, it shouldn't be a surprise" Mead answered.

They all nodded.

"What happens now?" Crofts asked.

"Obviously, we will see if the searches produce anything first" Bates replied, before adding "I've already set up the analysts with the task of finding out as much as possible about our new friend, Bob Pearson."

"I imagine you'll find out a lot of what he wants you to see quite easily, him being a successful local businessman" said Williams "But whether we find any clues to what he has done in this case, I very much doubt."

Mead nodded before adding "Me too, but we need to find out everything we can about this character. The info is in there somewhere."

"At least we have the forensic results" Mead said, "Any doubt that the result was wrong has now gone, hasn't it?"

"It certainly has" said Bates, as his phone started vibrating on the desk "Excuse me, that's the search team leader at his office."

He answered the call, and the others watched as his expression changed from questioning, surprise, to a smile, finally adding

"Thanks for that, carry on with the search and let me know if you find anything else."

He put the phone down and looked at the expectant faces. "Well, that was something I wasn't expecting" he said "The search team at his office found it quite a simple task, only a few items of furniture there, not much paperwork, as it is all stored centrally. About finished, when they moved his table, quite a large mahogany table?" He looked at Johnson, who nodded. "Anyway, as they move it, one of the searchers noticed that on the inside of one of the legs there was a join, only about six inches. They opened it and stored inside was a mobile phone and two credit cards!"

"Really?" Williams asked.

"Yes" replied Bates, "They're bringing it back for cybercrime to look at, but they've had a quick shuftie, and there's only three numbers on it."

"Go on" Williams urged.

"All three are online betting companies!" Bates replied.

"He's got money problems! We've finally got a motive" added Crofts.

"We certainly have" said Bates "It is all coming together nicely now."

"Apart from the most important thing" Mead said, "We haven't got a clue where he is."

Chapter 84

Now that she realised that her husband was obviously up to something, Wendy Pearson was a lot more helpful. She had made the whole search team hot drinks and sat in the kitchen at her laptop, trying to work out what Bob had been up to, and where he had gone. He had given her no clues that there was something up, and she could think of no reason.

The search teams carried on with their searches of various areas of the house. As was usual in their role, they were methodical, leaving no area unturned.

Martin Buller was sitting outside in the van, scrolling through his phone. He didn't see the point of sitting in the kitchen with the wife. Her initial hostility had now changed to a helpful mode as realisation had set in. He didn't want to make it worse for her.

He then heard a sudden shout "Hey, Sarge, come and have a look at this!" from within the double garage.

The search co-ordinator went over to have a look, before saying "Get a SOCO over to photograph it, before anyone touches it."

Buller jogged over to the garage.

"That's the fastest we've seen you move" the sergeant said.

"Very funny. What have you got?" Buller asked.

"There's a couple of bags and golf clubs in there. Nothing untoward, but then Andy spotted that one of them looked a bit odd and found a false bottom to the bag. Unzipped it and a small revolver and some ammunition fell out!" said the sergeant incredulously.

"You are joking?" Buller replied.

"I'm not. Just let the SOCO photo and deal with it forensically, and I'll let you see it" he replied.

Ellen Parsons had been sat along the road in her van, not expecting to be needed, when she got the call. She grabbed her equipment, put on her PPE, and headed into the garage to find Andy with a grin on his face, pointing at what he had found.

"That's a good find" Ellen told him.

"Just doing my job" he replied unable to stop smiling.

Ellen took some photos of the gun in its hiding place before removing it and securing it in a small cardboard box with a transparent plastic window. This would enable it to be protected, whilst still being on show to anyone who needed to see it, such as the incident room and for interviewers, if any offender was caught. She then did the same with the two small white boxes of ammunition, making a note of the numbers on the base, as well as photographing them. This would help the ballistics side of the enquiries.

She then took them out to show Martin Buller, who had a quick look at them before heading into the kitchen.

"Mrs Pearson, did you know if Bob had a gun at all?"

"Please call me Wendy, and no, of course he didn't."

"Well, we've found this in the garage at the bottom of one of his golf bags" Buller told her.

Wendy looked and exclaimed "Oh my god, what was that doing there?"

Buller shrugged, and continued "Not sure, but it may have something to do with why he has suddenly disappeared."

Wendy stood there, open mouthed, "Not my Bob, no! There must be some mistake. He would never have anything to do with a gun."

"Looks like we'll have to see" Buller stated, "can you honestly say that you have never seen these items?"

"No, I haven't, and I would also add that I can't imagine my Bob with them, either." Wendy replied.

"I believe you" Buller told her, "But up until an hour or so ago, you thought you knew where he was, and what he was doing, didn't you?"

"Yes" she replied, turning away as her eyes filled with tears.

Chapter   85

Crofts had the gun on the table in front of him as he prepared the lab submission form. He had just sent the photographs of the gun and the ammunition to Phil Jenkins. His mobile rang, and the ballistics scientist name showed on the screen. "Hello Phil, what do you think?" he asked.

"Hi, Simon. No doubt about it, the ammunition is the same as the empty cylinder you recovered, same markings. Once I've examined it, I'll be able to tell if they were fired by the same weapon. As for the gun itself, I obviously need to carry out the tests needed up here, but it is exactly the type of weapon I expected it to be." The scientist replied.

"That's good news. I'll be sending it up to you today, so will you be able to work on it tomorrow if you have time?" Crofts asked.

"Definitely will" Jenkins replied, "I can make it my priority. What's the story behind it?"

Crofts told him about the search finding, and his wife's reaction.

"That's a bit odd" Jenkins replied "Unusual for someone to have a gun and for their spouse to be unaware, but everyone is different!

Once I've done the tests, I'll also be able to tell you whether that weapon has been used in any other crimes, either solved, or unsolved."

"That's good" Crofts answered, "It'll be interesting to see whether this character has done this before, or whether it was a one off."

"Yes. I'm sure you're aware that nowadays due to the gun laws in this country, there aren't many guns available on the open market. How a plain accountant got hold of one will be interesting as well" the scientist told him.

"I know our intel people are trying to find out whether he has any connections with anyone in those circles" Crofts said, "Accountants do deal with people of all walks of life."

"I agree" Jenkins said, "However, there is a difference between carrying out some accountancy work for someone involved in gun provision, and actually getting a weapon."

"I know" Crofts said, laughing "What's that saying? – There's nowt as strange as folk?"

"There isn't" Jenkins replied "I've given up being surprised by what people do. It'll be great to get to the bottom of this though. Any update on where Pearson has gone?"

"Nothing" Crofts replied, "He has completely disappeared."

"I'm sure you'll find something about it soon" Jenkins said, and then added "Can't wait to look at this gun tomorrow, and hopefully give you some info that will help you."

"I'm sure you will." Crofts replied, before putting the phone down and carrying on with the paperwork needed to send the weapon off.

# Chapter 86

It had been a while since the briefing room was as full as it was on the Monday. Alison Williams had contacted all departments to ask as many officers as possible to attend. It had got to the stage in the enquiry that most units were able to stop what they were doing and attend that morning.

It meant a lot of noise and banter across the room. The briefings in the early days of the enquiry would be serious as everyone got on with their tasks, but now, with lots of the questions answered, it almost had an end of term feel about it.

The noise abated as Mead and Williams entered the room and sat down, and Mead asked everyone to introduce themselves.

He then said "I would like to say a big thank you and well done to all involved in this enquiry. We have covered a lot of ground and done it quickly to get to where we are now. There is still a lot of work to do, especially in tracing our main suspect, but I know we'll get there. So well done again.

Right the first update I want is from the forensic side of things. Before he says it, yes, this is another job that we couldn't have done without that side of things isn't it Mr Crofts?"

Crofts smiled "Yes, Guv it certainly is. I wasn't going to mention it" There were a few sniggers around the room before he continued, "The ballistics scientist, Phil Jenkins called me this morning with an update. The ammunition that we found at Pearson's house is the same as the empty casing we found in the main bedroom at the scene."

There were a few knowing nods around the room, before Crofts continued "After examining the weapon, he concluded that it was likely to be the same weapon that had fired the fatal shots. He then carried out test firing of the weapon, using some of the ammunition.

He then examined the empty cases and compared them to our one found at the scene." Crofts paused and looked around the room before adding "He has said that the striation marks on all of the casings prove that they were all fired by the same weapon, and that that weapon is the one recovered in Pearson's garage."

There was a cheer around the room, and a few people started high-fiving and the normal composure of a briefing disappeared for a few moments, before being brought back to normal by Kevin Bates saying "Calm down, everyone. We might have the weapon, but we have no idea where the man who fired it is," which managed to quieten everyone down.

Having got the most essential information into the meeting, the other departments then added their updates.

The financial side of the enquiry was heavily into Jimmy's business dealings. So far everything seemed legitimate. There was a lot of money involved, but he had been highly successful in his dealings within the property sector over the years. There was no obvious signs of any involvement with drugs at this stage, but that didn't mean that there wasn't any. Over the years they had found proceeds of criminal activities in a lot of companies that weren't obvious to the outsider. They would carry on working on their investigations.

The financial background to Bob Pearson was completely different. Although he appeared well off, he certainly wasn't according to his bank accounts. He was up to his limit on all his credit cards and was in that much trouble financially that he was in danger of losing his house. The cards and the mobile phone found hidden in his office showed that he had a betting habit that went back over five years. Every now and then there would be an individual win, sometimes quite substantial, but in general he was losing a lot.

He had only had dealings with the Fletchers over the last two years but had met up with them monthly according to his diary, although there was no record of where those meetings took place, apart from the fact that they weren't at his office. So they could have been at Jimmy's office or at his home, neither which would have been unusual in either of their business dealings.

There had still been no sightings of anyone or anything suspicious around the Cooden Beach area on the day. The ANPR systems had been checked for both Pearson's cars on the day in question, and neither had been registered anywhere outside Battle.

At the end of the briefing, Mead summarised "So we know the weapon that shot the Fletchers was found in the garage of Bob Pearson. We know he had money issues, and we also know that he was aware of how much money the Fletchers had. So we can only surmise that there is our connection. However, we have no reason Pearson had that gun and ammunition. We have no idea how he (or someone he knew) managed to carry out the shooting and not be seen by anyone, and we don't have any idea where he has gone" he paused looking around the room, "So we need to get right into this characters background" there were a few nods of agreement around the table, "There has got to be something hidden in his background that he has managed to keep hidden, so far. It is up to us to find it."

Mead nodded to Kevin Bates who continued "I have plenty of actions generated by the system for the outside enquiry team to start getting into. We need to know everything possible about Pearson, from the day he was born, to today. Every single piece of information could be vital. Somewhere in there will be a tiny piece of data that unlocks this case. Now go out and find it."

There was a murmuring as the officers stood up, recovered their notebooks, and left the room. In this case it was a confident buzz, as every one of them leaving that room were in no doubt that they would get their man.

Chapter 87

Martin Buller went straight back to interview Wendy Pearson formally. He wanted to know all about their lives together. He had gone right back to when they had first met. Going into detail about everything from how they had got together, even who introduced them, and what had happened from there onwards. It took a couple of hours, and Buller could see how upsetting it was for her, and he could tell that she was oblivious to anything that had happened outside their happy marriage. Apart from a few business trips that she had been a little suspicious about over the years, there was nothing that she could think of that was anything other than their normal life. Buller believed her.

Graham Johnson decided to go back to see Pearson's sister, Jenny Simpson. Having made an appointment to see her at her home, he remembered her wariness of the police once inside.

He had put her at ease straight away, by telling her that she wasn't in trouble or anything, they just wanted some background history of Pearson.

He sensed her ease as she heard that and answered the detective's question about their childhood.

They had both been born in Eastbourne, Jenny was two years older. As they grew up in the Langney Point area of town, they had a happy childhood, with loving, supportive parents, and both did well at school. Bob had always loved and been good at Maths. A fact that had helped her, as he was able to complete her homework even though he was two years her junior. He went on to college and was just completing his pure mathematics A Levels when the Falklands War happened.

Jenny remembered that he almost became obsessed by the news every night and pouring over the newspaper reports. It was so unusual as he had never been interested in anything military before that. He hadn't even been in the cadets. His only topic of conversation was about the various aspects of the conflict, and then he told them he wanted to join the military.

It was a shock for them all, but once he had made up his mind, there was no way he would change his mind. He went along to the careers office in Brighton, hoping to join the Paras or the Marines, as they were involved in the conflict. However, once he did the asymmetric tests, it was obvious to the recruiting sergeant that Pearson was highly intelligent and would be wasted as a foot soldier. He decided that it would be better for him to join the Army Pay Corps. Pearson wasn't overly happy, but the sergeant told him, that it was a great regiment for promotion, and that he could later apply for attachment to either the Paras or the Marines, where he could do their training course and end up wearing the maroon or green beret he so wanted.

As this was all he had been after, having watched those two units win the war, Pearson agreed, and signed up.

He left home a month later and he went off for his basic training. Twelve weeks later, Jenny and her parents went to Pirbright in Surrey to watch the passing out parade. Jenny remembered that he was a completely different person. He had matured and was now a confident young man who loved the military life.

Jenny remembered that she hardly saw him after, except for when he was on leave. He would spend most of his time home in various pubs in the town, she noticed he swore a lot, and that he tried to chat up all her friends. Something she didn't like, and most of her friends didn't, either.

He had finished his trade training, and joined his regiment in Germany, but the only thing on his mind was to get fit enough to join one of the units he so craved for. A year later he went to the commando training centre in Devon where he joined the all-arms commando course, along with members of several different regiments and naval ratings who wanted to be attached to the Royal Marines.

After six weeks of arduous training he passed the course and was awarded the coveted green beret. He was then sent to the commando logistic regiment in Plymouth. Jenny remembered him coming home on leave, and being even more cocky, loud mouthed, and drinking even more. In fact, the few times they went out together, she found him obnoxious, thinking he was god's gift to every woman in the pub. She could also see that he wasn't going down too well with the local men either, or it was only his commando forces sweatshirt that stopped people attacking him.

He didn't come home so often then. He said he had outgrown his friends at home, and that they were boring. He loved his life in Plymouth with his brethren, and so spent most of his leave there.

About a year later, he rang home to say that he would be home over that weekend and would be bringing his new girlfriend. They were all surprised, as he hadn't mentioned her before. So he turned up with Tina, a pretty blonde girl from Plymouth. They could see that he was besotted with her, and she seemed happy too. She had been brought up in the city, and so knew servicemen well. All the things that Jenny and her friends didn't like about Pearson; Tina seemed to encourage. Their parents took them all out for a meal, and they couldn't believe how the two of them behaved, they were so loud. In fact after they had finished, their father went back to the restaurant and apologised for their behaviour.

They were all glad when the couple left and went back to Devon.

Chapter 88

Jenny remembered that they hardly heard from Pearson after that for some months. Then one evening she was sitting at home watching the television when there was a knock at the door, and her dad answered it. She heard him say "Hello mate, what are you doing here?" and then Pearson walked into the room and dumped his bergen on the floor.

"What's going on?" their mother asked.

"I've quit the Army" he stated.

"But I thought you loved it?" his dad asked.

"I did, but I've now realised that they're a bunch of muppets, and I want a normal life again. I've had enough of travelling about with that bunch of dickheads. It's time to get back to the real world."

None of them could believe what they were hearing.

"What about Tina?" Jenny had asked.

"She's the same as all the Plymouth girls, she'll find another serviceman soon enough" he had replied.

He had then grabbed his pack, and went up to his bedroom, and didn't emerge from it for a few days. His mum made him meals and left them outside. They were all eaten, so that put her mind at rest.

A few days later, he disappeared out of the door, and came back in the evening with a smile on his face. He had been into the town and been to see one of the partners in a local accountancy firm. He knew him, as he had been one of his old bosses in Germany. He had told Pearson that the qualifications he had obtained during his training were good enough for him to take him on in his firm.

Pearson had started the following week and made a success of the role, gaining promotion within the firm, and then eventually becoming a partner, before starting his own firm in Hastings.

He never mentioned the Army again.

He met Wendy a couple of years later, and the rest of his life had been as everyone had seen it. Successful businessman, happily married man, and a pillar of the community.

"Did you ever find out why he left the army?" Johnson

"Not officially" Jenny replied.

"What do you mean?" he asked.

"You bloody detectives" Jenny replied, "You know how to get information out of people, don't you?"

Johnson smiled, "It is my job you know. So what did you hear?"

Jenny inhaled before replying "As I said, Bob never mentioned it, and never again talked about even being in the army, I don't think Wendy even knew that he had served. However, I knew a lad who was serving in Plymouth in the navy, and I got him to try and find out."

She paused, before continuing "From what he could find out, Tina was 'friendly' with lots of the lads based in Plymouth. They had moved in together into a flat near to Union Street, the main centre for the nightlife in the city. Bob had gone away on exercise for a few days on Salisbury Plain. For some reason he had driven back to Plymouth during the exercise and decided to pop in to surprise Tina" She took a drink of water before saying "It was definitely a surprise, as she was in bed with two American sailors!"

"Wow!" Johnson said.

"I know" Jenny replied, "There was a fight, and Bob got arrested by the military police. He was taken back to barracks and charged with assault. He was found guilty and fined. There was no way in the military environment that it was ever going to remain a secret and the ribbing started that day and got decidedly worse. Bob couldn't cope with it, and just walked into his commanding officer and requested to buy himself out of the army, and he agreed. It was all done very quickly due to the circumstances. That's why he suddenly turned up at home, unannounced."

She paused before adding "He has never mentioned it to any of our family."

The detective thought for a moment before saying "Thank you for that. It gives us a lot of leads to find out what he has done, and where he may have gone. All that information was unknown to his wife?"

"Yes, it was. I so wanted to tell her about it many times over the years, but as Bob never mentioned it, I didn't have the heart to tell her, and spoil their marriage. It looks like she is going to be finding out a few more secrets from her 'loving' husband" she said, looking sad.

"It certainly does" Johnson agreed.

## Chapter 89

On return to the major incident room, Johnson headed straight to Anita Marshall's desk and explained what Jenny had told him. The analyst took some notes and then started looking on her computer "Getting his military record is nice and simple" she told the detective.

"That's good. Once we have that, it might lead to other avenues of his life that he has kept hidden." Johnson told before heading along the corridor to the SIO's office.

Tom Mead and Alison Williams were both deeply engrossed in their computers but looked up at the sound of the knock on the door.

"Hi Johnno, what's up?" the deputy asked.

Johnson updated them with the information he had been given.

"That's a turn up for the books" Mead stated, "It does explain some of the case though, doesn't it?"

The others agreed.

Johnson added "It certainly does. The one thing that we couldn't work out was how the offender had managed to be so good at initially carrying out the shooting, and then leaving little evidence. I imagine commando training might have helped."

Williams nodded in agreement, "But why has he kept that hidden all this time?"

"I imagine that finding his so-called girlfriend in bed with two blokes was bad enough, the fact that they were American sailors even worse for a rugsy commando. The mickey taking amongst servicemen is terrible anyway, but with that sort of ammunition all he could see was that his life was going to be hell from that day on" Johnson replied.

"It happens in all walks of life" Mead said "You get someone who is the life and soul of the party, confident and popular. All is well while they are in charge of things. The minute the tables turn, and they become a laughingstock, they can't cope with it."

"Good at giving it out but can't take it back" Johnson added.

There was a knock at the door and the analyst was stood there, looking worried.

"Come in" Johnson told her "What have you got?"

Anita visibly reddened before telling them "I have his army records and they are exactly as his sister remembered. He joined in September eighty-two, served four years, and left in August eighty-six, at his own request. All the units are as she recalled."

"Did he have any further connection with the services after he left? Did he go on to the reserve list, or join the territorials?" Mead asked.

"No, nothing at all. No other military connection after he left" Anita stated.

"Seems like he really did just up and leave" Williams said.

"Still it gives us a start" Mead told her "Have a look at cross referencing any of that information with his client list, and friends. See if there's someone that he has stayed connected with?"

"Certainly, sir, although I know his wife said that he doesn't do social media such as Facebook or twitter" the analyst told them.

"I know, but he also told his wife a lot of other stuff that wasn't true, and completely forgot to tell her about four years of his life" Johnson said, "We can't believe anything he told her."

"I guess so. I'll start widening the parameters" Anita told them.

"Thank you, and clever work so far" Mead added before she left.

Williams went through to call Kevin Bates through from the main office and updated him with the information. Mead told him "I think the key to finding this character lies in that 'hidden' service background. Can you sort out some actions along those lines?"

"Certainly will, guv" the sergeant said before heading back to his desk to get to work.

Mead told Johnson "Well done Johnno, you might have cracked this one after all!"

Johnson shook his head and smiled "I'm never going to live that other one down, am I?" before adding, "But don't worry, I'm not likely to leave because of all the banter!"

The two senior detectives laughed, before Williams said, "You know we couldn't cope if you did?"

The three of them laughed together.

Chapter 90

Bob Pearson sat on a bench on The Hoe in Plymouth, sipping his coffee and looking out to sea. It was a great vantage point. He could see for miles and was watching the movements of the naval ships and fishing boats entering and leaving the harbour. He was thinking back over what had happened in the last few weeks, and he was also thinking that he had got away with it.

He had realised some months ago that he was addicted to gambling. He was also still in the gamblers mindset that the next bet would be the winner that would solve all his problems. As many others had found, it wasn't.

As he had borrowed more and more against the business and against his house, he had realised that there was a distinct chance of him losing both. He knew he couldn't face that, and he knew that Wendy would never have been able to either.

He also knew that if anyone started to investigate his accountancy work, they would find that he had been making quite a bit of extra cash through dealings that would not have stood up in court.

He was in trouble.

He was looking at several different ideas on how to make a large amount of money on the side when he met Jimmy Fletcher at the golf club. They hadn't really been formally introduced. He knew of him through other acquaintances and had seen him around the club.

Then one day Jimmy's group were a man short, and Bob had joined them. What started out as a normal round of golf had changed when Jimmy had asked Bob what he did for a living.

"I could do with a new accountant" Jimmy had told him, "Mine's retiring soon and looking to hand me down the line in his business, but I don't really fancy that. I'd rather use someone I choose. Someone who has similar interests to me, like golf!"

Bob had laughed, thinking that he was joking.

Jimmy realised straight away that he wasn't being taken seriously, so added "I don't joke about things like this. I have always used my gut reaction in business, and it has done me well over the years. I've heard of your reputation, and I think you can do a job for me. I can tell you, that it will be lucrative for you."

Bob was well used to doing business on the golf course but couldn't believe what Jimmy was telling him. They arranged to meet the following day at The Lamb, a country pub in the village of Hooe. Jimmy told him not to mention it to anyone as he didn't want anyone else involved at that stage.

The following day, over a long lunch, Jimmy had explained some of his business dealings, and how much money he would be moving about. Bob was used to working with this type of clientele and was able to give Jimmy the information that he knew he wanted to hear. Secretly, Bob knew that this might be the answer to his prayers. He just had to think of a plan.

They met several times after that first meeting. Jimmy kept insisting that no-one else was to know at this stage due to his current accountants association with him. Bob was gleaning as many details as possible, all the time noting what he could do with all the information.

It was when Jimmy mentioned about his 'secret stash' of cash at his house, and how much there was that Bob started to bring his plan to fruition.

He had realised about a year before that everything was going to pot. He knew that he was in too deep to ever pay all the debts off, so decided to plan a way out. He had spent many hours thinking about it and realised that the only way out was to disappear. That way he wouldn't have to face the fall from grace. It also meant that eventually Wendy would end up with the house and life insurances. It would take a while, but it would be hers.

He didn't feel any guilt about leaving Wendy. He did love her, but after all these years they were more like brother and sister. She had fitted the bill excellently when he met her. A nice, safe, loyal wife who enjoyed being married to an accountant. She enjoyed the social circle to which they belonged, much more than Bob did, although he always made sure it looked as if he was happy, it went with the job.

He guessed that when he went missing, they would uncover his debts and guess that he had gone off and taken his own life. Something that wouldn't be too unusual in the circumstances.

For the last year, he had slowly been syphoning insignificant amounts from various clients and putting them in a separate account that would be untraceable. None of the clients he chose would notice as they all trusted him with their money. Although it was only small amounts, it soon added up to a tidy sum, enough to invest in an apartment on the Barbican in Plymouth.

It was an area he had loved living in when he was younger. As well as being beside the sea, it was only a few miles away from the vast area of Dartmoor where he could spend as much time as he wanted. Whether walking, cycling, climbing, or camping, it was the largest free playground. It would suit him down to the ground. He loved the outdoors, something his job didn't allow him to do. With nothing else to do in life he would be able to go up on the moors whenever he wanted.

Chapter 91

The first thing he had to do was make up a new name and persona, something he managed to do very simply. He had been involved in quite a lot of cases of hidden accounting over the years and knew how easy that was to deal with the money side of things, now all he had to do was make up the name.

He tried the technique that was first mentioned in a spy book he had read many years before and had also been used by the police for their undercover officers at various times. It meant searching around local graveyards for someone who was born the same time as him.

After noting the name and date of birth, he then applied for a copy of the birth certificate which was duly dispatched to him. With that, under his new name of Paul Ward, he was able to open bank accounts, savings accounts, and all other personal memberships of random organisations.

He had them all sent to a PO Box in Plymouth which he collected once a month whilst on business trips. Once he had enough money syphoned off, he bought the apartment on the Barbican overlooking the sea. He knew all the transactions needed, and Paul Ward was able to pass through them all without causing any questions or any hold ups.

The only thing he needed was ready cash, and when Jimmy had told him about his money in the safe, it was all he needed to know. He was going to vanish soon anyway, so knocking off someone was the least of his worries. It had been a long time since he had served as a commando, but it had never left him, and it was a fitting end to Bob Pearson's life. He was looking forward to it.

He had joined the Senlac Gun Club in Hastings with his new name of Paul Ward. They were very tight on security, but it didn't take him long to learn the routines there, and he was able to get a revolver out and then some ammunition, over a few weeks.

It was the week before Christmas that he had met with Jimmy again, and he had told him about his and Natalie's plans over the festive period in detail. He had already realised that it was nearing the time for his disappearance, as Jimmy was getting close to the time that he would officially start using him. He didn't want any real connection to him, so would have to act soon.

He hired a car on the morning he knew that the Fletchers would be in and parked about a mile away from the houses on some beach land.

He purposely didn't carry a mobile phone or other electronic device. It was a risk, but also meant that he wouldn't be picked up on any networks. He then walked slowly along the beach amongst other walkers, slowing right down outside their house and hoping to attract their attention.

He couldn't believe his luck, Jimmy was stood at his large ground floor window with a coffee, looking out. He spotted Pearson, slid open the patio door and called him over. Pearson made a bit of a show of pretending he didn't know who it was before walking over to the fence. Jimmy invited him inside for a coffee, and they stood together admiring the views out to sea.

Pearson had told Jimmy that he didn't realise that was where he lived, and Jimmy had told him "And this is why I want to sign you up as my accountant."

Pearson had smiled and agreed to take him on. Jimmy had then gone looking for a pen, and when he headed into the utility room, Pearson had decided that this was his moment. He drew the gun and shot him at point blank range as he walked into the room. He fell forward into the room.

Natalie had shouted "What was that?" and started heading down the stairs. She was unaware that Pearson was in the house, as she had been showering and getting herself ready in the bedroom. He had the element of surprise and shot her twice on the stairs. He then started searching for the safe, which he found straight away, and guessed the combination using Jimmy's date of birth.

It was incredibly quiet now that the sounds of the gun had stopped ringing in his ears, but he could hear a faint noise somewhere above. He slowly headed towards the stairway, and then saw that Natalie was no longer where he had shot her. For a split second he panicked, and ran up the stairs two at a time, before seeing the blood trail, and Natalie halfway across the bedroom floor, slowly moving towards her mobile phone which was on charge in the far corner. He grabbed her and turned her over, shooting her between the eyes, so that he knew she was dead.

He swore at himself, knowing that he had nearly cocked up the whole plan by not checking her. Attention to detail, he had always been taught, but he hadn't this time, and he knew he had to switch on and get out of there still.

He picked up the empty cases upstairs and in the room downstairs. He then scooped up the cash from the safe before re-locking it and putting everything back in place. He didn't have time to count the cash, but he guessed about two hundred thousand in used notes. Just what he needed. He had then taken one of the patio door keys and let himself out and locked up after him.

He then walked casually along the beach, throwing the empty cases one by one into the sea, followed by the key. On arrival back at the hire car he drove to a secluded car park along the Marsh Road where he changed his clothing and shoes. He parked the car in a side street in Hastings before walking into the town centre, discarding the clothing in a large rubbish bin on the seafront, knowing it would be emptied that evening. He then caught a train back to Battle.

He thought about making his disappearance that day but decided against it. He knew that once the bodies were found a major enquiry would take place, and him going missing the same day might connect the two events. Living a normal life and then vanishing a few weeks later would be less likely to ring alarm bells, and the busy police would just treat his case as a missing person.

The visit from Johnson had meant that he had to bring his plan forward, but as everything was now in place, he was ready. He just walked out of his office, and drove his hire car off to Birmingham, where he left it as planned.

He then bought some casual clothes and Paul Ward checked into a Travelodge overnight. He left the next morning and caught the National Express coach down to Plymouth. Later that evening he was sat on his small balcony of his flat watching the fishing boats returning to port.

Chapter 92

Over the next few days he had hardly ventured out. Just stayed in the apartment and just got used to being Paul Ward. He scoured the news websites for updates on the murder of the Fletchers, but there wasn't much coverage now. As he was now living in a different part of the country it wouldn't be on the local news anyway.

He started to leave the house occasionally, just to get provisions from the local co-op shop. As he remembered, the Plymothians were a friendly bunch, and he was soon on nodding terms with various neighbours who he would see on his short treks.

He went online looking for a second-hand car, his only stipulation was that it was a four by four, so he could use it up on the moors. He soon found an old black range rover which fitted the bill, and paid cash for it. Even though he was sure there was no connection back to Bob Pearson, he was careful with what he was doing on the money side of things. He had to spend money like Paul Ward would.

Although he had somewhere to live and plenty of money in the bank, he had little income coming in.

He had made some investments which would bring him some money each month, but he would never get a pension now, so he had to be careful of the future. Once the summer came, he would find some cash in hand work somewhere on the boats or other tourist attractions and see what happened from then on.

He had checked that the real Paul Ward had died as a child, and so had no social media contacts, and few people who would have remembered him by now.

In his mind he had prepared a script for his Paul Ward.

From London originally, worked in insurance, wife had died, and he had retired to the west country on his own. All very plausible, and all easy for him to talk about if ever questioned.

He finally tried an evening out on the Barbican after a fortnight. He went to The Three Crowns, one of the biggest pubs on the quay side. He had a decent steak meal and sat and watched the other customers, quiet couples as it was a midweek evening. Then the peace was shattered by four loud young men who came in and stood at the bar. Ward could tell straight away that they were servicemen.

He watched them as they all tried to chat up the pretty blonde barmaid, who was loving all the attention. It reminded him of himself thirty years before, and he smiled to himself.

He heard the tallest one tell the barmaid that they would be going to The Navy after they had finished there. She replied, "I'll make sure I won't go there then." Which caused the other three to cheer and take the mickey out of their mate.

Ward had waited until after they had gone before finishing his pint and strolling around past The Navy pub. He told himself that it was on his way home, anyway. The music was loud, and the disco ball light was spinning on the ceiling. Two girls were crucifying 'Simply the best' by Tina Turner on the karaoke on the small stage. It was about half full, which surprised him for a Wednesday night, but then he remembered when he was based down there, and he was out every night. Servicemen always had enough cash for a night out.

He stood waiting to be served, and an attractive woman of a similar age to him came to serve him. "Alright my lover, what are you having?" she asked in the strong Plymothian accent he remembered so well. He ordered a pint of Stella which she duly served and then gave him a wink as she handed him the change. He felt himself redden and turned away quickly. No woman had treated him like that since he had last been down that way.

He almost felt like a twenty something squaddie again. He stayed for another drink and then headed home, as he thought that was what Paul Ward would have done. Along the road from his apartment was a row of shops that he hadn't really noticed before as they all looked closed down. However at night three of them were lit up, all selling fast food, he remembered that at the end of a night on the beer, they would always get what they called 'big eats' on the way home. So he wandered over and ordered himself a lamb doner kebab, something else he hadn't had for thirty years.

He got back to his apartment and sat on his balcony, chomping away on his kebab. He'd had a thoroughly good night out, and he was beginning to believe that he was going to like the world of Paul Ward.

Chapter 93

The chairman of the Senlac gun club, Alan Hardy, had contacted the police as soon as he realised there was a gun missing. He had contacted the Firearms Liaison Team who he usually dealt with monthly, but as soon as the clerk heard that it was a revolver missing in the Hastings area, she had put him in touch with the major crime team.

Martin Bullard was now in his office and listening to him telling him how everything was so tight on the security front, and how they had never had one go missing before.

Buller quickly shut him up by saying "But you have got one missing now, haven't you?"

"Er yes" he replied, looking down at the floor.

"I'm not too bothered about the other stuff, and I know you run a good club here, the firearms liaison guy told me that. All we need to do is find out who took this one, and how, and where he is now" Buller told him.

Hardy visibly relaxed, and started to take on an extremely helpful tone, realising that his beloved club was not going to be shut down.

"What can I do to help?"

"I want a full list of members, and their attendance dates to start with?" Buller told him "I'm guessing that if it was our man, he wouldn't have been in here since, would he?"

"Certainly, we do keep all of those type of things on record" Hardy replied going to his computer and printing off a couple of pages of lists.

They went through the lists together, Hardy being knowledgeable about all the members. After about fifteen minutes there were only five names left that hadn't visited the club since the murders.

"The easiest thing to do, is just ring them" Buller told him.

"What do I say?" Hardy asked.

"Just tell them you are updating your systems for the new year, and that you are just checking they still want to be members?" Buller said.

Hardy nodded in agreement and started making the calls. It took a while as each call wasn't just a yes or no. It ended up with a conversation about anything to do with guns. Buller excused himself and went outside to wait. Hardy came and found him. "All done, everyone accounted for except one, who's phone seems to have broken."

"Really? So what's his name then?" the detective asked him.

"Andrew Farrell" Hardy replied.

"Do you have any details of this Mr Farrell?"

"Yes, of course. I will get his file" Hardy told him.

He returned and gave the file to Buller who opened it. The first thing he saw was a copy of the photo ID of Andrew Fuller, and straight away the photo looked familiar.

"When did he join?" Buller asked.

"About a year ago" Hardy replied.

"What was he like?" Buller questioned.

Hardy thought for a moment before answering "He seemed a nice bloke, recently moved down from London, said he worked in insurance."

"Did he now" Buller said "Well, I can tell you he isn't who he said he was, and it does look like our suspect."

"Oh" Hardy responded, disappointedly, "We did the usual checks on him though?"

"I'm sure you did, however this man is clever" Buller told him, "He has managed to get away with a double murder, and is nowhere to be found at the moment, so faking his ID for your club would have been easy for him."

"I suppose so" Hardy said, "but I will need to find out how and what he did, so that we can stop it happening again in the future."

"I'm sure that when the dust settles, we'll be able to tell you that information. Can I take the copy of the registration form he filled in?" Buller asked.

"Of course you can, anything to help, but why do you need it?" Hardy asked.

"He had to fill it in by hand, so his fingerprints will be on it" Buller told him "We can get it chemically treated and get a copy of his prints on there. We can then run them against his marks when we catch him. It will tie him back to the club, and to the fact that was how he got hold of the gun used in the shootings."

"That's if you catch him?" Hardy asked.

"We will eventually, don't worry" Buller told him.

Chapter 94

A few days later, and it was Saturday. Paul Ward had had a good day so far. He'd got up early and went for a jog from his apartment, around the Barbican, before running up on to the Hoe, around the top of the front, round to the Stonehouse area, before heading back. His phone told him he had run four miles in total, and he felt good for it. He had a bacon sandwich from Captain Jaspers on the quayside, it was originally a burger van which had now turned into a thriving business, as the queue for food showed.

He then spent the afternoon reading a book on his balcony, before getting ready to go out. He had enjoyed his night out during the week and thought he would sample a Saturday night in his new hometown.

He had a stroll around the harbour area to a restaurant called Suphas, an Asian street food restaurant he had seen whilst out on his run. It was a brightly coloured restaurant, busy already, which was always a good sign. He was shown to his table, and he ordered a Tiger beer to drink while he looked through the menu. The smells were amazing, and the open kitchen in the middle of the restaurant was busy with three Asian ladies expertly cooking their specialities, all the time chatting to each in their happy singsong voices.

Ward sipped his beer and dipped the prawn crackers in the sweet chilli sauce before eating them. He decided to order coconut prawns for starters and then a whole crab in a sticky black pepper sauce as a main course with a side of noodles and fried rice.

The starter was served within ten minutes and Ward devoured it quickly. He hadn't realised how hungry he had been, and sat waiting for his crab, looking around and realising that this was his future, sitting on his own in restaurants. It felt strange. He couldn't think of a time when he would have been sat alone eating food. Most evenings he would eat with Wendy, but when he did eat out through business, it was always with a client or colleague. This was going to take some getting used to.

He wondered to himself if he could continue in this way, or would it be better trying to find some female company, but he realised that if he did, there would be many questions about his past, and he wasn't ready for that yet. He still had to get used to being Paul.

The crab was also delicious, and he finished off another two bottles of the beer with it. Feeling stuffed, he paid the bill and went for a walk around the quayside. He ended up in a pub called The Dolphin. He could tell from the photos on the walls, that this was an old established pub which had been there for many years. It would look dated in most towns, but here on the Barbican, steeped in maritime history this pub fitted in. He could tell by the fact that it was packed, that many people also liked it that way. The modern chain pubs would never be able to replicate the atmosphere that places like this enjoyed.

After three more pints, Ward decided that he was bored with his own company, and that he fancied a bit more life, so crossed over the road to The Navy, where he could hear the karaoke in full flow again.

It was a lot busier than it had been midweek. Ward stood at the bar waiting to get served, and the friendly barmaid from his previous visit spotted him, winked at him again and asked, "Hello lover, what are you fancying tonight?"

Ward knew she was flirting with him, and any other time he might have enjoyed it, but reminded himself that he didn't need a relationship yet. He asked for a pint of Stella, and quickly paid up and moved away from the bar just as a group of girls started to kill Gloria Gaynor's "I will survive."

He smiled to himself, it was a song that Wendy loved, and for a second, he found himself wondering what she was doing now but made himself think of something else straight away. This was no time to get all melancholic. He was never going to see her or be part of his old life ever again.

He was on his second pint, served by a young barmaid this time, when the door opened and four young men walked in, causing a quick lull in conversations around him. Ward looked over at them. They were obviously servicemen, but that wasn't why people had stopped talking around him.

They were all wearing matching t-shirts, and they were all maroon in colour, with the Airborne motif on the left chest. Ward knew that this was bound to cause trouble, as paras weren't welcome in a naval city, just as marines wouldn't be made welcome in Aldershot or Colchester, the garrison towns where the airborne fraternity ruled their little empires.

The four men strolled over to the bar and ordered their drinks as if there wasn't a problem. Ward could see glances around him from some of the other drinkers to each other and knew what was coming next. He decided that the last thing he needed was to get involved in a scrap between rival servicemen, so finished his pint and left.

He decided to finish his night with a brandy as a nightcap in another old pub called the Queens Arms, which was just approaching closing time, so noticeably quiet. He could hear sirens, and guessed that his hunch had happened, and the rivalry between the green berets and the red berets was still as strong as it had been when he had served.

He also made a mental note to himself that it was best he avoided Saturday nights in the busy pubs.

Chapter 95

A fortnight later, Crofts was sitting with Mead, Williams and Bates having their weekly management team meeting.

They were reviewing the forensic evidence, deciding what to send off to the lab for examination.

Crofts started with "I don't know about your thoughts, but I can't see anything that is worth sending off now?

The three senior detectives all nodded in agreement.

"As is stands, we have the evidence we would need to convict Pearson. We can prove he took the gun; we can prove that gun was used to kill Jimmy and Natalie, and we can put the gun to him. There's not much else needed forensically at this time, is there? Crofts asked.

Mead answered "No, there isn't unless we find something later."

Williams continued "We have the motive now, as well. The finance team have certainly unravelled his accounts. He was in debt up to his neck. In a few weeks' time he would have gone under. All because of gambling. Let that be a lesson to you Kev!"

"What do you mean?" Bates asked, "I have a little flutter every now and then, and never much more than a pound!"

The others laughed.

"That's how it all starts" Williams told him.

"I have read those financial reports" Bates told them, "I cannot believe anyone could bet such copious amounts on one horse, or one spin of a wheel, it's scary!"

"It certainly is" Mead added, "But it doesn't help us on this case. We have every bit of evidence needed to solve this case, and put him away, but we have no idea where he is."

Crofts looked at them all before saying "You do all realise that if Pearson doesn't do anything silly, and behaves himself, we may never catch him?"

"We do Simon, and you know I always give forensics the plaudits it deserves when it solves a case for us?" Mead said, "But although it was forensics that got us thus far in this case, I don't think it will be forensics that finds Bob Pearson now."

"I know" Crofts responded, "How do you think we'll find him?"

Meads thought for a while before answering "I don't know yet. He has been incredibly good so far, and lucky. It's only a matter of time before he makes a mistake, and we will track him down."

Bates added "There must be something in those pages and pages of evidence and statements that will give us a clue. We've just got to find it."

"We will" Meads replied.

*Two months later*

## Chapter 96

Pearson laid back on the bed in his cell in the remand wing in Lewes Prison and stared at the ceiling. It was visiting time, and Wendy had booked a slot to see him, but he had decided at the last minute that he didn't want to see her.

What was the point?

He knew she would be disappointed, but he also knew it was for the best, as she wouldn't be seeing him again. He knew he was going to be locked up for a long time, and he also knew that she wouldn't want to wait for him when she realised what he had done.

Not only on the crime side of things, as that was bad enough, but also in the fact that he had left her without anything. The house, the cars, everything would be taken from her because of him. If it hadn't already been taken.

He was trying to remember where it had all started to go wrong, where he had got the gambling bug from, but he couldn't pinpoint it. He remembered his dad and his mates used to frequent the betting shop when he was growing up, and how his dad taught him to write out a betting slip. When he was eighteen it meant that he could go into that shop and join in with all the regulars, but he wasn't that bothered by it.

He remembered the first time he had ever been to a casino. It was when he was in the army, and they went one night after the pubs closed. It was just a way of getting more alcohol in those days of stricter closing times. He remembered watching the blackjack and roulette but being a low paid squaddie at the time meant that he couldn't afford to play anyway and sat nursing his Bacardi and coke.

As he had got into building his accountancy business, gambling had never even entered his mind. He was too busy sorting out everyone else's finances to have time to, in the first place.

He would sometimes attend casinos with clients, but would always bet sensibly, especially in front of others. He didn't want those people important to him and his business, to think that he was a gambler. That would certainly make them look elsewhere for someone they could trust with their money.

He did sometimes go on his own if he was away on business, somewhere where he wasn't known, and he did enjoy the experience, but that wasn't where he became hooked. It was when the gaming laws changed, and he was able to bet online. It meant that he could do it wherever and whenever he wanted to and be anonymous about it. The fact that smartphones came on the market a couple of years later made it easier for him.

It hadn't taken a lot of thought on how to produce fictitious names and accounts several years before. His background then made it easy to apply for credit cards using these names. He had found that if there was proof of funds, none of the companies were that bothered in checking out his details.

That was where it had started to impact on his life. He found himself spending more and more each day as he became addicted. He would even gamble in-between clients. There was always a few minutes spare after someone left his office, where he would revise what had been decided during the meeting. He would then also grab a minute or two to get out his hidden phone and have a few more moments online. It was usually only stopped when the receptionist called him to say that his next appointment was due.

Even though he was an expert on dealing with other people's money, he wasn't when it came to his own.

It hadn't mattered at first, as he was comfortably off, and had quite a lot of spare cash in various accounts. Wendy would never notice, as she relied on him to take care of everything financial, and why wouldn't she? She enjoyed being the wife of a successful businessman, and all the trappings that came with it. She had never needed to want for anything since they had been together, so why would she worry?

It was this fact that upset him the most. Wendy had no idea of the predicament he had let himself fall into. As he started losing more and more, and started using funds from various sources, she was oblivious to it all. He made sure that if she ever asked for anything specifically, he would make sure that she was able to get it, thus leaving her oblivious to his plight.

Now she would be sitting in the visiting room waiting to see Bob, expecting him to come out and tell her that it was all some mistake, and that he would sort it out.

Unfortunately, that wasn't going to happen.

Chapter 97

It was eighteen months later when the Goldsons walked out of Lewes Crown Court to a waiting group of reporters, photographers, and camera crews.

There was a bit of pushing and shoving and people calling their names, but John and Julie just stood there holding hands, waiting for them to calm down.

John took out a piece of paper with a written statement on it he had prepared but didn't bother using it.

He knew what he wanted to say:

"Ladies and gentlemen, on behalf of myself and my wife Julie, we would like to thank DCI Tom Mead and his team for solving this and making sure we saw justice for our darling daughter Natalie and her husband Jimmy" He paused and looked at the group of reporters before continuing "From day one, the police have been so good to us as well as so professional in their enquiries. They stayed connected every step of the way. I would especially single out our family liaison officer, Louise Jacks" he paused again to look around for her and spotted her amongst the small group of officers stood to one side. Lou smiled at him and nodded "We met her on the day after our Natalie was killed, and she has been such a rock for us. Keeping us informed of every single development, answering all our questions however strange they might have been" He smiled at Lou before adding "You are a credit to your force."

Lou mouthed "Thank you" back to him.

"Losing your only daughter is something I hope never happens to anyone else. It feels as if someone has ripped your heart out, it honestly does. To find that she has been murdered in cold blood for something that doesn't involve her made it even worse" John paused to take a breath and compose himself before adding "But thanks to DCI Mead and his team, that evil man is behind bars, hopefully for the rest of his life."

Some of the reporters asked questions but then told to move out of the way by a couple of armed officers who ushered the Goldsons through and into a waiting black Range Rover, which then whisked them away at speed.

Tom Mead then gave his statement thanking his team of detectives for their professionalism, their thoroughness, and their tenacity throughout this investigation. He also thanked the forensic units both in force and those at the lab, adding "Without their team efforts, we would never have solved this case." He then added, "My last thoughts are with Jimmy and Natalie. They lost their lives through one man's greed. Fortunately that man is now serving two life sentences, one for each of the people that he gunned down in cold blood."

He then walked off, crossed the busy high street, and entered the White Hart Hotel, where several members of his team were already waiting. He looked around them before saying.

"Go on then, I will buy you all a drink!" before adding "You deserve it. Well done and thank you for all your work."

His words were hardly heard as the clamour towards the bar started for the thirsty detectives.

Crofts waited for a while before heading over to Mead, he took Jo Whatmore and Phil Jenkins with him "Hello Guv, thanks for the comments in your statement about forensics. We hardly ever get mentioned."

"That's okay" he said "You know I've always been a fan anyway, unlike some SIO's in the past. However in this case you really did solve it."

"I know, it's a great feeling" Crofts said.

"To be honest, in hindsight, without your work, I wonder if we would have solved it. No previous history meant that we might never have caught him if he had kept his nose clean" he looked around their faces before continuing "He did very well on the ID front, and on the financial front, which was to be expected really. He also did very well at the scene, except for one tiny mistake, not picking up that empty casing which rolled under the bed."

"The thing was, that without the familial connection we wouldn't have caught him, as he had been a good boy up until then with no police record" Crofts added nodding to Jo.

"I know, and I mentioned at the time how few results we get on with familial" the scientist continued "It surprised me that we got a result to be honest."

The others smiled, and then Jenkins said, "He was a bit unlucky there wasn't he?"

"Not as unlucky as he was later" Crofts said.

"Why what happened?" Jenkins asked.

"You really don't know?" Crofts asked.

"No, I only came down on the day I gave evidence and today, I didn't get to hear any more of the case."

Crofts explained how Pearson had escaped and changed identity, and how he set himself up in Plymouth as Paul Ward.

"So did he commit a crime then?" Jenkins asked.

"No!" Crofts and Whatmore replied laughing.

"So how did we catch him then?" said Jenkins, looking puzzled.

Crofts told him "There was fight in a bar in Plymouth which ended up with a young squaddie with serious head injuries, and a bleed on the brain. The bar was cordoned off for a crime scene examination. One of our many mundane tasks in jobs like that is to fingerprint and DNA all the glasses in the scene. It's to prove who was in the bar in case we don't get all the names through statements."

"Yes" said Jenkins, still confused.

"Well, Pearson had been in the bar earlier, and his empty glass was still on the side where he had left it. All the DNA samples were sent off to the lab, and his name came back as being there. It only took a bit of detective work to find him on CCTV that evening and follow him back to his new home and arrest him."

Jenkins stood open mouthed "I don't believe it, how unlucky was that?" he finally said.

Crofts said, "It definitely was unlucky for him, but it was certainly lucky for us."

"Indeed" Mead said, raising his glass to them.

THE END

Printed in Great Britain
by Amazon